CITY OF DARKNESS

Mystery Novels by Al Lamanda

John Bekker Mysteries

Sunset
(Edgar Award Nominee for Best Novel)

Sunrise
(Voted Best Crime Novel of 2013 by the Maine Writers and Publishers Alliance)

First Light
(Nero Award Nominee)

This Side of Midnight
(Nero Award Nominee)

With Six You Get Wally
(Winner of the 2017 Nero Award for Best Mystery,
and a Shamus Award Nominee)

Who Killed Joe Italiano

For Better or Worse

Western Novels as Ethan J. Wolfe

The Last Ride

The Regulator

The Range War of '82

Murphy's Law

All the Queen's Men

One If by Land

CITY OF DARKNESS

AL LAMANDA

Encircle Publications
Farmington, Maine, U.S.A.

Editor: Cynthia Brackett-Vincent
Book design: Eddie Vincent
Cover design: Christopher Wait
Cover images © Getty Images

Published by:

Encircle Publications
PO Box 187
Farmington, ME 04938

Visit: http://encirclepub.com

Printed in U.S.A.

One

———————

Eli Andrew Rico always did his ironing in front of the kitchen window. It faced the park across the street from his Bronx apartment and he liked to watch the kids playing baseball while he ironed.

Today was Sunday and his day off. He was ironing five white shirts for the coming week. White wasn't a requirement, but it made life a bit simpler if all his shirts for work were the same color.

His apartment was small, but comfortable and the view of the park from the fourth floor was excellent. Today the kids were playing a game of pickup baseball where teams were chosen at random. School was out for the summer and the kids made the most of it. Baseball, touch football, tag sometimes so the girls could play and when a fire hydrant was opened by the fire department it attracted the neighborhood kids by the hundreds.

He thought about a pet for company. The building allowed pets, dogs and cats, but his job took up so many hours it wouldn't be fair to an animal to be left alone so much of the time.

Eli finished the fifth shirt and hung them neatly in the bedroom closet. In the bathroom, he shaved carefully and then took a shower. The humidity was high so he turned on the bedroom fan and stood before it to air dry rather than towel off.

Then he dressed in white slacks, a pullover shirt, tan socks and loafers. In his right pocket he stuck some folding money, his keys and

1

old Zippo lighter in the left. Handkerchief in the left rear pocket, wallet in the right. Cigarettes in the shirt pocket. To his right ankle, he strapped on the .38 special snub nose revolver. The holster, gun and six extra bullets were heavy but he was used to the weight.

Before he left the apartment, as an afterthought, he tucked the five and a half inch long switchblade knife into his right pocket.

He wore his father's old watch, the only watch he had ever owned.

The heat and humidity outside was like a slap to the face. He crossed the street and entered the park. Mr. Peru, who sold Italian ices in the summer for as long as Eli could remember was in his usual spot at the gate.

Eli forked over a dime for a cherry flavored snow cone and found a bench to eat it and watch the game in progress. Nobody ever kept score. The games lasted until it was too dark to see the ball. Oftentimes fights broke out and delayed play until someone broke it up and play resumed. Sometimes in the middle of a game a kid got upset with his team and went to play for the other team.

It didn't matter to Eli who won or lost. The noise of kids playing was like fine music to his ears.

He ate the snow cone until all the cherry syrup was gone and then tossed the paper container into the nearest trash bin. He reclaimed his bench and lit a cigarette. The Zippo had seen better days, but it was thirty-two years old and was given to him by his father. He would use it until it no longer functioned and then store it someplace safe.

The heat and humidity wore the kids down and they called the game quits.

Eli stood and left the park. He walked two blocks to the Italian bakery on the corner and picked up two round loaves of bread, the crusty kind. Then he walked back to his apartment to retrieve his car that was parked at the curb.

It was still early, but the drive to his parent's home in New Jersey took forever. First he had to drive into Manhattan and then to the George Washington Bridge and cross over and drive south to Paramus.

He couldn't be late. His mother served dinner promptly at 6:30 every night except Sunday. Sunday was 5:00 on the nose and you felt her wrath if you were late. His sister Shelly, her husband Robert and their two girls would be there along with Mom and Pop.

His car, a '41 Ford didn't have a radio, so he hung a transistor radio from the rearview mirror. He turned it on and played with the dial until he found a ball game. The Yankees were playing Cleveland at home. The Yanks were up eleven to three in the fifth. Red Barber gave a quick recap as the sixth inning began. Joe DiMaggio had a home run and a double and Yogi Berra had two home runs. Unless there were some serious injuries on the team, the Yanks were a shoe-in to win the 1949 pennant and World Series.

By the time he reached Manhattan the game was in the seventh inning. He drove north to One-Seventy-Ninth Street to the entrance ramp of the bridge. Traffic leading to the ramp was backed up for ten blocks. The game ended as he reached the toll booths. He paid the seventy-five cents toll from the loose change he kept in the ashtray and crossed the bridge.

Seventy-five cents may seem a lot to cross each way, but it was the longest bridge in the world and hailed as an engineering marvel, so he really didn't mind the steep toll.

Once on the Jersey side, Eli drove south to Paramus.

Thirty minutes later, he arrived at his parent's home. The home, a modest, three-bedroom Tudor was the crowning achievement of his parents' lives. His father, Salvatore, arrived in New York from Italy in 1901 at the age of thirteen. Eli's grandparents spoke no English and his father just a few words. It was there, at the point they were identified by immigration agents incorrectly that the family name of Riggeo was recorded as Rico.

Eli's mother, Michele O'Rourke was born in The Bronx and was third generation Irish. Her great-grandfather came over in 1863 and fought in the Civil War. Salvatore and Michele met in 1913 and had to hide their romance from their families because an Italian boy didn't date an Irish girl without consequences. In 1914, they secretly married and when the marriage became known they were outcast from their families.

It didn't matter to Salvatore or Michele. They moved to a Bronx apartment and a year later Eli was born. Two years after that, Shelly came along. Salvatore worked for the Transit Authority and helped build tunnels and lay track. Later, he became a motorman and finally a conductor. Michele worked as a telephone operator for thirty-five years and retired just a year ago. Salvatore planned to retire in 1950.

They bought the house in 1939 when the price of homes was dirt cheap.

Shelly moved to Jersey with her parents. Eli stayed in The Bronx because he was into his second year as a New York City Police Officer.

In late '41, Eli took the exam for detective and made the grade the first try. He proved to be a brilliant detective and was on the brink of great things when the Second World War broke out.

He enlisted in the spring of '42 as did nearly twenty million other men.

Salvatore gave Eli his watch and Zippo lighter that he carried in World War One when he'd fought in Italy, France and Germany.

Eli returned home in early '46 and his job, as promised, was waiting for him. The war had depleted resources and by '47 he was promoted to homicide as a sergeant and just last year to lieutenant.

Sally, Robert and their kids were already there when Eli arrives at his parent's home. Robert drove a '47 Cadillac, his father a '43 Ford. He parked behind the Ford, grabbed the bread and prepared himself for the dinner conversations to follow.

Robert would subtly brag about his career as an engineer and how well he was doing financially. Shelly would discretely inquire about Eli's dating habits and try to set him up with one of her 'unmarried friends.' Ma would tell him for the thousandth time how she would sleep better at night if he had a different career, one that was safer. Pop would want to talk baseball. The Yanks, Giants and Dodgers. It would all go on for hours and nothing would ever get resolved except that everyone would eat too much and burp too much later on.

As Eli walked to the front door, it suddenly opened and his father stepped out.

"Your office called," he said. "They said it was an emergency."

* * *

Eli used the phone in the bedroom to call the office. He spoke to the dispatcher on duty for a few minutes and then hung up.

He went to the living room where the family had gathered.

"I have to go," he said.

"It's Sunday," his mother said.

"I know, Ma," Eli said. "I have to go."

"I'll walk you out," his father said.

At the door, Salvatore said, "Eli, be careful."

"And make sure you eat something," Michelle called after him.

5

Two

The drive back to Manhattan took about an hour. An accident on the GW closed two lanes and heavy Sunday traffic funneled into the remaining open lanes causing a bottleneck.

He fiddled with the radio and found the Giants game. They were losing and 'Stan the Man' had just hit a home run to crack open the game. He lit a cigarette and felt his shirt stick to the seat.

Traffic inched along the bridge.

The back of his shirt was drenched by the time he reached Manhattan. He drove to Broadway and then south and then to Central Park West to the Charter Arms apartment building on 81st Street.

Eli parked at a hydrant, opened the glove box for the Police on Duty sign and left it on the dashboard. He also took out a small notebook and pen.

The Charter Arms was thirty stories high of luxury living for the city's elite. Eli had never been inside the building, but had driven past it hundreds of time. The ornate and lavish lobby faced Central Park. The underground parking garage was located on the 81st Street side of the building.

A guard employed by the building was on duty in a little hut at the entrance to the garage. Eli showed him his badge on the way in. He walked the ramp into the garage and stopped for a moment to observe the scene.

Six police cruisers were parked in somewhat of a circle. A woman sat in back of one of them. An ambulance and the medical examiner's wagon were parked beside a Cadillac sedan. The sedan's driver's side door was open. A department photographer stood waiting for the word to go to work.

Eli approached the scene.

"Hi, Lieutenant," a patrolman said.

Eli nodded. "Did anybody touch anything?"

Another patrolman said, "Me and my partner took the call. Nothing was touched."

Eli nodded again. He walked to the medical examiner, an experienced doctor named Wilson.

"Did you check the body yet?" Eli asked.

"Waiting on you," Wilson said.

"Go ahead."

Eli looked at the woman in the back of a patrol car. "Who is she?"

A patrolman stepped forward. "That's my car, Lieutenant. She's the maid. She found the body. She says the victim is Roger Tanner, her employer."

"The maid?" Eli said.

"That's what she said," the patrolman said. "Her English isn't very good. I think she's a PR."

Eli walked to the patrol car, opened the rear door and sat beside the maid. He showed her his badge.

"I'm Lieutenant Rico," he said. "What is your name please?"

"Rosa Garcia."

"I understand you work for Mr. Tanner," Eli said as he jotted her name in his notebook.

Rosa nodded her head. "I am the housekeeper," she said in a thick Spanish accent.

"Why don't you tell me what happened," Eli said.

"What happened?"

"Yes, tell me what happened."

"Mister Tanner, he leave to go play cards like he do every Sunday night and he forget his cigars," Rosa said.

"His cigars?"

"Si. I mean yes."

Rosa picked up the leather cigar holder from the seat beside her. "His cigars," she said.

"What time did he leave the apartment?" Eli asked.

"Four," Rosa said. "He leave every Sunday at 4:00 to play cards."

"And how did you notice he didn't take his cigars?"

"Every Sunday I pack his case with six fresh cigars and leave it on the table beside the front door," Rosa said. "He forget them. I see them there and I rush to the elevator to try and see him before he drive away."

"What time was that?"

"Four. He always leave at 4:00 to go play his cards."

"So you grabbed the cigars and did what?"

"I go to the hallway to the elevators and I have to wait for the elevator," Rosa said. "Two, maybe three minutes and then it come. I ride down to garage and see Mister Tanner's car door open and he on the floor covered in blood."

"And what did you do?"

"I screamed. What would you do?"

Eli smiled. "Who called the police?"

"I ran up the steps to lobby and tell the guard," Rosa said.

"Did Mr. Tanner ever forget his cigars before?"

"Si. I mean yes. He forget things all the time. A few times he call from the card game and I go deliver them."

"Where do you live, Miss Garcia?"

"In the apartment in the maid's room."

Eli nodded as he jotted a few more notes. "Excuse me for a moment."

Rosa nodded.

Eli left the cruiser and went to Wilson. "What do you got?"

"I got a corpse on the floor of a parking garage," Wilson said.

"Funny," Eli said. "What killed him and when?"

"One large stab wound to the spleen," Wilson said.

"Jesus," Eli said.

"He didn't die from that, although he would have left untreated," Wilson said. "His neck is broken. Snapped like a dry twig."

Eli stared at the body of Roger Tanner for a moment. He was slumped on his left side. "Get his wallet and then go over the body with a fine tooth comb. Prints on the car, whatever. Check everything and I mean everything."

"Can I photograph the body now?" the photographer said.

"Every angle," Eli said. "Just don't touch it."

"Lieutenant, some reporters are here," a patrolman said.

"Keep them out," Eli said. "I want five two-man teams to knock on every door in the building and get statements. I'm taking Miss Garcia up to the apartment. Wait, I want statements from the guard at the garage security booth and from the doorman and like right now. Bring them to the apartment."

"You got it, Lieutenant," the officer said.

* * *

Rosa used her key to unlock the front door to the apartment. She opened the door and stepped inside and held the door for Eli. Before he entered, he glanced down the hall. As with most large apartments there was a servants' door down the hall.

9

The living room was as large as or larger than Eli's entire apartment. It was expensively furnished, including a set of Tiffany lamps.

"Let's sit on the sofa and talk for a bit," Eli said.

Rosa took a seat on the twelve-foot-long sofa.

Eli sat near her and opened the notebook.

"How long have you worked for Mr. Tanner?" Eli asked.

"Since 1942," Rosa said.

"Where are you from?"

"Cuba."

"When did you come to America?"

"I… what is the word… I can't think," Rosa said.

"I understand. You've just witnessed a terrible crime," Eli said. "Take your time."

Rosa nodded. "In Cuba, my family was put into the prison," she said.

"Why?"

"Politics. They believe in freedom."

Eli nodded. "I understand. Go on please."

"I work as housekeeper at hotel in San Juan," Rosa said. "The man who own the hotel say he own a hotel in New York and I can go there if I want. That's how I came, to work in the hotel. He sponsor me."

"And how did you come to work for Mr. Tanner?"

"One of the women at the hotel, she tell me about Mr. Tanner looking for a new housekeeper. She say I should see Mr. Tanner."

"And you did?"

Rosa nodded.

"He like me and hire me as housekeeper," Rosa said.

"How old are you, Miss Garcia?" Eli asked.

"Twenty-nine."

"Did you plan to work for Mr. Tanner much longer?"

"Until I have enough."

"Enough what?"

"Money saved. I have $15,000 in the bank."

"You have $15,000?"

"*Sí.* Yes. Mr. Tanner, he pay very well. $1,000 a month, and I live in the apartment. I show you."

Rosa and Eli stood and she led him to the large kitchen. She opened a door located on the back wall.

"See?" she said.

Eli looked inside the large studio apartment that was well furnished.

"You live here?" Eli asked.

"Si. Yes. I live here. I pay no rent so I save most of my money."

Eli nodded. "Where does Mr. Tanner keep his cigars?"

"In the cigar room. I show you."

Rosa took Eli to the den. The walls were lined with well-stocked books. The desk was oak, the chair leather. She opened a door and Eli looked inside. The room was lined with shelves of boxed cigars of every major brand, including Cuban.

"Let's go back to the sofa," Eli said.

"I can make coffee you like?"

"That would be fine," Eli said.

They returned to the kitchen where Rosa made coffee. Eli sat at the table until it was ready and then she filled two cups and sat opposite him.

Eli sampled the coffee. "Good," he said.

"Is Cuban coffee. I buy at the special store on Broadway."

"Miss Garcia, what did Mr. Tanner do for work?" Eli asked.

"Mr. Tanner no work," Rosa said. "He a...how do you say... wealthy."

"Do you know how he acquired his wealth?"

11

Rosa shook her head. "He never say about such things."

"What about friend and girlfriends?"

"Mr. Tanner have many friends. They play cards every Sunday night."

"Where?"

"The Park Plaza Hotel. They always play in room 1919."

"At what time?"

"He always leave at four. He get home around 1:00 in the morning."

"Are you sure?"

Rosa nodded.

"How long have you and Mr. Tanner been lovers?" Eli asked.

Rosa blushed and her eyes looked away.

"Your room looks as if it hadn't been slept in for quite a while," Eli said. "You're a very pretty woman and the average salary of a live-in housekeeper is around fifty dollars a week. It wasn't hard to figure it out, Miss Garcia."

Rosa looked at Eli. "He say one night he very lonely after his wife died," she said. "He say he want company. At first I not understand."

"That was when?"

"Five years ago, maybe longer."

"Well, there is no crime in being lonely," Eli said. "What about his enemies?"

"He have none I know of," Rosa said.

The phone rang. Rosa looked at Eli and he nodded. She stood and picked up the wall phone.

"Hello, residence of Mr. Tanner," she said.

Rose listened for a moment and then said to hold on. She looked at Eli. He stood and took the phone.

"This is Police Lieutenant Eli Rico, who is this please?"

"Michael Breck. Where is Roger?"

"Mister Breck, I'm afraid Mister Tanner is dead," Eli said.

"Dead? How could he be dead?" Breck asked.

"Somebody murdered him," Eli said. "Are you at the Park Plaza Hotel?"

"Yes, we're…"

"Stay until I get there," Eli said and hung up.

Eli looked at Rosa. "Did Mr. Tanner have a safe?"

Rosa nodded.

"Show me."

Rosa took Eli to the master bedroom and opened the walk-in closet door. Against the back wall stood a three-foot-tall safe. He entered the closet and tried the door. It was locked.

"Lieutenant?" a voice called from the living room.

Eli and Rosa returned to the living room.

Two crime scene investigators had arrived.

"Search everything," Eli said. "Find date books, notes, whatever and have someone from the department open the safe in the bedroom."

"What I do?" Rosa asked.

"For now, nothing," Eli said. "Just stay in the apartment and help my men with whatever they need. Okay?"

Rosa nodded.

"And have a uniformed officer stay with Miss Garcia until I return," Eli said to the two crime scene investigators.

*   *   *

Michael Breck answered the hotel room door. Eli had his badge and ID ready and showed it to him.

"I spoke to you on the phone," Breck said.

Eli entered and Breck closed the door.

"Who do we have here?" Eli asked.

Three men sat at the card table in the center of the room.

"John Potts, William Teal and Steven Roth," Breck said. "Now will you tell us what in God's name happened to Roger?"

"Gentlemen, let's talk," Eli said.

* * *

As he rode the elevator to Tanner's apartment, he scanned his notes. Roger Tanner was thirty-eight years old. The four men he played cards with the past decade were, as him, wealthy trust fund heirs. In Tanner's case, he inherited a trust worth three million, seven hundred dollars.

While it was true that Tanner didn't work at a regular job, he did have an advisement banker that managed his portfolio closely and he more than doubled his trust fund.

He married his high school sweetheart when they were both twenty-two years old. She died in 1940 from a freak accident in Central Park. She enjoyed riding her bicycle every morning in the park. It was the weekend of the Fourth of July. Some kids threw a pack of firecrackers in front of a horse-drawn carriage. The horse spooked and raced away from the driver. Horse and bicycle collided. The horse won.

Breck told Eli that Tanner barely left the apartment for close to a year after his wife died. After the bombing of Pearl Harbor, Tanner enlisted.

Or tried to.

He was deaf in the left ear from a childhood disease and was classified 4F.

He spent the war on the sidelines but did his part with fund raising events and donating money to military causes.

Breck and the others verified Rosa's story of her employment as far as they knew.

Breck told Eli that he spoke with Tanner recently concerning his relationship with Rosa. Breck said that Tanner was considering asking her to be his wife.

Tanner wasn't a small man. He stood six feet tall and weighed 190 pounds according to his driver's license information.

So how was he overpowered so easily?

And without a fight.

The elevator door opened and Eli walked to the Tanner apartment. A uniformed officer was in the hallway at the door.

"Is someone inside with her?" Eli asked.

The officer nodded. "Everybody in the building is asking what's going on?"

"They'll find out soon enough."

Eli opened the door and entered the apartment. A uniformed officer was sitting on the sofa and he stood up. "Hi, Lieutenant," he said.

"Where is Miss Garcia?" Eli asked.

"In the master bedroom," the officer said. "One second she's sitting on the sofa calm as a Hindu cow, the next she's hysterical."

"See any combat, officer?" Eli asked.

"5th Infantry."

"When the battle is over, that's when you breakdown," Eli said.

The officer nodded. "Two statements from the guard in the garage and the doorman," he said. "On the coffee table."

Eli went into the master bedroom. Rosa wasn't on the bed or anywhere else. The bathroom door was closed.

"Miss Garcia?" Eli said at the bathroom door.

"The door is no locked," Rosa said.

Eli opened the door. The bathroom was the size of his kitchen. The marble tub could hold four and was sunken. Rosa sat in the tub up to her neck in bubble bath.

"I'm sorry. Excuse me," Eli said.

"Is all right," Rosa said. "Sit on the bench, please."

There was a bench against the wall. Eli sat and looked at her. Her eyes were red and swollen from crying. A glass of wine rested on the tiles floor beside the tub.

Rosa sighed heavily. "What happen now?" she said.

"If you mean tonight, I'll head over to the office and review what we have," Eli said. "An officer will stop by tomorrow to escort you to my office to take your statement. I'll make sure an officer stays in the apartment overnight."

Rosa nodded. "I will have to find a place to live now," she said.

"Wait until a lawyer tells you that," Eli said. "For now you're my witness and I need you to stay put."

"I ask myself why this happen," Rosa said. "Mr. Tanner never hurt nobody."

"Listen, it's getting late and I haven't had anything to eat since breakfast," Eli said.

"Would you like me to cook for you?" Rosa asked.

"That would be nice," Eli said. "I'll wait in the living room."

Eli returned to the living room where the officer was in a chair, reading a newspaper. He stood when Eli entered the room.

"Were you here when forensics left?" Eli said.

"I was. They took everything but the kitchen sink."

"What time does your shift end?"

"In about an hour."

"You're from the four-two?"

The officer nodded.

"Head back to your house and tell your captain I asked for an overnight watch," Eli said. "I'll wait here until your people show up."

"One for the hallway?"

"If there's manpower."

The officer nodded and left the apartment.

Eli picked up the two reports and went to the kitchen. He used the phone on the wall and called the medical examiner.

Wilson answered after three rings. "Medical Examiner," Wilson said.

"It's Eli."

"I figured you'd call," Wilson said. "Tanner's on the slab as we speak."

"And?"

"Too soon. Stop by in a couple of hours."

"I will. Thanks."

Eli hung up and touched the pot of coffee on the stove. It was still warm and he opened a cabinet, removed a mug and filled it. He found an ashtray in a drawer and took it to the table where he lit a cigarette.

How was Tanner overpowered so easily and quickly, he mulled over? From the time he left the apartment to the time Rosa found him was a matter of minutes. He read the reports from the guard in the garage and the doorman.

The guard claimed and his log book verified his statement that no one drove into or left the garage one hour prior to Tanner's murder. A record of the log showed that seven residents of the building had left and entered the garage prior to four o'clock.

The doorman said that only building residents had left and entered the building during his shift that started at 10:00 am and ended at 6:00 pm.

"What would you like?" Rosa asked as she entered the kitchen.

She had changed into white slacks, a yellow blouse and wore

slippers. Her dark hair was pinned up. Her face, especially around the eyes was puffy and swollen. She had been crying again.

"Anything would be fine," Eli said.

"That coffee is old," Rosa said. "I'll make fresh."

Rose emptied the pot and went about making a fresh pot.

"That door there, is that the second entrance to the apartment?" Eli asked and pointed.

"Yes. The servants' door," Rosa said.

"Rosa, how is the trash removed?" Eli asked.

"The trash?"

"Yeah, the trash."

"I leave it in the hall and the… what is the word?"

"The building superintendent," Eli said.

"Yes. He come and pick it up."

"What days?"

"Monday, Wednesday and Saturday."

"Not Sunday."

"No."

"Does he live in the building?"

Rosa nodded.

"Can you call him on the phone and ask him to stop by?"

Rosa went to the phone, dialed a number and then spoke in Spanish. She hung up and looked at Eli. "He be right up."

Eli nodded.

"The coffee take a minute," Rosa said.

"No hurry."

The doorbell rang.

"I'll get it," Eli said.

He stood and went to the living room and opened the door. "I am Victor Sanchez, the super," Sanchez said in a thick accent.

"Come in," Eli said.

"I already talk to police before," Sanchez said.

"I know. I have a few questions though. In the kitchen."

Eli and Sanchez went to the kitchen.

"Hello, Rosa," Sanchez said. "I am so sorry about Mr. Tanner."

Rosa nodded. "Have some coffee with us."

Eli and Sanchez sat and Rosa filled three cups and then sat next to Eli.

"Mr. Sanchez, tell me about the garbage," Eli said.

"The garbage?"

"Yes. How do you remove it and where does it go?"

"The tenants leave it outside the servants' door and I pick it up in a cart and bring it down to the basement and fill the cans," Sanchez said.

"On Monday, Wednesday and Saturday," Eli said.

"Yes."

"If a tenant has something they want to get rid of on say Tuesday or Thursday, what then?" Eli asked.

"They can call me or take it down themselves," Sanchez said. "The private elevator is never locked."

"Can you show me?" Eli asked.

"Sure."

"Rosa, I'll be right back," Eli said.

Eli and Sanchez went out to the hallway through the servant's door in the kitchen. Sanchez led Eli down to the end of the hall where the private elevator was located. Sanchez pushed the call button and after a few seconds the door opened. A large and empty laundry cart was in the elevator car.

Eli and Sanchez got on and Sanchez pushed the button for the basement.

"I keep an empty cart on the elevator for me to use," Sanchez said. "And for people to put their trash in if they no want to go downstairs."

The elevator arrived in the basement. The door opened and Eli and Sanchez got off. The basement was large. Thirty garbage cans lined the walls. Workbenches were filled with tools.

Eli pointed to a door.

"Where does that go?" he asked.

"The garage," Sanchez said.

Eli opened the door and looked into the garage. "Is this door ever locked?"

"Never."

"How do you bring the cans to the street?" Eli asked.

"Here," Sanchez said and walked to another door at the end of the basement.

"Is this door ever locked?" Eli asked.

"No, never."

The door opened to a courtyard. Eli and Sanchez stepped into the courtyard. There was a tunnel that led to the street. They walked the tunnel and it ended at the sidewalk about forty feet to the left of the parking garage.

Eli looked to his left. The guard on duty at the garage wasn't visible.

"Mr. Sanchez, I suggest that from now on you lock those doors," Eli said.

* * *

Eli returned to the apartment to find a large Spanish omelet waiting for him. Rosa had prepared a second, smaller one for herself.

"This is delicious," Eli said.

"Thank you," Rosa said.

"I need you to do something for me," Eli said. "Several things, actually. The first is that you speak to no one concerning Mr. Tanner.

The second is when an officer arrives tomorrow to take you downtown to make a statement you be as thorough as possible. The third is you rack your memory for any information you can remember about friends, enemies and whatever. Okay?"

Rosa nodded.

"In all likelihood, I will see you tomorrow," Eli said.

Three

Eli looked at the body of Roger Tanner on the examination table.

"He's a fit man, isn't he?" Eli said.

"He was," Wilson said. "A mite over six feet tall, a solid 191."

Wilson rolled the body over. "The stab wound on the left side goes directly to the spleen. Painful, mortal given enough time, but not fatal in this instance. His neck is snapped in two like a twig. That's what killed him and in my opinion, instantly."

Eli looked at the stab wound.

"What kind of knife?"

"Haven't identified it yet," Wilson said. "It's one I haven't seen before. It's at least fifteen inches long, though."

"I'll have the lab get on that," Eli said. "Any other evidence on the body?"

"Clean. Look at the throat, tell me what you see."

Eli examined Tanner's throat. It was crushed at the Adam's apple but there wasn't a mark on it.

"How is that possible?" Eli asked.

"You tell me," Wilson said.

"It takes time to crush a man's throat, even if you're twice the size of the victim," Eli said.

"Maybe he stabbed him first to weaken Tanner?" Wilson said.

"Maybe?"

Eli stared off into space for a moment.

"What are you thinking?" Wilson asked.

"Nothing. Call me if you figure out the knife," Eli said. "The lab boys will be by later to take a look."

* * *

Eli called Art Howe, the captain of his division and asked him to meet him in the office. Howe was a tough, no nonsense cop with thirty years on the job. He fought in Germany and France in the First World War and was as fearless as he was fair-minded.

While Howe looked at the crime scene photos, Eli drew a little diagram on a legal pad.

"The killer enters through the street tunnel that leads to the basement where the garbage cans are stored," Eli said. "He opens the door to the parking garage, kills Tanner and slips out the same way sight unseen."

"This fucking city," Howe said.

"The killer knew exactly where Tanner would be and exactly at what time," Eli said. "That took some planning."

"What do we have on the victim?" Howe asked.

Eli gave him the rundown on what he had so far.

"This is going to take some legwork, Eli," Howe said. "A guy worth seven million doesn't walk through life without some enemies and a lot of friends."

"Agreed," Eli said.

"What about the murder weapon?" Howe asked.

"The murder weapon was the killer's hands," Eli said. "The stab to the spleen didn't kill him, a broken windpipe did."

Howe sat on the edge of Eli's desk.

"The press?" Howe asked.

"Nothing yet."

"I'll call a press conference in the morning," Howe said.

"Will you need help on this one?" Howe asked.

"If I do, I'll pull Jack Bannon and Tyler," Eli said.

"The City doesn't like its millionaires getting murdered, Eli," Howe said. "Solve this one."

"I'll do my best, Art," Eli said.

Howe stood up. "Do more than your best," he said. "Do a miracle."

* * *

After Howe left, Eli sat in his chair and mulled things over in his mind. The killer knew Tanner's habits. That required surveillance and lots of it.

Unless he was close enough to Tanner that he was familiar with Tanner's regular routines.

The killer didn't use a gun because in the confines of the underground garage a shot would have sounded like a bazooka and alerted the guard.

Motive?

There had to be a motive.

The phone rang and Eli picked it up. "Lieutenant Rico."

"It's Roscoe in the lab. We got the safe open."

"Be right there."

* * *

The crime lab was located in the basement. Roscoe was the lead crime scene investigator, a twenty plus year veteran.

The contents of the safe were spread out on a table.

Eli looked at them.

"Jesus Christ," he said.

"And then some," Roscoe said. "Let's start with the cash. $50,000 in stacks of $10,000 a stack. One ring box containing one wedding and engagement ring. Some pretty expensive women's jewelry. An insurance policy for two million dollars. His..."

"Wait," Eli said. "Who is the beneficiary?"

"Rosa Garcia," Roscoe said. "As of a month ago. Prior to that it was blank."

"Blank?"

"That's what I said, Lieutenant. Blank."

"What else?"

"His portfolio of investments and statements," Roscoe said. "He was worth close to eight million dollars. Bank records of transactions, that kind of stuff. One key that I believe is for a bank safe deposit box."

"Is that it?"

"That's it."

"What bank?"

"Manhattan First, according to the stamp."

"Let me have the key," Eli said.

Roscoe gave him the key.

"I'll take the insurance policy, bank records and rings," Eli said. "I'll have my guys bag the rest into evidence."

Roscoe nodded. "Anything else?"

"You can count on that," Eli said.

*   *   *

Eli read the insurance policy at his desk. Tanner purchased the policy five years ago, but hadn't included a beneficiary until recently when he added Rosa Garcia's name.

His initial thoughts on the rings proved incorrect. His first reaction was the rings belonged to Tanner's wife and he saved them as keepsakes. However, the rings were new, less than two months old and purchased at Tiffany's for $6,000 according to the receipt folded inside the box.

"Six grand?" Eli said aloud. "It takes me ten months to make six grand."

He read through the financial reports. Most of it didn't make sense to him. A lot of buying and selling of stocks and commodities. He would have to get in touch with the financial banker to spell it all out.

Eli made a note of the banker's name. Leo Carson Jr. His office was on Park Avenue South.

Eli stood for a moment and stretched. He lit a cigarette and went to the window. A wino was asleep on a bench across the street in the tiny park that faced headquarters.

There was a knock on the door and a detective named Tyler entered carrying a cardboard box. "The stuff we gathered from Tanner's apartment," he said and set it on Eli's desk.

"Anything interesting?" Eli asked.

Tyler shrugged.

"Okay, thanks," Eli said.

Tyler left the office and closed the door.

Eli emptied the box on his desk. There were two date books. One for business, the other personal. The business date book had regular appointments with Carson Jr., along with appointments with a real estate agency. There was no name, just the name of the agency. The West Side Real Estate Agency, located on West 57th Street.

In the personal date book, Tanner wrote everything down. Everything from haircuts to trips to his shirt maker to what brands of cigars he wanted to buy.

It was apparent to Eli that Tanner forgot more than his cigars on a regular basis and needed to write everything down to remind himself.

Eli opened the photo album. There were dozens of family photos of his parents and his wife. Nothing unusual and nothing out of the ordinary.

He picked up the large envelope marked contents of pockets and dumped it. $1,000 in twenty dollar bills rolled and held in place with a rubber band. $500 in his wallet. His driver's license and a New York City issued gun permit. His checkbook with $100,000 in the account. A gold Zippo lighter, the real thing.

Eli picked up the phone and called the squad room. Tyler picked up.

"Hey, get in here," Eli said.

Tyler came in a few seconds later.

"His car keys, where are they?" Eli asked.

"They weren't on the body or in the car," Tyler said. "Or on the ground."

"He has a gun permit, does he own a gun?"

"I don't know, Lieutenant."

"Find out."

"It's ten o'clock at night," Tyler said.

"In the morning then."

Tyler nodded and returned to the squad room.

Eli took his chair and lit a fresh cigarette.

Who wanted to kill this guy?

What was the motive?

Where are his keys?

Where is his gun?

Eli picked up the phone and called Wilson.

"Don't you ever go home?" Wilson said.

"On his body, did you find a set of keys?" Eli asked.

"If I had I would have already given them to you," Wilson said.

"Thanks."

Eli hung up the phone.

'In the morning then' sounded like a good idea.

Four

The apartment was a fucking oven. There was no other way to describe it when Eli opened the door and stepped inside.

He went to the kitchen and turned on the wall fan. He took a bottle of milk from the fridge and filled a glass and added two ice cubes from the freezer, sat at the table and took out his cigarettes.

Eli sipped icy cold milk, lit a cigarette and thought for a while.

Tanner wasn't robbed.

He was killed for another reason.

Money?

Power?

Lust?

Envy?

Revenge?

A rainbow of motives.

None of them on the surface seemed to fit.

On the surface.

Tomorrow was another day.

Tomorrow he would start to scratch below the surface and look for the pus that always bubbled up.

Eli finished the glass of milk, turned off the fan and went to the bedroom. He turned on the fan beside the bed, stripped down to his T-shirt and underwear and flipped down the sheets.

The fan cooled his body, but even so he was sweating heavily. Exhaustion won over sweat and he felt his eyes grow heavy and Eli drifted off to sleep.

*   *   *

The fucking Germans just wouldn't quit. Eli's unit, the 1ˢᵗ Ranger Battalion invaded Sicily with the idea of capturing the town of Butera and the harbor at Porto Empedolce.

The fighting went on for days. The Germans just wouldn't quit. They had to know the war was lost, but they just wouldn't surrender. In the end, his unit took seven hundred prisoners and killed four times that amount.

Afterward, when the smoke cleared and the fighting ended, Eli and his unit had to do the unthinkable.

The German Army used more horses than any other force. They had more than a million horses in military service. The Rangers had to kill the wounded horses on the battlefield.

Screaming horses in pain, limbs missing, stomachs blown open, they would simply end their misery with a shot to the head.

Eli remembered crying with each horse that he killed.

There was no reprieve, either.

Rangers took far longer to train so reinforcements were few and far between.

Rest was out of the question for Rangers. His unit, along with eight other Ranger units was sent to join the 29ᵗʰ Infantry at Omaha Beach for the D-Day invasion.

The Navy bombed the shit out of the beach before the landing, but overall it was inadequate in accomplishing the goal.

The Germans had eighty-five machine guns scattered throughout the beachhead and they put them to good use.

Hundreds died in the water without ever setting foot on sand.
Hundreds more died on the beachheads.
The engineers suffered forty percent casualties.
The Rangers captured the beachhead but at a great cost.
One soldier near Eli took a German .25 caliber bullet in his penis.
He lay in the sand crying for someone to please kill him. Eli crawled to
him and called for a medic.
The soldier screamed he didn't want a medic; he wanted Eli to shoot
him. Begged him to shoot him.
Because, how can I go home to my wife without a dick?
Eli crawled back to his men and the soldier took out his .45 caliber
pistol and put a bullet in his brain.

* * *

Eli woke in a cold sweat.

The sheets were soaked.

The fan blowing on him gave him chills.

He went to the kitchen for another glass of milk. At the table, Eli smoked a cigarette and sipped the milk.

The car door was open, but Tanner didn't have his car keys.

He had fifteen hundred dollars and a gold lighter in his pockets.

He was stabbed in the spleen and died of a broken neck.

The attacker knew exactly where and when Tanner would be on Sunday at four o'clock in the afternoon.

The kitchen was stifling. He took the milk to the window for a breath of air. Even at 2:00 in the morning the street was lit up by traffic lights, street lamps and even traffic.

He forgot his cigars; maybe he forgot his keys as well?

But the car door was open.

The motive for the attack wasn't robbery. The damn lighter cost more than Eli's suits.

That he was attacked from behind meant Tanner didn't know his attacker.

Unless he did know him and Tanner turned his back on the man to allow him to get into the car.

Rosa would have mentioned it if Tanner was meeting someone. That someone would have been seen entering the building and wasn't.

Eli turned away from the window and put the empty glass in the sink.

He returned to bed and smoked another cigarette in bed in front of the fan. He wanted to sleep, needed the sleep, but he was afraid of another bad dream. The war had been over for more than four years, but he still lived it nearly every day.

The dead.

The destruction.

The wounded.

The battles he fought in, the men he killed, it lived in his mind as if it all happened just yesterday.

Over there killing was expected. It was your duty to kill. Back home it was a terrible crime punishable by life in prison or death.

Eli crushed the cigarette out in an ashtray and went back to sleep.

* * *

Eli was out of bed at 5:30, a habit he acquired as a Ranger that he couldn't seem to break. He made a small pot of coffee and drank two cups at the table and smoked two cigarettes.

As the sun broke, he performed his daily routine.

One hundred push-ups.

One hundred sit-ups.

One hundred squats holding a sixteen-pound medicine ball.

He attached the portable pull-up bar to the bathroom door frame and did fifty pull-ups, followed by fifty chin-ups.

On Saturday, he did the routine twice, in the morning and in the evening.

Then he shaved, took a shower and dressed in a summer suit, charcoal grey with a dark tie.

He only had breakfast in the apartment on weekends.

On the way to his car, Eli stopped at the corner coffee shop and picked up a bacon and egg sandwich and a container of coffee and ate on the drive into Manhattan.

* * *

The captain who lived a short distance from headquarters was already in his office by the time Eli arrived.

"I'll be running down leads most of the day," Eli said. "Okay if I team Bannon and Tyler to tie up some loose ends for me?"

"Do whatever you have to," Howe said. "After I hold a press conference the press will have a field day with this one."

"I'll call in with my locations," Eli said.

He left Howe's office and went to the squad room. Jack Bannon and Tyler were at their desks.

"Jack, Tyler, a moment," Eli said.

Bannon and Tyler followed Eli to his desk.

Eli handed Bannon the safe deposit box key. "Jack, two things," Eli said. "Head over to the bank and check the contents of this box and bag it into evidence. Then run down Tanner's gun permit."

"You got it," Bannon said.

"Tyler, see what you can find out about the knife from Wilson," Eli said. "Then head over to Tiffany's about the rings."

"Okay, Lieutenant," Tyler said.

"Meet me back here around four," Eli said.

* * *

Rosa Garcia wore white slacks and a sleeveless blouse when she opened the door to Eli.

Her eyes were still puffy and swollen, but she put on a small smile for Eli.

"Do you have some time for me?" Eli asked. "I have some questions that need to be asked."

"Please come in," Rosa said. "I just made coffee."

They went to the kitchen. Rosa filled two cups with coffee and they sat at the table.

"I think most of last night and again this morning about what you say," Rosa said. "I can think of no one who would hurt Roger."

Eli nodded as he took out his pad and pen.

"I have a few details I need to clear up," Eli said.

Rosa nodded.

"Mr. Tanner's car keys were not found with his body," Eli said.

"His keys?"

"The suspect didn't take anything from his clothing, so I doubt he took the keys," Eli said.

"Come," Rosa said.

Eli followed her to the master bedroom.

"The little box on the dresser," Rosa said. "He keep his tie pins and cuff links in the little box. Every night he put the car keys in there. He always forgets his keys and have to come back for them. Like his cigars. He very forgetful all the time."

Eli opened the box. Mixed in with the tie pins and cuff links was a set of keys.

"The car door was open," Eli said.

"He never lock the car when in the garage," Rosa said.

They returned to the kitchen.

Eli lit a cigarette and Rose put an ashtray on the table.

"Rosa, I have reason to believe that Mr. Tanner was about to ask you to marry him," Eli said.

Rosa stared at him. Her bottom lip quivered a bit, but she held her composure.

"Had he asked, what would you have said?"

"I would have said yes," Rosa said. "Roger was a very kind man. A woman could do worse than marry a wealthy man who love her and who is very kind."

"He told you he loved you?"

Rosa nodded. "Many times."

"Did you love him?"

"Not at first," Rosa said. "But, yes, I love him. He tell me he wanted children. I would have given him many. He used to say I have the hips for children."

"It's too complicated to go into right now, an attorney will do that, but Mr. Tanner left you well taken care of," Eli said.

"I don't… what that mean?" Rosa said.

"In his will," Eli said.

Rosa sighed and held back her tears.

"Mr. Tanner owned a gun," Eli said. "Did you know that?"

"Yes, I know that," Rosa said. "He only carry it when we go out together to dinner or a show. He say he bring it to protect me."

"He never carried it otherwise?"

"No."

"Do you know where he kept it?"

"The medicine cabinet," Rosa said.

"The… show me."

They returned to the master bedroom and entered the large bathroom. Above the sink was a wall-mounted, large medicine cabinet.

"Open the door," Rosa said.

Eli opened the door. It held the usual stuff.

"On the right is a button. Push it," Rosa said.

Eli felt for the button, pushed it and a hidden door opened. On a shelf was a gun box and a box of ammunition.

Eli removed the gun box and opened it. Inside was a .32 caliber revolver.

"I'll have to take these with me," Eli said.

Rosa nodded. "Is okay," she said. "I never touch them."

Eli took the gun box and ammunition with him when they returned to the kitchen.

"More coffee?" Rosa asked.

"Yes, thank you."

They sat at the table and Eli lit another cigarette.

"I'll be seeing Mr. Tanner's attorney this morning," Eli said. "His name is Gitter. I will ask him to call you."

"You have been very kind," Rosa said.

* * *

Sometimes life is kind and throws you an unexpected bone. Gitter's office was on the twelfth floor in the same Park Avenue South building as Tanner's banker, Leo Carson Jr.

As Eli rode up on an elevator, he wouldn't have bet himself that lawyer and banker knew each other quite well.

Gitter's office door was frosted glass. His name Martin Gitter was etched into the glass and painted in gold.

The receptionist asked Eli if he had an appointment.

Eli showed her his badge. She picked up the phone and made a call. When she hung up, she smiled and said, "Mr. Gitter is in."

She took Eli down a long hallway to an office and opened the door.

"Is it true?" Gitter asked. "What I just heard on the news about Roger Tanner."

"It's true," Eli said. "That's why I'm here."

Gitter was around sixty years old, had graying hair and wore thick glasses.

"Please sit and tell me what happened," Gitter said.

"What you heard on the news is what happened," Eli said.

"Jesus Christ, why?" Gitter said.

"I can't get into that," Eli said. "I'd like to know about his insurance policy and his will. I saw the policy for two million. You as his lawyer witnessed it. What's in his will?"

Gitter picked up his phone. "Bring me the complete file on Roger Tanner please," he said.

"When did you last see Mr. Tanner?" Eli asked.

"About two months ago when he amended his will," Gitter said.

The door opened and the receptionist entered with a large folder and set it on the desk. "Will that be all?"

Gitter nodded.

He opened the file and removed the documents.

"Basically half of Tanner's worth goes to various charities," Gitter said. "The other half goes to Rosa Garcia."

"Including the two million insurance policy?"

"She gets all of that plus the half," Gitter said. "He loved her. He was going to propose to her on her birthday."

"Did he tell you that?"

Gitter nodded.

"Is she… is she a suspect?" he asked.

"Not at the moment," Eli said. "Can you make me a copy of the will?"

Gitter nodded.

"When will you contact Rosa Garcia about the contents of the will?" Eli asked.

"As soon as you tell me it's okay to do so," Gitter said.

"In a few days," Eli said. "Do you know Leo Carson Jr.?"

"Of course," Gitter said. "I recommended him to Roger years ago."

"What about enemies Mr. Tanner may have had?" Eli said.

"This city is full of people who despise the rich," Gitter said.

* * *

"I just heard the news driving in to the office," Leo Carson Jr. said when Eli entered his office. "I can't believe it. Roger Tanner. Jesus."

"When did you see him last?"

"Couple of weeks," Carson said. "We had an appointment for this Friday."

"I saw that in his date book."

Carson wasn't what Eli expected. For one thing he was about seventy years old and the use of the title junior gave Eli the impression of a much younger man.

"Mr. Carson, what did you do for Mr. Tanner?" Eli asked.

"It's not complicated, really," Carson said. "I helped him manage his money and investments. Stocks, bonds, properties, things like that. In the past five years we've doubled his wealth."

"You said properties," Eli said. "Such as?"

"We talked about him buying a home on Long Island for him and Miss Garcia to live in after they were married," Carson said. "And he was interested in buying property in the city for investment purposes."

"With the West Side Real Estate Agency?" Eli said.

"Yes, exactly," Carson said. "My job is to manage Mr. Tanner's funds so that he can grow his wealth while at the same time buy the things he needs and wants."

"It doesn't sound so simple to me," Eli said.

"What about you, detective? Do you have anything besides your pension for your retirement?" Carson said. "I can set up an account for you. A nest egg, if you will."

"When I'm finished with this case, maybe I'll come see you," Eli said.

"You do that," Carson said.

"Would you happen to know how much Mr. Tanner paid for rent at the Charter Arms?" Eli asked.

"$2,000 a month," Carson said.

"Every month?"

"That's correct. Every month."

"My car cost half a month of his rent," Eli said.

"Let me open an account for you and you could drive a better car," Carson said.

"Can you think of any enemies Mr. Tanner may have had?" Eli asked.

"Anyone in this city who doesn't like rich people," Carson said.

* * *

The West Side Real Estate Agency was located in the Flatiron Building on Fifth Avenue and 23rd Street. Part of the triangular building faced Fifth Avenue, the other part faced Broadway.

The West Side Real Estate Agency was located on the eleventh floor facing Broadway.

The real estate agent handling Tanner's affairs was a woman named Pamela Kohn and she reminded Eli of his mother.

"I heard the news just a little while ago," Kohn said. "To say it's shocking is an understatement. I'm at a loss for sure."

Eli looked around the large room and counted a dozen empty desks. "Are you the only one here?"

"I'm the boss," Kohn said. "All of my agents are in the field, so to speak. Let's go to my office."

Eli followed Kohn into her office. The windows faced Broadway. They were closed to keep out the noise of traffic. An overhead fan cooled the room.

Kohn took her seat behind her desk. Eli took a chair facing it.

"The radio said Mr. Tanner was murdered in the parking garage of his building," Kohn said. "Who the hell would want to kill Roger Tanner?"

"That's what I intend to find out," Eli said. "What did you do for Mr. Tanner?"

"He was interested in a home on Long Island," Kohn said. "He wanted to surprise Miss Garcia with it as a wedding gift. He planned to drive her to the house and propose to her in the living room. When he told me his plans I nearly cried."

"I was told he was interested in real estate as investments," Eli said.

"Yes. He invested in several buildings in Manhattan," Kohn said. "He was about to purchase an eight-story building as a condo."

"What's a condo?" Eli asked.

"A condominium."

"Okay, what's a condominium?"

"Each apartment in a building is for sale like homes," Kohn said. "Instead of buying a home a person buys the apartment. Every tenant owns their apartment and a fee is paid to a board every month for maintenance of the building."

"And Mr. Tanner was interested in buying an apartment?"

"Good heavens, no. The entire building," Kohn said. "We would then sell each apartment for a tidy profit."

"How much for the building?"

"The one he was interested in was in the West Village," Kohn said. "About $80,000, I believe."

"He was a smart man, Mr. Tanner," Eli said.

"As smart as they come when it came to business," Kohn said. "But more than that. He was honest and fair man. Smart, honest and fair are hard to come by."

"Did you know if he had any enemies?" Eli asked.

"If he did, I wasn't aware of any," Kohn said. "Except for people who don't like the rich."

* * *

On the way back to his office, Eli stopped at the diner on Seventh Avenue and 23rd Street and grabbed a burger. The afternoon edition of the newspapers were out and he grabbed a copy of *The Daily Mirror*.

He ate at the counter and read the lead story on Tanner's murder. Apparently the entire city was shocked over the incident. Last month seven winos were rolled and killed on The Bowery and nobody batted an eye.

Tanner was rich. The winos were not. Tanner got the headlines. The winos got lost in the shuffle and buried at the city's expense.

The diner had good looking apple pie and Eli had a slice for dessert.

* * *

Bannon and Tyler were waiting for Eli when he returned to the office.

41

"The captain wants to see us," Bannon said.

Eli made his report first.

"I hate it when the victim comes off looking like a saint," Howe said. "The fucking newspapers harp on it for all its worth."

Bannon went next. "I ran down his gun permit. Issued out of Albany. He belonged to a gun club in Westchester County where he purchased the .32 caliber revolver. The safe deposit box at First Manhattan had original documents of all his stuff. His will, finances, things like that. No cash, no jewelry, just documents. I have it in evidence."

"You said original documents," Howe said.

"It's easy to make as many copies as you want using the mimeograph machine," Eli said. "They are as good as the original. They say by 1950 this company called Xerox will come out with a self contained copy machine."

"As fascinating as that is, it tells us what about a suspect?" Howe said. He looked at Tyler. "What do you got?"

"I went to Tiffany's about the ring," Tyler said. "He bought it for the woman all right. Cost a bundle. Then I headed over to see Wilson. He still doesn't know what type of knife was used, but I have a theory. Wilson said the wound went in just over fifteen inches. So I went home and checked my souvenirs."

"Your souvenirs?" Howe said.

"I was in the 101st Airborne," Tyler said. "We got dropped all over the fucking place on D-Day. Everywhere except the drop zone. It was a total fucking mess. You should have been there."

"Detective Tyler, my blood pressure is high enough," Howe said. "Get to the point, please."

"I brought home a bayonet I took off a Kraut I killed on D-Day," Tyler said. "I measured it and it's exactly fifteen and a quarter inches long. I got it in my desk."

"Get it," Howe said.

While Tyler left Howe's office, Eli lit a cigarette.

"What do you think?" Howe asked.

"I've seen a lot of German bayonets," Eli said. "It could fit."

Tyler returned with the bayonet in a paper bag. He removed the bag and handed the bayonet to Howe.

"Did you show this to Wilson?" Howe asked.

"Not yet," Tyler said.

"Get it over to him, see what he says," Howe said.

"Jack, what's that gun club in Westchester?" Eli asked.

* * *

Driving back to the office from the Westchester Rod and Gun Club in Yonkers, Eli replayed his conversation with the manager in his mind.

Roger Tanner became a member a little more than a year ago. He told the manager he was interested in learning to shoot, but wanted nothing large. The manager showed him the .32, which he later purchased.

At first, Tanner couldn't hit a barn from six feet away. With practice over time, he became a pretty good shot. He purchased the .32 directly from the club.

When in the club, Tanner rarely spoke to anyone except the instructors.

The manager was sorry to hear what happened to him.

Except for Tyler, the office was empty when Eli arrived in the squad room.

Tyler was at his desk, typing a report.

Eli sat on the edge of the desk and lit a cigarette. "How did you make out?"

"Wilson said the Kraut bayonet is the murder weapon, no doubt," Tyler said.

"Not an American bayonet?"

"You carried one, same as me. Ours are very different," Tyler said. "Ours is only ten inches long tip to handle."

"Is that what you're typing?"

"Yeah. Almost done."

"Tomorrow, you and Jack call every pawn shop and Army/Navy store in the five boroughs," Eli said. "See who bought and sold German bayonets."

"A lot of guys brought back their own same as me," Tyler said.

"I know, but we can't knock on the door of every GI in the city and ask to see their war trinkets," Eli said.

Tyler removed the report from the typewriter and set it on the desk. "I'm going home," he said. "I'm bushed."

Alone, Eli went to his desk, picked up the phone and made a call.

"This is Mavis," the woman on the other end said.

"It's Eli. Are you free?"

"I'm free," Mavis said.

"I'll be right over," Eli said.

"I'll have a hot bath waiting," Mavis said and hung up.

Five
_____

Eli rested his head against the rim of the large, sunken bathtub. The weariness in his bones seemed to fade away as the hot water penetrated his skin and muscles.

Mavis Waite was a high-class call girl who operated out of her East Side apartment located on Fifty-Second Street and 1st Avenue. The apartment was on the twentieth floor with a balcony that faced the East River. Sometimes they sat on the balcony and just watched the river.

Eli had been a client of Mavis since late '46.

He returned from the war with a problem. All across Europe and Africa, whenever possible the men engaged the services of prostitutes. Most of the men figured they wouldn't make it home and sought comfort in the arms of a woman.

Any woman.

Even if it was for just a short while.

As an officer, Eli resisted such temptation until he nearly was killed in Africa by a German grenade.

After a while, wherever his unit went, prostitutes were always close by and he began to partake.

Eli lost count, but by the time he made it home in early '46, he must have engaged the services of a hundred women. Africa, Sicily, Paris and finally Germany. The price was cheap. Fifty cents to two dollars. In Germany, the whores would fuck you for a chocolate bar. As cheap as a human life in a war zone.

The problem Eli brought home wasn't physical. It was mental, so said the department shrinks.

He couldn't get or keep an erection with a woman unless he paid for it. With a normal woman he was impotent.

The shrinks showed him ink blots and talked about his mother and after a dozen visits, Eli told him he was cured just to be rid of them.

How he came to Mavis was by chance. In the spring of '46 he investigated the murder of a man on the Lower West Side. The man had her phone number in his wallet.

Eli went to speak with her and she identified the man as a client.

Two months later, after he dropped the shrinks, Eli called her for an appointment.

Mavis charged twenty dollars a session. Eli could only afford two visits a month. He usually called when he was working a high stress level case.

In the first visit all they did was talk. He told her about his problem. She told him she'd seen it before with returning veterans. They talked in the second and third sessions as well. She understood what war did to men after they returned home.

In the fourth visit, Mavis told him he was spending his hard-earned money on chitchat. She saw the nervous anxiety on his face and told him she understood and would be gentle.

To his surprise, Eli's erection was immediate and although it was over in just a few minutes, the relief he felt at having performed nearly brought him to tears.

"Hey, where are you?" Mavis asked.

Eli opened his eyes.

Naked, Mavis walked toward the tub, a glass of white wine in one hand, a scotch and soda in the other.

She handed Eli the scotch and then slowly entered the tub and sat opposite Eli with her breasts above the water.

"I heard on the radio about this millionaire who was murdered in a garage," Mavis said. "As soon as you called me I knew it was your case."

Eli sipped scotch. "It is," he said.

Mavis sipped wine.

"There is something you should know," she said. "I turn thirty this September."

"I remember," Eli said.

Mavis told him last year that she would quit when she turned thirty and leave the city and move home to Ohio.

"Do you want to stay the night?" Mavis asked.

"I can only afford twenty," Eli said. "We homicide cops don't make much."

"Don't be silly," Mavis said. "I wouldn't charge you if I asked. And I enjoy your company."

Eli sipped and looked at her.

"So, are you staying or not?"

"Can you wash my shirt?"

"Of course. I can feed you, too."

"Good, cause I'm starved."

* * *

Eli knew that it was just an act for his benefit, but Mavis made it appear so real that sometimes he almost believed it. The way she dug her nails into his back and arched her own, moaned so softly and then gripped him so tightly he barely could breathe.

An act, all of it, for the benefit of his fragile male ego.

As the lay in bed afterward, he lit a cigarette and she snatched it away the way a wife or girlfriend would do when she is comfortable with her man.

Eli lit another.

Mavis blew a smoke ring and said, "What would you like me to cook for you?"

"What have you got?" Eli asked.

"I have two nice steaks waiting to be pan fried in butter," Mavis said.

"Sounds good."

Mavis sat up and reached for her robe. There was a small white scar on her upper right back and Eli reached up and touched it.

"Don't bring back bad memories," Mavis said.

She stood and went to the kitchen.

A few years ago in early winter, Eli called for a session, but when he arrived he found Mavis bloody and beaten. Her previous client wanted to play a little too rough and she refused. He played anyway.

At first she didn't want to tell Eli who beat her, but he persisted and she finally broke. He was a cop, a patrolman from The Bronx.

Eli tracked the patrolman to his precinct in The East Bronx and confronted him in the parking lot after dark

"She's just a fucking whore," the patrolman said.

"She's also a human being," Eli said.

"She got paid," the patrolman said. "That's all fucking whores care about, anyway, getting paid."

Eli stared at the patrolman. "I saw how you did beating a woman. How are you dancing with a man?"

"You mean you?" the patrolman said.

"Having any?"

Eli put the patrolman in the hospital for two weeks. The patrolman never talked so Eli was never charged. Soon after that, the patrolman quit and the incident forgotten.

Eli tossed on his shorts and T-shirt and went to the kitchen. Mavis was at the stove, pan frying two large steaks. He went to her, pulled down the robe to expose the cigarette burn scar and gently kissed it.

"I told you not to think about that," Mavis said. "Go toss the salad."

Eli went to the counter to toss the salad. When it was tossed, he added oil and vinegar, salt and pepper.

"It's a beautiful night, Eli. Why don't we eat on the balcony?" Mavis said.

They ate at the table on the balcony and watched garbage ships, tug boats and small vessels sail up and down the East River.

Afterward, over coffee and pie, Mavis said, "There's a nice girl on Seventy-First and 2nd I can set you up with come September."

"No, don't do that?" Eli said.

"She really nice. A redhead," Mavis said.

"Please, no."

"More coffee?"

"Yes."

Mavis went inside to the kitchen and returned with the pot and filled both cups.

"I put your shirt in the washer," she said. "I'll need your shorts and T-shirt."

"As soon as we finish our... Eli said.

Mavis sat on his lap and looked him in the eyes. A strange little smile crossed her lips as she lifted herself a few inches, reached under and pulled Eli's shorts down to his ankles.

"I feel something hard," she whispered in his ear.

"You are an evil woman," Eli said.

"Don't talk," Mavis whispered.

Eli entered her and it was like floating in a vat of warm oil.

"Oh God," he whispered.

"He's got nothing to do with this," Mavis said. She opened her robe and jutted her breasts. "Kiss," she said.

* * *

Eli opened his eyes at 5:30, entangled in Mavis's legs and hair. He quietly freed himself, got up and went to the kitchen.

Next to his cigarettes was a note.

Coffee pot is ready. Just turn on the stove.

While the coffee percolated, he grabbed a quick shower and put on his clean underwear, T-shirt, pants and clean shirt.

The coffee was ready and he drank a cup on the balcony and watched the horizon slowly lighten.

He wished it could stay this way forever, that little window of time caught between light and dark where the air was cool and smelled fresh and the rats weren't visible.

Eli lit a cigarette and watched a garbage scow sail west on the river.

Something he never told Mavis, or even the shrinks, popped into his mind. It happened in late '44 after Paris was liberated. His squad of Rangers was sent to support a tank division ordered to destroy a German stronghold near the border.

They entered a small village that was mostly destroyed. A church was intact, though and Eli and some of his men checked it out before calling for a rest.

They entered the church.

A GI was raping a woman on the altar.

On the fucking altar.

His hands were around her throat and he squealed like a pig as he thrust inside the woman.

Eli handed his grease gun to one of his men, drew his .45, walked to the altar, put the .45 to the man's head and blew his brains out.

Calmly, Eli holstered the .45, took back his grease gun and walked out of the church.

His men stared at him.

"Fubar," one of the men uttered.

Later, in Germany, Eli found out the rapist was a captain and the woman was a French nun.

Fubar.

Maybe that was why he reacted so strongly to the patrolman who beat Mavis?

Eli finished his cigarette and coffee, went inside and closed the balcony door.

He left Mavis sleeping as he went downstairs and drove to work.

Six

The squad room was empty when Eli arrived with his egg sandwich and coffee. He sat in the quiet and ate and pushed Mavis out of his mind and thought about Roger Tanner.

The man wasn't so much murdered as executed.

Why?

Robbery wasn't the motive.

There didn't appear to be a jealous husband or boyfriend on the horizon.

A grudge perhaps?

Against what?

Held by whom?

Tanner's murder took careful planning and perfect timing.

It wasn't a chance encounter by any means. Weeks, maybe even months of surveillance went into the execution of the murder.

Eli lit a cigarette and sipped his coffee.

It wasn't a professional hit. A pro wouldn't use a knife or need to get close enough to break a man's neck.

They just shoot you in the back of the head and walk away.

Still, every angle needed to be investigated.

By 8:30, the squad room was filling up.

Bannon and Tyler stopped by his desk.

"Still want us to work the pawn shop angle?" Tyler said.

"Yes. Wait. Tyler, get started on that," Eli said. "Jack, I want you to dig deep and see if Roger Tanner has any mob connections. No matter how remote, check it out."

"That's whistling in a graveyard, Lieutenant," Bannon said.

"I know, but no stone left unturned and all that," Eli said.

Bannon and Tyler went to their desks.

Eli went in to see Howe.

"I'll be at The Charter Arms for a while," Eli said. "I need a uniform."

"Grab one out of roll call," Howe said.

"Right."

"Are you running a lead or going to see that woman?" Howe asked.

"Neither," Eli said. "Think time."

* * *

Mavis woke up a bit after 9:00. As she usually did during the spring and summer months, she took the first cup of coffee on the balcony. She allowed herself a cigarette, a habit she's been trying to break unsuccessfully for years, although she smoked just a handful a day now.

She watched a few small ships on the river as she sipped and smoked and thought about Eli.

It was odd how after he left she could always smell his scent on the pillow. She could never remember any other man's scent on the pillow except his.

She thought about Art Howe, Eli's captain and boss. He was one of her first customers going back to '42. He was a captain in Vice back then and knew how to make connections to the girls not on the street. She was new in town and eager to build up a client base so she took him on.

Howe claimed that his wife had physical problems and wasn't able to satisfy his needs. His visits were once a month at first, then every other week and finally weekly. She never asked where the money came from and he never volunteered the information.

Howe was as strong as a bull, the equal to Eli and he could go all night if given the opportunity. He wasn't rough, but he wasn't gentle either.

And he had a mean streak that she didn't see until a year ago.

He called for an appointment and she told him she was quitting the business. He told her it was a particularly bad week and he needed the relief. She was adamant and told him she could refer him to a friend of hers, a nice redhead.

That's when he got nasty and told her he didn't want a redhead, he wanted her. Again, she refused. He told her one last time or he would tell Eli that he was a client. How awkward would that be around the office, captain and lieutenant both fucking the same whore, especially given the fact that Eli was in love with her.

How he knew that about Eli was anyone's guess as Eli never spoke about his work.

Mavis agreed to one last visit.

He never spoke of the incident to Eli, but she often wondered if it was true that Eli was in love with her. Sometimes he didn't act like it. Other times he was so sweet she almost forgot he was a client.

None of it mattered, not really.

She went inside to take a shower.

* * *

Eli walked into the precinct two blocks away from headquarters and told the desk sergeant he needed a uniform for a few hours.

Roll call had just ended, the desk sergeant said, see who is available.

Patrolman Joseph White, a Back man and twelve-year veteran of the department was working alone because his partner was out with the flu. White was as tall as Eli, though nowhere near as stocky.

"What do you need, Lieutenant?" White asked.

"Company," Eli said. "My car is parked outside."

Eli stopped for containers of coffee at the donut shop on West 14th Street before proceeding north to The Charter Arms.

"So what do you need from me?" White asked.

"I'm not sure," Eli said.

"This has to do with that millionaire killed last week though, doesn't it?"

"It does," Eli said. "But don't ask me what."

"I won't. Okay if I smoke?"

"Go right ahead."

White lit a cigarette and he and Eli sipped their coffee as Eli drove north. When they reached the Charter Arms, Eli showed his badge to the guard on duty at the garage and he parked in a vacant space near Tanner's car.

After White and Eli exited Eli's car, White looked at the chalk outline beside Tanner's car.

"Man killed with a guard a few hundred feet away," White said.

"Stand beside the car," Eli said. "By the driver's door."

White stood facing the door.

"Open it," Eli said. "It was open when the body was discovered."

White opened the door.

"Now just stay there a moment," Eli said.

Eli stood behind White. Directly behind Eli was an iron support beam. Eli stood behind the beam.

"Go to the elevator and walk to the car. Close the door," Eli said.

White closed the door and walked to the elevator, turned and walked back to the car.

"Did you notice me?" Eli asked.

"Yeah, but only because I knew you were there," White said.

"Open the car door again."

White opened the door and Eli stepped forward, shoved his left finger into White's back and encircled his neck with his right arm.

"Fuck, Lieutenant, you could a warned me," White said.

Eli released White. "I doubt Tanner had much warning," he said.

White nodded. "Over in two, three seconds," he said.

"Except that you knew it was me," Eli said. "Had the attack been real, you would have fought like hell to survive. Even with the bayonet in your side you wouldn't have given up so easily."

"I see what you mean," White said. "The newspapers didn't say about the bayonet, just that he was killed."

"The captain put a restriction on information," Eli said. "To discourage a copycat."

"Like that strangler back in '43," White said.

"I was somewhere else in '43," Eli said. "Let's do the attack thing again."

White turned and faced the car. Eli got behind the iron support beam and noticed a spent cigarette on the floor. He stared at the butt.

"Hold on, Joe," Eli said.

White turned. "What?"

"Cigarette butt," Eli said. He looked at the iron beam. "Shit."

"What?" White said again.

"Wait here and don't touch that butt," Eli said.

Eli went to his car and opened the glove box where he always kept a roll of nickels. He took the roll and walked up the ramp past the guard to the street to the pay phone on the corner.

"Roscoe, it's Eli. Grab your bag and meet me in the parking garage of The Charter Arms," Eli said.

"What's going on, Lieutenant?" Roscoe asked.

"Bring a couple of your guys," Eli said. "Make it quick."

"Be close to lunch time by then," Roscoe said.

"I'll buy. Just get over here," Eli said and hung up.

* * *

Roscoe used a tweezers to pick up the cigarette. "Camel unfiltered," he said. "How did we miss it the first go round?"

"Everybody focused on the victim and the car," Eli said. "And nobody looked at this."

Eli pointed to the iron support beam. "If he smoked a cigarette behind the beam, he may have…"

"Touched it," Roscoe said. He turned to his two technicians. "Dust every square inch of that fucking beam. Jesus Christ, I'm a Goddamn idiot."

* * *

"It could take a while to get a match on prints," Roscoe said. "If he's even on record."

"What about the cigarette?" Eli asked.

"Must be a half million who smoke Camels just in this city," Roscoe said.

"Let's grab some lunch," Eli said.

Roscoe turned to his two men, "Get back and start processing prints."

"He said lunch," one of the men said.

"For me, not you. Get going," Roscoe said.

"Meet us at the coffee shop on Sixty-Third and Broadway," Eli said.

* * *

Eli, White and Roscoe had burgers, fries and Coke at the counter of the busy coffee shop.

"How many sets of prints came off that support beam?" Eli asked Roscoe.

"Hard to say," Roscoe said. "Not many people go out of their way to touch a support beam in a parking garage."

"He had to have touched it," Eli said. "He's standing there. Waiting. He's early and smokes a cigarette. He probably wasn't even aware he touched it like when you're talking to someone and lean against the wall or a desk. He touched it."

"Why do you think the victim didn't fight?" White asked.

"Element of surprise is my guess," Roscoe said. "My cousin is a mailman in Queens. He keeps a sharp eye out for dogs when he approaches a house to deliver the mail. It's the dog you don't see that bites you."

"Could be," Eli said. "What do you think, Joe?"

"I'm just a beat cop," White said.

"That doesn't mean you don't have an opinion," Eli said.

White washed down a bite of his burger with a sip of Coke to clear his throat. "Surprise is a big factor in a fight," he said. "The guy who throws the first punch in a bar fight usually wins, even if the other guy is bigger and stronger. Only in the movies does John Wayne get off the floor and kick ass after getting sucker-punched. Add in the knife and Tanner never had a chance."

"I don't disagree with you, Joe, but it still doesn't explain why he put up no fight at all," Eli said. "There were no signs he struggled in the least. The medical report says he died instantly from a broken neck. Tanner was no small man and should have put up some sort of battle, even a weak one."

"I saw some cherry pie behind the counter," Roscoe said. "Let's grab some."

* * *

Tyler and Bannon were at their desks when Eli entered the squad room.

"Who knew there was so many pawnshops and Army/Navy stores in this stinking city," Tyler said.

"And?" Eli said.

"And every last one of them has German bayonets for sale," Tyler said. "I'd need a dozen men working this angle to cover it all."

"You don't have twelve men," Eli said. "You have you. Jack?"

"Still digging," Bannon said. This guy Tanner is as close to perfect as I've ever seen. A regular saint in shining armor."

"I think you mean knight in shining armor," Tyler said.

"Who knows what I mean?" Bannon said. "I don't even know anymore."

Eli went to his desk, sat and lit a cigarette.

Art Howe came out of his office wearing his suit jacket, something he did only when he was leaving for a meeting or to go home.

Howe sat on the edge of Eli's desk. "How was your morning?"

"Couple of things we missed," Eli said. "A cigarette butt behind an iron support beam near Tanner's car and fingerprints on the beam," Eli said. "I had Roscoe's team dust for prints and he has the butt at the lab."

Howe nodded. "It could be his prints are on file. Good work, Eli."

"Headed out?" Eli said.

"Meeting with the chief and commissioner at the mayor's office," Howe said.

"See you later, Art," Eli said.

After Howe left, Tyler approached Eli's desk. "Got a pawnshop in Times Square sold a German bayonet a few weeks ago. I think I'll head over and talk to the guy."

Eli nodded.

"How many people you know smoke Camel unfiltered cigarettes?" Eli asked.

"Only everybody."

After Tyler left the office, Eli called the lab and asked for Roscoe.

"Got something interesting," Roscoe said. "Come take a look and bring donuts."

"Donuts?"

"The boys are still pissed you didn't take them to lunch," Roscoe said.

"You kicked them out," Eli said.

"A dozen mixed should do," Roscoe said. "No sprinkles. Nobody likes sprinkles."

* * *

Eli set the box of donuts on Roscoe's desk and walked over to the examination table where Roscoe was waiting for him. A microscope was on the table.

"Take a look," Roscoe said.

Eli placed his right eye to the lens and looked at the Camel cigarette.

"See those ridges on the end of the butt?" Roscoe said.

"I see them. What are they?" Eli said.

"That's what I said," Roscoe said.

Eli looked up. "To who?"

"To myself. It's how I work. I ask myself questions."

"What answer did you give yourself?"

"Look on the counter," Roscoe said.

Lined up beside the microscope were various plastic and metal cigarette filters.

"Very popular in movies of the thirties," Roscoe said. "The woman would always put her cigarette in a holder, the rich guy, too. Keeps your fingers from getting stained, especially if it's an unfiltered cigarette."

"A filter made those ridges?" Eli asked.

"I'm about to test the patterns to see what brand filter makes those kind of ridges," Roscoe said.

"Should I wait?"

"I'll call you."

* * *

"Lieutenant, I'm headed home," Bannon said. "Tanner is as clean as they come as far as I can tell."

"Work with Tyler tomorrow on the bayonet angle," Eli said.

Bannon nodded. "Are you sticking around?"

"Waiting on a call from Roscoe," Eli said.

"Good night then," Bannon said.

After Bannon left, Eli lit a cigarette and put his feet up on the desk. He felt weary and drained. He was about to reach for the phone when it rang.

"Lieutenant Rico," Eli said when he picked up the call.

"It's Roscoe. The cigarette filter is made by a company called Apex Plastics and is marketed under the name Filt-ease."

"Catchy," Eli said.

"They are sold pretty much anywhere you can buy a pack of butts."

Eli scribbled the name Filt-ease on a slip of paper and said, "Thanks, Roscoe."

"Thanks for the donuts," Roscoe said and hung up.

Eli sat for a few more minutes and rolled things around in his mind.

The suspect smoked Camel unfiltered cigarettes and used a Filt-ease plastic filter. He used a German bayonet. He finished his victim by crushing his windpipe. He was meticulous and a careful planner. He was also very smart.

"I'm going home," Eli said aloud.

Seven

The Generals were caught *with their pants down. After the success of D-Day, they were lulled to sleep believing Hitler's Arms was defeated and in disarray.*

They were all wrong. All except Patton, who wanted to keep rolling his tanks all the way to Berlin.

Eli's unit of Rangers was attached to the 101st Airborne and when the German Army shocked the world on December 16th, 1944 by staging the Battle of the Bulge, the Allied forces were caught completely off guard.

Eli's unit was in Bastogne when the German Army surrounded the entire town. Fighting was fierce and non-stop and by December 21st, Allied ammunition was restricted to just ten rounds of artillery per day.

Fighting, at times was hand-to-hand.

Eli got in the thick of it with a tall, powerful German soldier inside a bombed out church. Neither had ammunition for their weapons. Both drew bayonets. The German got in a few good licks and bloodied Eli's forearms, but Eli got the upper hand and used a technique called a Ranger Choke Hold to break the man's neck.

On the 26th of December, Patton and his Army rolled in and opened up the gates to Bastogne and every German tank was destroyed.

* * *

Eli opened his eyes and got out of bed. He was drenched in sweat and went to the kitchen. He turned on the lights, then the wall fan and filled a glass with milk and ice cubes.

He reached for his pack of cigarettes on the table. His brand was Chesterfield filtered and he lit one using his father's lighter.

The son of a bitch used a Ranger Choke Hold on Roger Tanner.

The hold was taught in Ranger School, drilled into each and every member of the squad until killing by snapping a neck came as second nature.

Eli used it on a German soldier in Bastogne.

Death was instantaneous.

The reason Tanner didn't put up a fight.

But why the German Bayonet?

The attacker obviously didn't need it to kill Tanner.

Eli gulped cold milk until the glass was empty. He finished the cigarette and returned to bed.

He tossed, turned and finally fell back to sleep.

* * *

After his morning workout, Eli shaved, showered and dressed. He left the apartment just after 7:00 in the morning.

On the way to his car, he went into the large candy store on the corner that opened at 7:00 due to the early bird newspapers.

He picked up the *News* and *Mirror* and a pack of Chesterfield Cigarettes.

"Do you carry Filt-ease cigarette filters?" he asked the clerk behind the counter.

He set a box of ten filters on the counter. "Forty cents a box."

Eli paid the extra forty cents and went to his car that was parked across the street.

He sat behind the wheel and opened the new pack of cigarettes. He read the package of Filt-ease cigarette filters. It claimed to remove harmful chemicals from the cigarette, prevent stains on fingers while not changing the flavor of your brand.

Each filter was good for ten cigarettes before you had to switch it out for a new one. Eli opened the package and removed one filter. It was black and about an inch long.

Eli lit a cigarette and attached the filter. It was an odd feeling, the plastic between his lips instead of the cotton and paper filter, but the draw was easy and the flavor seemed unchanged.

He started the car and drove to work.

*   *   *

As was the usual, Eli was first in the squad room. He sat at his desk and ate an egg sandwich and scanned the newspapers.

Tanner's murder had been moved off the front page and he couldn't find a reference to it anywhere in the *News*. The *Mirror* had a short, two paragraph story on page thirty-seven just before the Op-ed Page.

By 9:00, Howe, Tyler, Bannon and most of the detectives had arrived.

From his desk, Tyler said, "Lieutenant, line one for you."

Eli picked up his phone and punched the button for line one.

"Lieutenant Rico," he said.

"Is me, Rosa Garcia," Rosa said.

"Miss Garcia, how are you?" Eli said.

"The lawyer Gitter call like you say," Rosa said. "He want to see me at 11:00 this morning."

"I talked to him the other day," Eli said. "He seemed like a fine lawyer and decent man."

"Yes, but it all so much for me," Rosa said. "Can you go with me to talk?"

"I'm a police detective, Miss Garcia," Eli said. "That's not my place."

"I know that. Please, I no drive and I don't know where the office is," Rosa said. "Can you do this for me, please?"

Eli sighed. "I'll pick you up at 10:00."

"Thank you. Thank you so much."

After he hung up, Eli went in to see Howe.

"Something I want to run by you," Eli said.

"Grab a chair," Howe said.

Eli sat in the chair opposite the desk. He told Howe about the cigarette and filter and showed him one.

"Our boy is a smoker," Howe said. "Narrows it down to half the city."

"A lot less if you factor in the plastic filter," Eli said. "I never even heard of them until yesterday."

Howe held the filter. "See a lot of these in old movies from the thirties."

Eli nodded. "Art, I think our man is military or ex-military."

"Again, half the male population of this city alone," Howe said.

"Art, Tanner was killed using a Ranger Choke Hold," Eli said.

Howe stared at Eli. "Are you sure?" he said. Then he nodded. "Yeah, I guess you are at that."

"Of course, you don't need to be a Ranger to learn the hold, but the odds are that's where you learn it," Eli said.

"If you're right, that's one major shitstorm," Howe said.

"I know," Eli said. "I'd like to keep that confidential for now."

Howe nodded. "It's your case, but I agree anyway."

"I'll be at Tanner's lawyer's office for about an hour," Eli said. "I'll leave the number with dispatch."

*   *   *

Eli parked curbside in front of The Charter Arms and waited for Rosa on the sidewalk. He was ten minutes early and smoked a cigarette, using the plastic filter.

He thought about the Ranger Choke Hold, or more specifically where one would learn it without the benefit of being a Ranger.

He took out his pocket notebook and made a note in pencil.

Check karate schools.

The doorman opened the lobby door for Rosa and Eli put the notebook and pencil away.

As she approached his car, Eli opened the door.

Rosa smiled at him. "Thank you, Lieutenant," she said.

She wore a simple, sleeveless blue dress with matching shoes and carried a small, black handbag. Once she sat, Eli closed the door and got behind the wheel.

"The lawyer say Park Avenue South is his address," Rosa said. "I wrote it down."

Eli started the engine and pulled away from the curb. "No need, I know where it is," he said.

Rosa was silent as Eli headed south for a few blocks.

"The lawyer, what he going to say?" she asked as Eli skirted east through Central Park.

"My guess is he's going to read Tanner's will and tell you what he left you," Eli said.

"Left me?"

"In his will," Eli said. "From what I could determine Roger loved you very much."

Rosa nodded. She misted up a bit, but choked it back and smiled.

"I love him, too," she said. "But not for his money. He was a good man and he treat me like a woman and not a servant."

"He was, by all accounts, a good man. Mind a few questions?"

"No."

"We've interviewed his friends from the card game," Eli said. "Can you think of any other friends he might have had that didn't play cards with him? Someone outside that circle."

Rosa thought for a moment. "No, I don't think so. Did you check his date books? He like to write things down."

"We checked," Eli said. "Maybe someone casual? Someone he wouldn't write in his appointment book?"

Rosa shook her head. "I don't remember him talking about someone like that."

"It was just a question," Eli said. "We're almost there."

*   *   *

"I no understand what all this means," Rosa said. "What are you saying?"

From behind his desk, Gitter looked at Eli and Rosa.

"In short, Miss Garcia, you have inherited half of Mr. Tanner's wealth," Gitter said. "More than four million dollars in all. There is considerable paperwork to sign if you are up to it."

"Can I have some water please?" Rosa asked.

Gitter looked at Eli.

"There's a cooler in the hallway," he said.

Eli went into the hallway and filled a paper cup with water and brought it to Rosa. She gulped and emptied the cup. "Thank you," she said.

The phone on the desk rang. Gitter picked it up, listened, pushed a button and said, "Line two is for you, Lieutenant. You can take it across the hall."

Eli went back to the hall, entered an office, and picked up the phone.

"Lieutenant Rico," he said.

"It's Tyler and we got another one," Tyler said.

"Where?"

"Village on Bleeker Street," Tyler said. "Jack's with me. Address is 147."

"Keep a lid on the place," Eli said. "I'll be there in twenty minutes."

Eli hung up and returned to Gitter's office. Rosa was crying in her hands.

"Police emergency," he said. "I have to go."

"I'll see Miss Garcia gets home by cab," Gitter said.

* * *

Four cruisers were parked curbside in front of Milo's Jazz Club on Bleeker Street. Several patrolmen stood with Tyler and Bannon out front.

"What is this place?" Eli asked.

"A jazz club for jivers," Tyler said.

"Jiver?" Eli said.

"A place for those that wear turtlenecks to gather, smoke reefer and listen to live jazz," Tyler said. "The musicians are all black, but the patrons are all white."

Eli looked at the sign. "Who is Milo?"

"He was the owner," Tyler said.

"Was? What is he now?" Eli asked.

"Dead," Tyler said.

* * *

Milo Magrady lived in the apartment above his jazz club. It wasn't

69

a large apartment, but had a bedroom, kitchen, living room and a small den. There was a balcony in the bedroom that overlooked a courtyard garden.

Magrady was face down on the living room floor in front of the door that connected to the kitchen. He was completely naked. A dried stab wound was in his left side, but Eli didn't need a medical report to see he died from a broken neck.

Kneeling beside the body, Eli said, "Did you call Wilson and Roscoe?"

"Right after we called you," Tyler said.

"He's been dead since last night or early this morning," Eli said.

"Looks it," Tyler said.

"Wilson and Roscoe are here," Bannon said.

Wilson took one glance at Magrady and said, "He makes it number two."

"Number two, what?" Bannon said.

"Stabbed in the side and killed by a broken neck," Wilson said.

"Jack, Tyler, have a look downstairs," Eli said.

While Bannon and Tyler went downstairs, Eli had a look around the apartment. The bedroom was larger than expected and filled with clutter, mostly books on jazz and music. The closet held pants on one side, shirts on the other, and shoes in the middle.

The dressers were full of underwear, T-shirts and socks. A wood box on the dresser contained cuff links, watches and rings.

He checked the bathroom. The medicine chest held the usual stuff, shaving soap, razors, aspirins. A towel was hung over the bar that held the shower curtain in place. The towel was damp. He moved the curtain and checked the tub. It was dry to the touch.

The kitchen was cramped and full of stuff on the counters and table. More books on jazz, sheet music, records and magazines.

A book was open face down on the table. The spine was cracked.

Someone had recently been reading the book and set it down too hard.

The book was on the history of jazz in contemporary America.

He checked the refrigerator. It was fairly well stocked but the odd thing was a three-pound coffee can behind the milk. Eli removed the can and opened the lid. It was full of marijuana. He replaced the lid and set the can back into the fridge.

At least he wasn't killed by dope fiends.

Eli continued to hunt and peck around the kitchen and found the trashcan in a slide-out cabinet under the sink. He checked the garbage and found coffee grinds, egg shells, two empty packages of frozen foods and three cigarette butts.

He scooped out the butts.

They were Camel unfiltered.

"Roscoe, get in here," Eli said loudly.

Roscoe opened the kitchen door and stepped inside.

Eli held out his hand and showed Roscoe the butts.

"Hello," Roscoe said.

"Take them down to lab and let me know," Eli said. "I don't think Magrady was a smoker. No ashtrays in the apartment."

"My guys have dusted the living room, bedroom and his little den," Roscoe said. "Just the kitchen is left."

"Go ahead," Eli said.

He returned to the bedroom and checked the balcony door. It was unlocked and he went out to the small balcony. It was maybe fifteen feet high and overlooked a small garden that was protected by a brick wall.

The balcony was also protected by an iron fence about five feet high. It was painted green and Eli noticed fresh scratch marks in the paint.

"Roscoe, get out here," Eli shouted.

After a few seconds, Roscoe appeared. "What?"

"Those scratch marks in the paint, I want them analyzed," Eli said.

Roscoe looked at the marks. "What are you thinking?"

"I don't know," Eli said.

Wilson appeared on the balcony. "Well, this is cozy," he said. "No doubt, Lieutenant, Magrady was killed in the identical fashion."

"It can't be a copycat," Roscoe said. "Details were left out of the newspapers."

"It's no copycat," Eli said. "Finish up and I'll talk to you later. Oh, Roscoe, there's a coffee can full of dope in the fridge. I want it analyzed for something other than marijuana. I don't think Magrady smoked it himself. I think it was for patrons in the club."

Eli left the apartment and took a stairway off the living room that led down to the jazz club.

Bannon and Tyler were at the bar talking with five black men.

"Boys, this is Lieutenant Rico," Tyler said. "Lieutenant, this is tonight's jazz band."

"Who would want to kill Milo, man?" one of the musicians asked.

"I don't know, do you?" Eli said.

"Course not," the musician said.

"Are you sure?" Eli said. "Jack, you and Tyler take statements from these gentlemen regarding every and anything they know about Milo."

Tyler sighed.

Eli looked at the musicians. "I already found his dope, so don't skip details."

"You heard the man," Tyler said.

Eli returned to the apartment. "This is the only way up here from the club," he said.

"That's because this building was constructed as a two-story home and converted later on," Wilson said. "I once lived above a grocery store as a kid. Same setup."

"What about time of death?" Eli asked.

"Between 3:00 and 4:00 in the morning," Wilson said.

"Sign at the bar says last call at 2:00 am," Eli said. "The night is over, he comes upstairs and the murderer is waiting for him."

"Appears that way," Roscoe said. "We can find no signs of a struggle or forced entry."

"He took a shower," Eli said. "The tub is dry but the towel is still damp."

"We'll take the towel to the lab," Roscoe said.

Eli looked at the kitchen door. "After his shower, still naked, Magrady goes to the kitchen and is surprised by the killer waiting for him behind the door. He panics and turns to run. He makes it to the living room where he is murdered and left on the floor outside the kitchen door."

"Sounds about right," Wilson said.

"I got everything I need," Roscoe said. "I'm heading back to the lab."

"Tell my guys to get up here," Eli said.

"I'll be leaving, too," Wilson said.

Eli nodded as he lit a cigarette and went into the kitchen. A few moments later, Tyler and Bannon walked in.

"We got their statements and cut them loose," Tyler said.

"He stood right here and waited," Eli said. "Longer than he anticipated. He got bored and read the book on jazz on the table and smoked three cigarettes. I found the butts in the trash under the sink."

Bannon and Tyler looked at the book on the table.

"Jack, get back to the office and start looking for a link, a connection, something that ties Roger Tanner to Milo Magrady," Eli said. "Find out everything there is to know about Magrady."

"These guys are night and day, Lieutenant," Bannon said.

73

"Not to our killer," Eli said. "He picked them for a reason. Tyler, get started on the jazz club. Finances, employees, musicians, anything you can dig up."

"Jesus, Lieutenant," Tyler said.

"I know," Eli said. "I'll assign you both some help as soon as I get back to the office."

Bannon and Tyler both sighed.

"Go," Eli said.

Alone, Eli returned to the bedroom and the balcony. He examined the scratch marks on the railing. He looked below at the courtyard wall.

"Fuck," he said aloud.

Eli left the apartment and took the stairs down to the club. Tyler was in the small office in the hallway opposite the bathrooms.

"This guy was pretty well organized," Tyler said.

"The door to the courtyard is where?" Eli asked.

Tyler came out of the office. "This is the only hallway," he said.

Eli looked down the hallway at the door marked *Emergency Exit*. He and Tyler walked to the door and Eli pushed it open.

"This is the only way," Eli said.

"Appears so," Tyler said.

The courtyard was about thirty-by-thirty and the brick wall surrounded every square inch.

Eli stood beside a section of the wall.

"How high would you say the wall is?" Eli asked.

"Ten feet," Tyler said.

Eli looked up at the balcony.

"That's a long way up without a ladder," Tyler said.

"Yeah, it is," Eli said.

* * *

"You forgot this," Eli said and handed the book to Roscoe.

"Prints?" Roscoe said.

Eli nodded.

"The same markings on the cigarettes and the towel contain nothing but water and soap residue," Roscoe said. "The marijuana is still being analyzed."

"The markings on the balcony railing?"

Roscoe walked over to a table where blow up photographs rested on a table.

"Scratch marks," Roscoe said. "But I haven't identified what made them."

Eli picked up the photographs and looked at them carefully, then set them down.

"Keep trying," he said.

"I'll call you later," Roscoe said.

* * *

"There's no doubt," Wilson said. "Roger Tanner and Milo Magrady were killed in the identical fashion. Even the stab wounds match."

Eli looked at Magrady's body on the examination table.

"Height and weight?"

"Six-one, 155," Wilson said. "He was a skinny fellow."

"Blood?"

"Vodka and orange juice. No drugs of any kind," Wilson said.

"Was he intoxicated?"

"Hardly. He had one drink and it was hours before his death."

"If there's anything else, call me," Eli said.

* * *

"I told you to solve the first one, not go out and find a second," Howe said.

Eli lit a cigarette and looked at Howe.

"It's the same man, Art," Eli said.

"You don't know that," Howe said.

"Details were kept out of the papers," Eli said. "Yet both were murdered exactly the same way."

"I'm not willing to say serial killer just yet," Howe said. "That would panic the city and set the papers on fire."

"The hell with the papers, Art," Eli said. "This guy is going to keep rolling."

"Then stop him," Howe said. "I'll put everything at your disposal to get the job done."

"I want to show you something," Eli said.

"Show."

"Not here. Later tonight."

Howe sighed. "Where?"

"I'll pick you up around 10:00."

"My wife is asleep by 10:00," Howe said. "She isn't well."

"I know," Eli said. "Meet me in front at 10:00."

"I better be losing sleep for a good reason," Howe said.

* * *

Eli stopped by Bannon's desk.

"Anything useful, Jack?" Eli asked.

"Not yet," Bannon said.

"Tomorrow is another day," Eli said. "Tyler call in?"

"About ten minutes ago," Bannon said. "He's locking up the jazz club and going home. He expects to go back in the morning."

"You, too, Jack. Clock out," Eli said.

After Bannon left, Eli sat at his desk and smoked a cigarette. Howe exited his office and stopped by the desk.

"Are you going to tell me what this is about tonight?" Howe asked.

"Hard to explain," Eli said. "Better you just see it."

Howe nodded. "See you at 10:00."

* * *

On the drive home, Eli stopped at the hardware store a few blocks from his apartment. After parking his car, he went to see the superintendent of his building.

"I need to borrow a ladder," Eli told him. "Six foot if you got it."

Eight

"**I don't think I'll** make dinner on Sunday, Ma," Eli said.

He was at the kitchen table, using the wall phone. He lit a cigarette and blew a smoke ring at the fan.

"Twice, Eli," Michele said.

"Can't be helped, Ma," Eli said. "I'm working an important case."

"More important than your family?"

"Nobody said that," Eli said.

"Your sister has this friend she wants you to meet," Michele said.

"Ma, I wish Sally would mind her own business," Eli said.

"It's not healthy a man your age isn't married," Michele said. "Your sister loves you. She's looking out for you. Don't you understand that, Eli?"

"I'll try to make it, but no promises," Eli said. "Right now I'm still working and I got to go."

Dressed in blue dungarees, a white T-shirt and windbreaker to hide the .38 revolver on his hip, Eli left the apartment at 8:30.

Traffic was heavy and Eli remembered that it was Friday night and people went out to dinner and the movies on Friday night. Earlier he tied the ladder to the roof using two long pieces of rope he picked up at the hardware store.

Art Howe lived in a nice building on Riverside Drive and 73rd Street. Eli stopped at a deli on Broadway for two containers of coffee and arrived a few minutes before 10:00.

Howe was waiting on the sidewalk. He got in and Eli handed him a container.

"Okay, let the show and tell begin," Howe said. "And don't bother to tell me what the ladder is for, I like surprises."

They drank their coffee on the drive south to the village. Eli parked in front of Milo's Jazz Club beside a hydrant and put his police sticker in the window.

They exited Eli's car and faced the club.

"The only way in is through the front door," Eli said. "Milo Magrady lived above the club in an apartment. Access is through the club down a hallway. So, how did the killer gain access to the apartment on the second floor?"

"Not with a six-foot-tall ladder," Howe said.

Eli removed the ladder from the roof of his car and a black bag from the trunk.

"Around the back," Eli said.

Howe followed Eli around to the rear of the club through an alleyway.

"This wall surrounds the courtyard," Eli said. "If you look up, there's a balcony about fifteen feet high."

There was just enough street light and light from the moon to see. Eli placed the ladder against the wall.

"The ladder is for you to climb over the wall," Eli said.

He opened the bag and removed the twenty-foot-long rope and grappling hook he purchased at the hardware store earlier.

"I'll go over first," Eli said.

He tossed the hook over the wall, tugged to make sure it was secure and then climbed the wall and went over.

Howe climbed the ladder and clumsily maneuvered his body over the wall. He hung by his arms and dropped four feet to the ground.

"You okay," Eli asked.

Howe nodded.

"That's how he got into the courtyard and this is how he got into the apartment," Eli said.

Eli swung the rope and tossed the hook up to the balcony. He tugged several times to make sure it was tight.

"This is Ranger School 101," Eli said and climbed the rope to the top in a few seconds. When he reached the top of the balcony, he gracefully scooted over the railing.

"Son of a bitch," Howe said.

"That door leads to the bar," Eli said. "I'll be right down to open it."

While Eli went inside, Howe took the rope and tried to climb it. He got about one foot off the ground before he gave up.

The door opened and Eli said, "Come in, Art."

Eli led Howe up to the apartment to the bedroom and out to the balcony.

"See the scratches here on the railing?" Eli said as he took out his small flashlight.

"I see them," Howe said.

Eli removed the grappling hook and pulled up the rope.

"Now look at the marks I just made," Eli said.

Howe looked. "They're identical scratch marks."

"Our boy is a Ranger, Art," Eli said. "That's who we're looking for, a US Army Ranger."

"The shit storm just got worse," Howe said. "A whole lot worse."

* * *

They sat in Eli's car in front of Howe's building. Riverside Park across the street was dark and quiet.

Eli lit a cigarette.

"That Ranger theory of yours, that stays between us until I talk to the chief and the mayor," Howe said.

"It's no theory, Art," Eli said.

"Everything is a theory until you can prove it," Howe said. "And right now you can't."

"When will you see them?"

"First thing in the morning," Howe said. "Go home, get some sleep."

After Howe left the car, Eli drove to Broadway and stopped at 72nd Street where a long bank of pay phones was lined up outside the subway entrance.

He grabbed some nickels from the glove box and went to a pay phone.

Mavis answered the phone on the fourth ring. "Hello," she said.

"It's Eli. Did I wake you?"

"No, I was just reading."

"Are you alone?"

"I'm alone."

"I'm calling… this is sort of awkward," Eli said. "You know what, I'm sorry to bother you."

"Spit it out, Eli," Mavis said. "It's silly to be shy with me after… well, just after."

Eli sighed. "I need a favor. A really embarrassing one."

"Are you in the City?"

"Yes."

"Come over. I'll fix you a drink and you can tell me your favor."

*   *   *

"You're all sweaty," Mavis said.

"Been working," Eli said.

81

"Sit on the sofa in front of the fan while I fix you a cold drink," Mavis said.

Eli went to the sofa, removed the windbreaker and took a seat in front of a large rotating fan.

Wrapped in a sheer robe, Mavis returned from the kitchen with a tall glass of rum, Coke and ice.

"It's mostly Coke with a tiny splash of rum for flavor," she said.

Eli took the glass and sipped. "It's good. Thank you."

"So, what's this mysterious favor?" Mavis said.

Eli took another sip and set the glass on top of a coaster on the glass top coffee table.

"I need a pretend date for dinner," Eli said.

"A pretend date? I don't... what exactly is a pretend date?" Mavis said, smiling just a bit.

"I need... my family is after me to get married," Eli said. "They don't know about my... problem. I never told them. If you could... pretend to be my dinner date just for a few hours, I'll pay you for three sessions."

"Don't be an asshole," Mavis said.

"I don't... what?" Eli said.

"You asked for a favor," Mavis said. "I don't agree to do a favor and then charge for it. I'm kind of insulted you implied that."

"But I thought..."

"I know what you thought," Mavis said. "What do you need me to do?"

"Just pretend to be my date for dinner at my parent's house," Eli said. "A couple of hours at most."

"All right, I'll do it as a favor," Mavis said.

Eli stood up. "Thank you. I'll call you tomorrow with more details."

"What are you doing?" Mavis said.

"Going home."

"Why?"

"I… I don't know," Eli said. "I don't have enough cash on me to…"

"Jesus Christ, it's impossible for you to be this stupid," Mavis said. "Go take a shower. You stink of sweat."

* * *

Mavis rocked on top of Eli until he exploded inside her. When that happened, she leaned forward, pressed her breasts against his chest and moaned until he was finished.

Winded, she rolled off him and they both looked at the ceiling while they regained their breath.

"Be right back," Mavis said, got up and went to the bathroom.

She returned in a few minutes with a wet washcloth.

"Hold still," she said and used the washcloth to clean Eli up. "That's better," she said and returned to the bathroom.

Eli sat up and reached for his cigarettes and lit one.

When Mavis returned, she had two frosty bottles of Coke.

"I'll trade you a cigarette for a Coke," she said.

Eli lit a cigarette for Mavis and they sat against the headboard, sipped ice cold Coke and smoked.

"So what are the details?" Mavis asked.

"For Sunday? I'll pick you up at 3:00, we drive to my parent's house and have dinner," Eli said.

"Just like that, huh?" Mavis said.

"I don't…"

"We'll need a cover story, dumbo," Mavis said. "Unless you think there won't be dinner conversation and questions from your family."

"Yeah, you're right about that," Eli said. "My sister is especially nosey."

"I didn't know you had a sister," Mavis said.

"Nosey and constantly trying to fix me up with one of her friends," Eli said. "And every one of them resembles a pack mule."

"So they don't know about your problem?"

"Jesus God, no," Eli said. "A man doesn't tell his mother he's impotent with all women except…"

"Call girls," Mavis said.

Eli sighed.

Mavis smiled. "It's all right, Eli," she said.

Eli sighed. "I didn't mean to insult you, I'm sorry."

"You didn't and it's alright," Mavis said. "So let's think of a suitable cover story."

* * *

Eli and his unit of Rangers stood on a hill and watched the German tanks burn. The siege of Bastogne was over and the German Army defeated.

Ammunition was at a premium after days of non-stop fighting, Eli and his Rangers attached bayonets and walked down from the hill to the battlefield to check for German survivors.

Any survivors were stabbed to death with bayonets.

Most of them begged for their lives. Cried like babies at the end.

Some even spoke some English.

One German, shot through the gut, spoke English like a native.

Eli stood over him with his bayonet at the ready.

"Please," the German said. "I love American. Camel Cigarettes, Coca Cola, Mickey Mouse. Babe Ruth. Joe D.

Eli stared at him.

"John Wayne," the German said. "Please… I have three daughters. They wear Levi's. Jimmy Stewart."

Eli stabbed him through the heart.
The German was there to kill him.
He was there to kill the German.
When he pulled the bayonet out, the German exhaled loudly and
slowly closed his eyes.

* * *

Eli gasped and woke with a start and Mavis held on to him and gently rocked him in her arms.

"It's okay," she whispered. "It was just another bad dream."

"What time is it?" Eli asked.

Mavis glanced at the alarm clock on the nightstand. "2:30," she said.

"Do you have any milk?" Eli asked.

"Milk? Yes. Come to the kitchen."

Eli slipped on his shorts. Mavis tossed on her sheer robe and they went to the kitchen. She filled two glasses with milk and set them on the table.

Eli's pack of cigarettes and lighter were on the table. He lit two and passed one to Mavis.

"Can you talk about it?" Mavis asked.

"The dreams?"

Mavis nodded.

"I don't think it's anything you want to know," Eli said.

"Do you know how I got into the business I'm in?" Mavis asked.

Eli shook his head.

"I came to New York in '39," Mavis said. "I was going to be a dancer, a Rockette and dance at the Radio City Music Hall. Back home, I danced in school and studied in Cleveland."

"Is that where you're from, Cleveland?" Eli asked.

"From a small town along the Ohio River," Mavis said. "I just went to dance school in Cleveland. I came on the bus to New York in May to audition. I won the role of understudy. Know what that is?"

"If someone gets sick, you take their place," Eli said.

"That's right," Mavis said. "I was an understudy for three years. I had to practice seven days a week along with the regular lineup and never got to perform once. I lived in a roach-infested apartment on Forty-Fourth Street and 10th Avenue with three other understudies. I made fifteen dollars a week. My share of the rent was five. I worked as a waitress on the night shift at the Carnegie Deli so I could afford to eat."

Mavis paused to sip milk and take a puff on her cigarette.

"So what happened?" Eli asked.

"In June of '42, during rehearsal, my left knee gave out," Mavis said. "And there was no more dancing for me. I was in bed for two months recovering. No income, borrowing food money from my roommates and no career prospects in dancing on the horizon ever."

Eli sipped milk and waited.

"So along comes one of the understudies," Mavis said. "The redhead I told you about. She says she makes a hundred and sometimes even more a week and so could I if I was interested."

Mavis paused to take another sip of milk and then looked at Eli.

"I wasn't, but I also wasn't interested in starving, either," she said. "I was no virgin, but my experience was limited to a few clumsy guys and the manager of the understudies who kept promising me a spot in the line if I played ball with him. He was a no good bastard."

"Most of us men are," Eli said.

Mavis chuckled. "In a few months, I'll be returning to Ohio with

$50,000 in the bank, while the Rockettes are breaking their ass six nights a week for forty-five dollars a paycheck."

"What do you plan to do there?" Eli asked.

"Live," Mavis said. "Well, we finished our milk and cigarettes; let's try to get some sleep."

* * *

Mavis kept a man's razor and shaving soap in the bathroom for clients to use. While Eli shaved, she ironed his shirt after laundering it.

Before they got out of bed, they made love again and it was sweet, tender and unhurried. Before he jumped into the shower, he could smell breakfast cooking. He wondered if this was what it was like to be married.

By the time he was fully dressed, Mavis had breakfast on the kitchen table.

Bacon, eggs, hash browns, toast, orange juice and coffee.

"You went to a lot of trouble," Eli said.

"I usually have just toast and coffee in the morning because I have no one to cook for," Mavis said. "So whenever I have the chance to cook a full breakfast I sort of enjoy myself. Sit down and eat."

As they ate they talked about Sunday.

"I'll pick you up at 3:00," Eli said. "My parents live in Jersey, so it will be close to 4:00 by the time we arrive. Dinner is at 5:00, so be prepared for an hour long session of non stop questions."

"It won't be that bad," Mavis said. "I might even enjoy myself.'

"I'll owe you a favor," Eli said.

"Can you fix a parking ticket?"

"Actually, I can't."

"I'll think of something," Mavis said. "Seeing as I don't own a car."

Eli glanced at his watch. "I need to get to work," he said.

Nine

Eli had the squad room to himself for about an hour. He sat at his desk with the newspapers, a container of coffee and smoked a cigarette while he waited.

By 8:30, most of the scheduled detectives had arrived, including Bannon and Tyler.

"Jack, keep working the angle of a common link between Tanner and Magrady," Eli said. "Maybe their paths have crossed at some point."

"I could use some…" Bannon said.

"Grab whoever isn't working an active case," Eli said. "Where's Tyler?"

"He called. He's on the way to the jazz club," Bannon said.

Eli returned to his desk and called Roscoe.

"You'll be happy to know or maybe you won't be, but the marijuana contains nothing but marijuana," Roscoe said.

"Thanks," Eli said and hung up.

A moment later, the phone rang and he scooped it up.

"Eli, it's Howe. Get over to the mayor's office on the double."

"Be right over," Eli said.

Eli stopped by Bannon's desk on the way out. "Jack, I'll be with the captain at the mayor's office."

"Good luck," Bannon said.

* * *

The Mayor of New York City, William O'Dwyer, stared across his desk at Eli. Standing behind O'Dwyer, Howe also looked at Eli.

"I've looked over your record, Lieutenant," O'Dwyer said. "You are an excellent detective with an outstanding record of achievement."

"Thank you, sir," Eli said.

"Captain Howe tells me that you believe the same man murdered Roger Tanner and Milo Magrady, is that correct?" O'Dwyer said.

"Yes, sir, that's correct," Eli said.

"Captain Howe also tells me you believe this murderer of two is an Army Ranger," O'Dwyer said.

"Also correct, sir," Eli said.

"Because both victims were killed in the same fashion?"

Eli looked at O'Dwyer.

"Because of the way they were killed," Eli said.

"He couldn't just be some crazy karate expert who likes to kill?" O'Dwyer said.

"Crazy karate… there isn't a Karate school in the country that would teach the Ranger Choke Hold," Eli said.

"How do you know that?" O'Dwyer said. "Maybe there's a book on…?"

"A book?" Eli said. "Mr. Mayor, with all due respect, you haven't a clue what you're talking about."

"Lieutenant Rico, I won't…"

"The Rangers are unlike any other fighting force in the country," Eli said. "We're not engineers, we don't build things. We're not infantry supporting tanks or liberating towns. We're not a MASH unit there to save lives. Our purpose is one and one alone, to kill by any and all means possible. Our training is second to none. We are taught things others are not. Several things we are taught is to scale heights using a grappling hook and to kill when necessary using the choke hold. This man did both and seemingly with ease."

O'Dwyer glanced at Howe, and then looked at Eli. "Have you ever used this choke hold?"

"In the war, sir," Eli said. "I would never use it in the line of duty or anywhere else back home."

O'Dwyer sighed. "Lieutenant, do you know the circus it would create if we let it known our suspect might be a former Army Ranger?"

"Yes, I do," Eli said.

"The FBI and the Army would get involved," O'Dwyer said. "The newspapers, the radio coverage, our city would be in chaos and our citizens panicked."

"I realize that, sir," Eli said.

"Captain Howe happens to believe you're theory is correct," O'Dwyer said. "I am authorizing as much overtime as is needed to catch this bastard. Captain Howe will lead a special task force with as much manpower as he needs, but you will be the lead investigator. Understood?"

Eli nodded. "Yes, sir."

"That's all, Lieutenant," O'Dwyer said.

"Sir?" Eli said.

"What is it, Lieutenant?" O'Dwyer said.

"He's not going to stop, sir," Eli said. "For whatever his reason is, he's not going to stop until we catch him."

"Then catch him," O'Dwyer said. "And do it quickly and without publicity."

* * *

Eli used a pay phone on the corner of the next block from City Hall.

"Detective Bannon, Homicide," Bannon said when he picked up.

"Jack, it's Eli. Is Tyler still at the jazz club?" Eli said.

"He is," Bannon said.

"I'll be headed over there if you need me."

"Want I should forward calls or take messages?"

"Take," Eli said.

Eli returned to his car and drove to the village and parked in front of a hydrant and put his police sign in the window.

He walked to the front door. A sign was posted. *Closed Until Further Notice. New York City Police Department.*

Eli banged on the door. After a few seconds, Tyler appeared in the glass and unlocked the door from the inside.

"Lieutenant, did you bring donuts and coffee?" Tyler said.

"I did not," Eli said. "But that's not a bad idea. Be right back."

One block away was a coffee shop and Eli picked up two containers of coffee and a half dozen donuts.

Tyler was in the open doorway when Eli returned.

"I'm set up in the office," Tyler said.

They went to the office where Tyler sat behind the desk and Eli took a chair. Tyler opened the donut box and grabbed a chocolate frosted one.

Eli opened the lid on his container and took a sip. "So, how are you doing?"

"This guy Magrady cleared forty grand last year from this place," Tyler said. "He's no Roger Tanner, but forty grand is nothing to sneeze at. I talked to all his employees and they all say the same thing, the guy loved jazz more than anything."

"What about the dope in the refrigerator?" Eli asked.

"His bartenders claim Magrady never used it himself," Tyler said. "It was for the musicians. The better the dope, the better group of musicians. He never charged them for it either."

"This doesn't make much sense," Eli said. "Tanner and Magrady have nothing in common except they were both killed the same way. Did you go through his personal belongings?"

"I started a file," Tyler said. "His bank account has about $50,000 in it. A few grand in his checkbook. A small insurance police with his mother as the beneficiary. She died a year ago and he never got around to changing it."

"What about the accounts for the bar?" Eli asked.

"I've checked the ledger books and checking account for the bar," Tyler said. "The bar grossed about a hundred thousand before payroll and expenses. It seems on the up and up."

"Women?"

"He was married and divorced," Tyler said. "I found the divorce papers in a file. The bartenders claim he didn't have a steady girlfriend, but dated casually."

"Where's his wallet?" Eli asked.

"Box in the corner."

Eli stood, went to the box and found the wallet, returned to his seat and opened it. He started with the driver's license. According to his birth date, Magrady was just thirty-four years old. His height was sixty-eight inches or five-foot-eight. His weight was 138 pounds.

Eli flipped through the various items in the wallet and found Magrady's Select Service Card. He was classified 4F due to being severely underweight. Eli stared at the card for a few seconds and felt almost a buzzing in his ears.

"Are you all right, Lieutenant?" Tyler asked.

Eli looked up. "Yeah. I'm taking his draft card. Mark that down."

"Sure, but why?"

"I'll tell you later at the office," Eli said.

* * *

93

"Where's the captain?" Eli asked Bannon upon returning to the squad room.

"His office."

"Come with me," Eli said.

Eli knocked on Howe's door, opened it and he and Bannon stepped inside.

"I think I found something," Eli said. "A link between Tanner and Magrady."

"Close the door," Howe said.

Bannon turned and gently shut the door.

Eli set Magrady's draft card on the desk. Howe looked at it.

"Both Tanner and Magrady were 4F," Eli said.

"That could be just coincidence," Howe said.

"I don't think so, Art," Eli said. "I think the use of a German bayonet is a message."

Howe picked up Magrady's draft card, looked at it closely and then set it down. "The message being?" he said.

"I can't get in the guy's head, Art. That's a job for the shrinks," Eli said. "But I think he resents Tanner and Magrady missing the war because they were 4F. The German bayonet is what they missed."

Howe sighed. "Say your theory is correct," he said. "Do you know how many men were classified 4F just in New York alone?"

"I don't, Art," Eli said. "And neither should he, unless he has access to classified information."

"Oh, fuck," Howe said.

"I'm right, Art," Eli said. "You know I'm right."

Howe looked at Bannon. "What do you say, Jack?"

"I think it fits, Captain," Bannon said. "I trust Eli's judgment."

"I'm sorry to say I agree with you," Howe said. "What do you want to do, Eli?"

"Talk to the department shrinks," Eli said. "Then I need you to get me into the Department of Veterans Affairs."

"You heard what the mayor said," Howe said.

"He said to catch him," Eli said. "And I hate publicity."

"I'll make some calls," Howe said.

*   *   *

Doctor James Becker was surprised to see Eli in his office after a year. He assumed incorrectly that Eli wanted to discuss his old sexual problem and Becker set aside an hour for him.

Becker's office was on the fourth floor of the department headquarters building.

"How have you been, Lieutenant?" Becker asked when Eli took a chair.

"Fine," Eli said. "I'm here to…"

"Last time we spoke you said your sexual problems had cleared up. Have they returned?" Becker said.

"I'm not here about that," Eli said. "I want your opinion on something."

"Oh?"

Eli spoke for thirty minutes and as he talked, Becker made notes on a legal pad.

"So, what is your opinion, Doctor?" Eli asked when he was finished.

"With just two examples, it's difficult to make a diagnosis," Becker said.

"Give it a shot," Eli said.

"Well, I would say that this man has a seething rage inside him and it's directed at men who didn't serve in the war because of their draft status," Becker said. "He suffered in the war and resents those who didn't. The use of a German bayonet is his way of telling them so. He's a very sick, tortured and angry man."

Eli looked at Becker.

"Is that how you see it, Lieutenant?" Becker asked.

Eli nodded. "He's going to keep doing this, isn't he?"

"Count on it," Becker said. "So, Lieutenant, how is your problem?"

* * *

Tyler was at his desk when Eli entered the squad room.

"Jack went home and the Captain said to tell you he's working on the situation, whatever that means," Tyler said.

Eli sat on the edge of the desk and lit a cigarette.

"Are you finished with the jazz club?" Eli asked.

"I think so, yeah. The guy was clean except for the dope and he wasn't using or selling," Tyler said. "So what's with the draft card?

Eli gave Tyler a quick rundown.

"It can't be a coincidence, can it?" Tyler said.

"We'll know for sure when number three pops up," Eli said.

"I think you are right," Tyler said.

"Go home," Eli said. "We'll pick it up in the morning."

"Tomorrow is Saturday, but the Captain gave us the okay to come in if we want to," Tyler said.

"I lost track of time, I guess," Eli said.

After Tyler left, Eli went to his desk and called his parents.

"Eli, is everything all right?" Michele said.

"Yes, Ma," Eli said. "About Sunday, if I can make it is it okay if I bring a date?"

"A date? Do you mean a woman?"

"Of course a woman," Eli said.

"Your sister is bringing one of her friends for you to meet,"

Michele said.

"Ma, please. No more of Sally's friends," Eli said. "You tell her that or I won't make it."

"What kind of woman are you bringing?" Michele said.

"The female kind," Eli said.

Michele sighed. "Don't be late," she said.

* * *

Eli stripped down to his underwear and went through his routine in his apartment. He added a few extra sets of push-ups, pull-ups and chin-ups before ending with a long session of sit-ups.

He ran the tub and soaked in hot water and let the heat penetrate deep into his muscles.

He closed his eyes and allowed his mind and thoughts to wander.

Police work, especially a homicide investigation was tedious and long hours spent doing leg work and repetitive tasks until something broke. More often than not the break came from a tip or just plain luck.

He wasn't going to stop.

"Count on it," Becker had said.

"He suffered in the war and resents those who didn't," Becker had said.

Eli reached over and picked up his cigarettes off the floor and lit one.

Everybody suffered in the war. Some with lost limbs, others with their lives and many with emotional scars.

That's what Doctor Becker said happened to him and caused his inability to perform with women.

Emotional scars.

Becker said long-term prisoners had similar problems when

released and returned to their wives.

Performance anxiety, Becker called it.

The inability to perform with a woman caused by an emotional problem that leads to impotence.

So said Doctor Becker.

Doctor Becker didn't go to war. Doctor Becker didn't blow someone's brains out, or stab them in the heart, or snap their neck like a dry twig.

Doctor Becker spent the war telling other people what their problems were.

Eli stood up and grabbed a towel. He toweled dry and tossed on clean underwear and a T-shirt.

In the kitchen, he poured a glass of milk and sat at the table to drink it. He lit a cigarette and drifted off again.

The guilt at having to kill and surviving the war while others didn't weighs heavily on a man's mind, so said Doctor Becker. The use of prostitutes in a war zone is understandable, but coupled with guilt, the high stress of combat and returning home to a normal life can and does create such problems as performance anxiety.

So said Doctor Becker.

Eli stood and went to the window. The air was cooler and less humid and for once he wasn't covered in sweat.

He knew Becker was right about his emotional and physical problems. Was he right about the killer's seething rage against those who didn't serve because they were 4F?

Eli didn't know the answer to that question.

What he did know was that Becker was right in that he wasn't going to stop killing. His rage needed to be fed, but once fed, the rage only grew hungrier and needed to be fed more often.

He went to the living room, put the radio on, and found a station that played soft music.

He sprawled out on the sofa and didn't move until he opened his eyes in the morning.

Ten

Eli was alone in the squad room. He ate an egg sandwich and skimmed the newspapers at his desk.

Bannon arrived a few minutes past 9:00.

"Morning, Lieutenant," he said.

"Jack," Eli said.

"I figured I'd put in a few hours on paperwork," Bannon said. "Catch up for Monday."

"Want some coffee?" Eli asked. "I think I'll take a walk to the coffee shop around the block."

"Sure. Tyler should be in, too," Bannon said.

"I'll grab one for him," Eli said.

Eli left the squad room and walked around the corner to the coffee shop where a pay phone was in the vestibule. He dropped in a few nickels and dialed Mavis's number.

She answered after three rings.

"Mavis, it's Eli. Did I wake you?" Eli said.

"I'm a fairly early riser, Eli," Mavis said. "And I was hoping you would call."

"Have you changed your mind about tomorrow?"

"No, silly. But, I have an idea," Mavis said. "Instead of picking me up tomorrow afternoon, why not stay over tonight and save yourself some time?"

"That's not a bad idea," Eli said. "If it's not putting you out."

"It's my idea, Eli," Mavis said. "I wouldn't have brought it up if I thought it was putting me out."

"I have some work to do," Eli said. "Is late this afternoon okay?"

"Sure. Call from the lobby when you get here," Mavis said.

"I'll see you later then," Eli said.

He hung up, entered the coffee shop and got three containers to go and six donuts. Tyler was sitting on the edge of Bannon's desk when Eli returned to the squad room.

"We're just hashing things out, Lieutenant," Tyler said.

Eli set the paper bag on his desk and removed the containers of coffee.

"So, what do we got?" he said as he opened a lid on a container.

Tyler reached for a container and passed it to Bannon, then took the last container for himself. Bannon reached into the bag for a chocolate donut. Tyler grabbed a plain donut and looked at Eli.

"Jack and I both figure luck is going to solve this one," Tyler said. "Our man is going to keep rolling until he makes a mistake and opens a door for us."

Eli lit a cigarette. "He already has made mistakes," he said. "And we know exactly who we're looking for."

Tyler sipped some coffee.

Bannon did the same.

"He's tall, very powerful, is right-handed, is in all likelihood an ex Army Ranger and is mentally disturbed," Eli said. "He probably saw a great deal of action and is emotionally scarred and holds a grudge against those who were 4F and didn't serve. He's smart, knows how to plan and is very patient. He smokes Camels unfiltered and uses a plastic filter that leaves a mark. He uses a German bayonet, probably one he brought home. If we sit around and wait for him to make a mistake, we could all have long grey beards by then."

101

Bannon nodded. "So how do we go about finding him? We got five million people in this city alone, half of them men. We can't exactly look at the service record of every GI who served in the war."

"No, we can't," Eli said.

"And we can't check every guy who was 4F, it would take a team a year or more," Tyler said.

"We have to narrow the field," Eli said.

"How do we do that?" Bannon asked.

The phone rang and Tyler answered the call. "Hold on," he said and held the phone to Eli.

Eli took the phone. "Lieutenant Rico," he said.

"Eli, it's Howe. I arranged a meeting with the VA for Monday, ten o'clock," Howe said.

"Thanks, Captain," Eli said.

"See you Monday early," Howe said. "If you dead end kids find something new and useful, call me at home."

"Will do," Eli said and hung up.

He looked at Tyler and Bannon. "Our break might come on Monday," he said. "The Captain set up a meeting with the VA."

"This choke hold, is it taught to anybody besides Rangers?" Tyler said. "We never heard of it in the hundred and first."

"As far as I know only Rangers get that kind of training," Eli said.

"We had hand-to-hand in the infantry, but nothing like what you described," Bannon said.

"Finish what paperwork you have and head out," Eli said. "There's nothing we can do until Monday."

* * *

Mavis smiled broadly at Eli when she opened the door to him.

"I have something to show you," she said.

Eli held a small overnight bag in his left hand. She took his right hand and walked him into the living room.

"Look," she said.

Eli looked at the square cabinet against the wall opposite the sofa.

"Do you know what that is?" Mavis asked.

"Looks like a bar," Eli said.

Mavis went to the cabinet and opened the swinging door to reveal a thirteen-inch television set.

"It's a TV," she said. "My first one. It was delivered yesterday."

"I'm seeing them everywhere now," Eli said.

"It's a Philco," Mavis said. "The store said there are at least fifty thousand of them in New York alone."

Eli set his bag down. "Did you want to watch something?"

Mavis took Eli's right hand again. "No, I want to make love," she said and guided him to the bedroom. "And not to the TV."

* * *

Mavis sat behind Eli in the bathtub full of bubble bath and oils and washed his hair.

"That stuff smells pretty good," Eli said.

"It's Richard Hadnut," Mavis said. "It has egg in it that gives your hair shine. Rinse."

The tub was large enough for Eli to comfortable dunk under and rinse his hair. When he surfaced, Mavis said, "Now you can do me."

Mavis turned her back to Eli and he picked up the bottle of shampoo from the ledge and squirted some on her long dark hair.

"Work up a good lather," she said.

Eli rubbed in the shampoo until it formed a soapy lather.

"About tomorrow," he said.

"Quit worrying," Mavis said. "It will be fine."

"You never met my family," Eli said. "My mother is Irish, my father is Italian and both have stubborn tempers. My sister Sally thinks it's her obligation to play Cupid to anyone who isn't married and she specializes in me."

"They sound wonderful and quit worrying," Mavis said. "Scoot over a bit, I have to rinse."

Eli gave her room and she dunked under to rinse her hair. Eli stared at her, at her perfect breasts, slim waist and hips and her opening.

Mavis sat up and looked at Eli's erection.

"Jeez, Eli, we just did it," she said.

"Sorry," Eli said.

"Don't be sorry," Mavis said. "Save some for later. Like dessert."

*   *   *

"Where are we going?" Eli asked.

"I told you, to dinner," Mavis said.

She wore casual slacks with a cream-colored blouse and flat, black shoes.

Eli reached for his car keys on the coffee table.

"Won't need them. We're walking."

One block north and two blocks west, nestled at the end of the 53rd Street sat a cozy little restaurant called Backstreet. Inside seating held twelve tables. Outside in the garden held another six.

As they walked, Mavis linked her left arm through Eli's right arm and she guided him along.

"Miss Waite," the host said as they reached the front door of the restaurant. "It's been too long."

"It has," Mavis said. "Can we have the garden?"

"Certainly."

The host led them through the restaurant to the courtyard gardens where the six tables were empty.

"Take your pick," the host said. "In another hour all will be full."

They chose the table closest to a tree that afforded privacy.

"How are the prices here?" Eli asked.

"If you need to ask you can't afford them," Mavis smiled.

Eli looked at her.

Mavis smiled. "This was my idea, it's my treat."

"I can't allow that," Eli said.

"Then we'll go Dutch."

Ninety minutes later, as they walked back to her apartment, Mavis took Eli's hand in hers.

"It's not against the rules to hold my hand, Eli," she said. "God knows, you've held everything else."

"I didn't want… I mean I wasn't sure if you… I…" Eli said.

"You're tripping over your tongue again," Mavis said. "It's cool tonight. Let's sit out for a bit."

Mavis's apartment building had a backyard garden with patio furniture and lawn chairs.

They chose lawn chairs and Eli lit a cigarette that Mavis snatched away from him. He lit another and they were silent for a few moments.

"Can you talk about the case you're working on?" Mavis asked.

"Not really, no," Eli said.

"It's bad though, right?"

"It's bad."

"That's why you came to see me," Mavis said.

"What do you mean?"

"Stress," Mavis said. "You needed a release. You always come to see me when you're under a lot of stress."

Eli looked at her. The courtyard lights were on and her skin glowed in the pale light. "Do you know that you are really beautiful," he said.

"Well, that only took you three years to spit out," Mavis said.

"I don't... what only took me three years?"

"That was the first time you complimented me on my looks," Mavis said.

"I didn't know I... really? The first time?"

"Really. The first time."

"I'm sorry," Eli said. "The truth is I think you are amazingly beautiful, but I was afraid to tell you."

"Why?"

"I figured you hear it all the time and I didn't want you to think I was full of it," Eli said.

"I don't think that, Eli," Mavis said. "If I thought you were full of it I would never have agreed to tomorrow."

"Why did you agree to tomorrow?" Eli said.

"Because you're sweet and I like you," Mavis said. "We call girls have feelings, too, you know."

"I know that," Eli said. "I want you to know how much you've helped me. More than the shrinks ever did."

"There is nothing wrong with you that the right woman couldn't fix," Mavis said. "Let's go upstairs and see if we can help each other one more time with some dessert."

* * *

Mavis woke up when Eli moaned in his sleep. His skin was hot; his face was covered in sweat.

He was having one of his nightmares. She knew not to try to wake him or ask what it was about in the morning. He wouldn't tell her. She knew it was bad, though. Over the past two years, she had picked up bits and pieces when he talked in his sleep.

She couldn't imagine the things he had to do in the war, but she knew they were horrible, terrible things. The kind of things that will haunt a man all the rest of his days.

The moaning stopped. She settled in beside Eli and held him against her chest.

She wondered if she should tell him how much in love with him she was.

How would he react?

There was only one way to find out.

Eleven

If she didn't see how nervous, how important dinner with his parents was to Eli, Mavis would have found the entire situation laugh out loud funny.

He was more a nervous little boy than a former Army Ranger and present day Homicide Lieutenant Detective on the country's largest police force.

As he drove them across the George Washington Bridge, she looked at his hands on the steering wheel.

"Eli, if you hold the wheel any tighter it's going to break off in your hands," Mavis said.

"Sorry," Eli said. "I'm just a bit nervous about this."

"A bit?" Mavis said.

"Okay, a lot," he admitted.

She touched his arm. "Try to relax," she said. "And have a little trust, okay?"

Eli nodded.

Mavis looked out her window so he didn't see her grin.

* * *

Eli parked behind his father's Ford.

"That new Cadillac you see there belongs to my sister's husband

Robert," Eli said.

Mavis looked at the shine on the Cadillac. "I haven't met him yet, but I would bet he's the type that never leaves hairs in the sink after he shaves."

Eli took a deep breath. "Ready?"

"Of course," Mavis said. "Let's go."

Salvatore answered the door. He looked at Mavis and spoke one word in Italian.

"Dad, this is Mavis," Eli said. "Mavis, this is my dad Salvatore."

"Call me Sal," Salvatore said. "Please, come in."

Eli and Mavis followed Salvatore to the living room where Sally and Robert were having a drink.

"My daughter Sally and her husband Robert," Salvatore said. "Eli, I'll get your mother."

Sally looked at Mavis with surprise and shock in her eyes. Robert's expression was more minor lust.

"Hey, sis, where are the kids?" Eli asked.

"We got a sitter," Sally said. "After dinner, Bob and I are taking in a show in the City."

Michele, Eli's mother, followed Salvatore into the living room and she looked at Mavis. "Goodness," Michele said.

"Ma, this is Mavis," Eli said.

"Would you look at this woman," Michele said.

"Look at her hips, mother," Salvatore said. "Like yours. Hips just made for kids."

"Jesus, Dad, we just got here," Eli said.

"Mavis, do you cook?" Michele said.

"Yes, I do," Mavis said.

"Come help me in the kitchen," Michele said.

"Sure."

Eli sighed.

Robert wandered over to Eli. "Good one, Eli," he whispered.

"I heard that," Sally said.

"Sally, go help them set the table," Salvatore said.

*   *   *

Mavis sat next to Michele at the table. Salvatore occupied the end seat as family patriarch.

"So, Mavis, what do you do?" Michele asked.

"Ma," Eli said.

"I'm just making conversation," Michele said.

"You accent is Northern Ireland," Mavis said to Michele.

"Yes, it is," Michele said. "My family is from there. I still have many relatives living in the old country."

"Do you speak the old language?" Mavis said in Gallic.

"Yes, I do," Michele answered in Gallic.

The table was shocked into silence, none more shocked than Eli.

"My mother was from the old country. She taught me when I was a little girl," Mavis said in Gallic.

"My son the Army Ranger and big shot police lieutenant is a bit clumsy around women, isn't he?" Michele said in Gallic.

Mavis laughed. "Yes, he is," she said in Gallic.

"Ladies, English, please," Salvatore said.

"Sorry, dear," Michele said. "I haven't spoken the old language in years."

"You were about to tell us what you do," Sally said to Mavis.

"I was a Rockette for three years until I hurt my knee," Mavis said.

"A Rockette at the Radio City Music Hall?" Robert said.

Under the table, Sally kicked Robert.

"What?" Robert said.

"You said was, what do you do now?" Sally asked Mavis.

"I coach new dancers on the routines," Mavis said. "It's a lot of hard work, but when a new girl catches on it's very rewarding."

"I'll bet," Robert said which earned him another kick under the table.

"Are we going to eat or let all this food go to waste?" Salvatore asked.

* * *

After Sally and Robert left, Mavis and Michele washed the dishes in the kitchen.

"He's a good man, my son," Michele said.

"Yes, he is," Mavis said.

Michele, washing, handed a plate to Mavis who dried.

"He needs somebody in his life," Michele said. "He went through hell in the war. Oh, he doesn't talk about it, but it shows on his face and he has nightmares. And being a homicide detective doesn't help matters much I suppose."

"He won't talk about it," Mavis said. "The war."

"No, he wouldn't," Michele said. "It's not like him."

Mavis took the last dish, dried it and placed it on the counter where the others were stacked.

Michele looked at Mavis. "Don't hurt my son," she said. "He already has far too many scars."

"I won't," Mavis said.

"The coffee should be ready," Michele said. "Shall we join the men in the living room?"

* * *

As Eli drove across the George Washington Bridge to Manhattan,

Mavis said, "They are really nice people and I enjoyed myself very much. Thank you for thinking of me, Eli."

"I'm the one who owes the thank you," Eli said. "You were pretty terrific with my family. They really liked you a lot."

Mavis looked out the window for a moment. "Are you taking me home?"

"I'll take you anywhere you want to go," Eli said. "You earned it."

Still looking out the window, Mavis said, "I want to go to your place."

"My place? My apartment?" Eli said.

Mavis turned and looked at him. "You said anyplace."

"I know, but…"

"But, what?"

"My apartment is the size of your living room," Eli said. "There's nothing there."

"You're there," Mavis said. "That's something."

Eli sighed. "All right, my place it is."

* * *

"This seems like a really nice neighborhood," Mavis said as she and Eli walked along the Grand Concourse to his apartment.

"It is," Eli said. "It's not the East Side of Manhattan, but it's a good neighborhood for families."

"Everything doesn't have to be Manhattan, Eli," Mavis said. "You should see the town in Ohio where I'm from."

Eli paused. "Well, this is my building."

* * *

"It's not so small," Mavis said as they entered the kitchen.

Eli clicked on the wall fan and then opened the window.

"My whole apartment is a closet," Eli said.

"Show me the bedroom," Mavis said.

Eli took her to the bedroom, turned on the lamp beside the bed, the fan and opened the window.

"Hold still," Mavis said. She looked up at Eli. She was a tall woman, about five-foot-eight inches tall, but Eli was a half-foot taller.

"What are…?" Eli said as Mavis reached for his shirt and unbuttoned the top button.

"No talking," Mavis said as she opened the second button.

* * *

After so heavy a meal with Eli's parents, neither of them was overly hungry after making love, but they craved a snack and Eli made a pot of coffee and they sat at the kitchen table with slices of pound cake he had in the refrigerator.

They sat naked at the table, something that only couples who are comfortable with each other would do.

Mavis decided the time was right to tell Eli her true feeling.

"Something I want to say," she said.

"Sure."

"Don't say anything until I'm finished, okay?"

Eli nodded.

The wall phone rang.

Eli looked at the phone. "It's too late to be my parents."

Mavis watched as Eli reached for the phone and answered the call. She knew the caller on the other end had bad news.

"Call detectives Travis and Bannon at home," Eli said. "Tell them to meet me in front of headquarters."

Eli hung up and looked at Mavis.

"You have to go," she said.

"Sorry," Eli said. "I'll drop you off on the way."

Mavis dressed while Eli took a quick shower. She sat on the bed and watched him get dressed. Slacks, white shirt, black shoes.

Then an amazing thing happened.

He pinned his gold shield to his belt and then reached for his gun and holster. As he clipped it to his belt, Eli the clumsy, insecure man vanished and she could see the Army Ranger and Homicide Detective take his place.

The transformation was both hypnotic and frightening at the same time.

"You can tell me what you were going to say on the drive," Eli said.

"Nothing," Mavis said. "It's not important."

*   *   *

At her building, Eli parked the car for a moment.

"I'm sorry about this," Eli said.

"Don't be. It's your job," Mavis said.

Eli nodded. "Can I…?"

"What?"

"Nothing. I have to go," Eli said.

Mavis nodded and opened her door.

"Wait," Eli said. "I had a really wonderful time with you."

"Me, too. I would like to do it again," Mavis said.

"With my parents?"

"I meant like a real date like people do. Dinner, a movie, like that," Mavis said.

"I'm not sure when I'll be free," Eli said.

"I copied down your number when you were in the shower,"

Mavis said. "I'll call you this time. Right now you have to go to work."

About to step out of the car, Mavis paused, turned and kissed Eli sweetly on the lips.

"That was a real kiss," Eli said.

"I know, silly," Mavis said. "Because this was a real date."

Twelve

Tyler was alone on the steps of headquarters when Eli arrived just before 10:00 pm. He was drinking from a container of coffee and smoking a cigarette.

Tyler stood, tossed the cigarette and approached Eli's car. From inside, Eli opened the door.

"Where's Bannon?" Eli said.

"Dispatch couldn't locate him," Tyler said. "They said they'll keep trying. So what do we got and where are we going?

"Midtown south took the call," Eli said as Tyler got in and closed the door. "One dead male killed as our first two. Address is Twenty-eight West 28th Street."

As Eli pulled away from the curb, Tyler looked at Eli and said, "Wait. Hold up, Lieutenant."

Eli stopped alongside the curb. "What?"

"Do you know what that address is?" Tyler asked.

"I know where, I don't know what," Eli said.

Tyler was suddenly sweating and a nervous wreck.

"What?" Eli said.

"That's the Everard Bath House," Tyler said. "A Turkish bath house."

"Okay, it's a Turkish bath house," Eli said. "We have a corpse waiting on us, so we better…"

"For gay men. Homosexual men," Tyler said.

"So? They're entitled to the same protection under the law as anybody else," Eli said.

Tyler stared at Eli.

"What?" Eli said.

"I'm… a client, Lieutenant. A patron," Tyler said.

Eli sat back in his seat and looked out the windshield. "You're homosexual?"

"What were you expecting, lipstick and a tutu?" Tyler said.

"Jesus Christ, Tyler," Eli said. "Why didn't you ever tell me?"

"Tell you what, Lieutenant? Do you know what the department would do to me if they found out? I'd be bounced off so fast my head would spin."

"Harry Truman made it mandatory that discrimination against…"

"Harry Truman? Harry fucking Truman? Are you serious, Lieutenant?" Tyler said. "Do you know how many jokes I hear in the squad room in a given day? Fags, queers, perverts, the guys would make sure I'm bounced. The shrinks would recommend that a homosexual man is mentally unfit to be a police officer."

Eli lit a cigarette and exhaled loudly.

"When I was in England with the 101st right before the drop, I was in a bar with my squad and this British soldier comes up to me and asks if I can spare a fag. I nearly decked the guy until one of my guys told me they call cigarettes fags for some reason."

"What do they call homosexuals then?" Eli asked.

"In England? Most call them buggers," Tyler said. "Ass bandit, bum bandit and for some reason a Nancy."

"Nancy?"

"I'd rather be a Nancy than an ass bandit," Tyler said.

Eli cracked up laughing.

Tyler shook his head. "Jesus, Lieutenant, I got fourteen years in."

"You're a great detective, Tyler," Eli said. "You wouldn't have made homicide otherwise. As far as I'm concerned nothing has changed. If the department finds out it won't come from me."

"Thanks, Lieutenant," Tyler said.

Eli shrugged. "Hey, it's almost 1950," he said. "Pretty soon nobody will care anyway. Now can we please go to work?"

* * *

Three patrol cars were parked in front of the Everard Bath House when Eli and Tyler arrived. Eli parked at a hydrant and both men got out.

"We cleared the building, Lieutenant," an officer said.

"Anybody from forensics or the ME's office here?" Eli asked.

"Only a detective can make that call, Lieutenant," the officer said. "We just guard the scene."

"I'll call from inside," Eli said. "Nobody else in or out. Where's the victim?"

"Second floor steam room."

"Who found the body?"

"Janitor. He was getting ready to close the place down."

Eli and Tyler entered the building through the revolving front doors. The lobby was lavish and ornate. There was a check-in desk similar to a hotel reservations desk.

"How does this work?" Eli asked.

"Don't bother with the registration book," Tyler said. "No one ever uses their real name and everybody pays cash."

Eli glanced at the registration book on the desk. Names were scrawled and illegible.

"Up those stairs," Tyler said.

The second floor held several private rooms, a sauna, steam bath, a small gym and a cafeteria.

Eli opened the door marked steam room and he and Tyler entered. The room had seats and benches for a dozen occupants.

The victim, a white male was face down on the wood floor. A stab wound was visible on the left side and it was obvious his neck was broken.

"Where do they keep their clothes and valuables?" Eli asked.

"The locker room on the third floor," Tyler said.

"See what you can find while I call Roscoe and Wilson," Eli said.

* * *

"For crying out loud, it's Sunday night," Wilson said.

"And almost Monday," Eli said. "What do you think?"

"One look at this guy and I can tell you he's victim number three," Wilson said.

Roscoe entered the sauna. "My guys are working the entire building, Lieutenant, but it would take a minor miracle to find anything."

"Have every ashtray and trashcan checked for cigarette butts," Eli said. "We might get lucky."

"Right," Roscoe said. "But I wouldn't count on a decent set of prints."

Tyler entered the sauna. "The Captain's here."

Wilson said, "I'll have my guys take the body as soon as you release."

"Did we find identification yet?" Eli asked Tyler.

"I had to send for a bolt cutter," Tyler said. "A lot of the lockers have padlocks on them."

Howe entered the sauna, looked at the victim and said, "You

gotta be kidding me. This ones a fruit. Why kill this one?"

"He's 4F, Captain," Wilson said.

"How do you know that?" Howe asked.

"He has flat feet," Wilson said.

Everybody looked at the victim's feet.

"He's right, Captain," Eli said.

"Well, who the fuck is he?" Howe asked.

"I'll let you know in a few minutes," Tyler said.

"I saw a cafeteria across the hall," Eli said. "Let's talk there. It's hot as hell in here."

Eli and Howe crossed the hall and entered the cafeteria.

"For God's sake, Eli. Do you know what this place is?" Howe said.

"I didn't. I do now."

"The whole building is a clubhouse for queers," Howe said.

"I don't see what that has…" Eli said.

"Got it," Tyler said as he entered the cafeteria holding a wallet.

Eli, Howe and Tyler took chairs at a table. Tyler gave the wallet to Eli. Eli opened it and removed the driver's license.

"Bruce Boxburger," Eli said. "Age is thirty-four. Lives on West 59th off Eighth Avenue."

Eli handed the license to Howe.

"He's got some photos here," Eli said and set them on the table.

"He's got a mother, father, two sisters," Howe said. "Wonder if they know he's a flaming queer?"

"He wasn't killed because he's homosexual," Eli said as he removed Boxburger's draft card. "He was killed because of this."

Eli set the draft card on the table. It showed he was 4F.

"There is no way to keep this quiet anymore," Eli said.

"Goddammit," Howe said.

"Tyler, tomorrow morning you and Bannon check Mr.

Boxburger's apartment," Eli said. "Find out what he did for a living, who his friends were, the usual."

Howe sighed. "Eli, talk to his parents. I never was any good at that. Wait until we get confirmation on the victim. I'll wake the mayor up and tell him we can't keep the newspapers out any longer."

Eli nodded. "Our meeting at 10:00?"

Howe nodded. "We'll meet at the VA Building at 9:30."

Eli nodded.

"And make sure this building is under lockdown until I say otherwise," Howe said. "Any complaints direct to me and I'll deal with them."

"Tyler and I are going to poke around a bit," Eli said.

"Just don't be late in the morning," Howe said.

* * *

Eli stood behind the desk in the lobby and scanned the guest book.

"What are you looking for, Lieutenant?" Tyler asked.

"Sunday night was a slow night," Eli said. "Just eight guests."

"They close early on Sunday. Ten o'clock," Tyler said.

"What are the odds our man walked in the front door and signed the book and went upstairs where anybody can see him?" Eli said.

"I'd say none," Tyler said.

"Let's find out how he did it," Eli said.

They went to the second floor where a window was located at the end of the hallway. It wasn't locked and Eli slid it open. Outside the window was a fire escape that went from the ground floor to the roof.

Eli and Tyler looked down.

"The ladder at the bottom is descended," Eli said. "It faces the rear of the building and Ninth Avenue. There's a fence. He has no trouble getting over, lowers the ladder and climbs up to the second floor where he finds Boxburger in the sauna. In and out in a matter of minutes."

"So how did he know where Boxburger would be at the exact time?" Tyler asked.

"Same as the others," Eli said. "He had them under surveillance. When you check his apartment and friends, find out all his habits."

"All, Lieutenant?"

"All that pertain," Eli said. "Let's get this place locked down and I'll drive you back to your car."

* * *

"What do you think the Captain would do if he found out about me?" Tyler asked.

"I don't think he would do anything," Eli said.

"You heard him. Fruit. Queer," Tyler said.

"I don't think he's aware of what he's saying or how it sounds," Eli said. "He's just talking how people talk these days."

"That's the problem," Tyler said. "It's like throwing the word nigger or wop or Mick around. People aren't aware of the pain it inflicts if the word describes you."

"That's not going to change," Eli said. "Hell, growing up I was a wop and a Mick both. I remember coming home from school one day in the first grade. I was crying because the kids were teasing me, calling me a wop mutt. I told my father. He said to punch them in the nose. My mother, though, she sat me down and told me people only have power over you if you allow them to. If you ignore them and what they say they have no power over you."

Eli pulled his car curbside to the headquarters building.

"So what did you do?" Tyler asked.

"I punched the kid in the nose," Eli said. "I was six. What would you have done?"

Tyler grinned and opened his door. "Goodnight, Lieutenant."

* * *

Eli smoked a cigarette in bed and watched the smoke rise and vanish into the stream of air coming off the fan.

He tried to keep his mind on the latest murder victim.

His thoughts kept drifting off to Mavis.

It was a possibility that he was falling for her, ridiculous as that sounded.

The one word in Italian he father uttered at the door was 'Jackpot.'

But then again dad didn't know what she did for a living.

Eli put the cigarette out in an ashtray, turned off the lamp and went to sleep.

He dreamt, not about the war, but about Mavis.

Thirteen

The administrator of the Manhattan Chapter of Veterans Affairs, John Rook, looked across his desk at Howe and Eli.

"You can't possibly expect me to comply with such a request, Captain Howe," Rook said. "Even if you are investigating a murder."

"Multiple murders at this point," Howe said. "And we suspect all committed by the same man."

"That may well be, Captain, but classified federal military records can only be declassified by a federal court order," Rook said. "I suggest you take the matter to a federal judge for review."

"Do you know what it takes to get such a court order?" Howe asked.

"I do," Rook said. "My advice is to quit wasting time here and start looking for a federal judge to give you one."

* * *

Mayor O'Dwyer stared hard at Howe and Eli from behind his desk. Both Howe and Eli stood.

"In fifteen minutes I have to meet the police commissioner and chief of police on the steps of City Hall," O'Dwyer said. "We're going to make a statement in front of every reporter in the city, print and radio. Even the new television news people will be there. Every man who was rejected for military service will feel they have a target on their backs and for good reason, they will. Two minutes after the press conference concludes, this city will go into a panic. We'll be in a fucking shit storm the likes of which this city has never seen."

"We understand that, Mr...." Howe said.

"Shut up, Captain," O'Dwyer snapped.

Howe and Eli glanced at each other.

"I expect the both of you to be at the press conference and I expect the both of you to keep your mouths closed unless I tell you to open them," O'Dwyer said. "Am I understood?"

Howe and Eli nodded.

"After the meeting, you two plus the chief and district attorney will see a federal judge about a court order," O'Dwyer said. "That's all, gentlemen. I'll see you on the steps."

* * *

Howe and Eli waited on the top of the steps for the press conference to begin. Two hundred or more reporters had gathered at the bottom of the steps in front of a podium.

Eli lit a cigarette. "I get the feeling his honor is looking for a hat to pin this on," he said.

"O'Dwyer is worried about votes," Howe said. "He's a politician."

"Do you think we can make a case to the district attorney to request a court order from a judge?" Eli asked.

"We can make a case," Howe said. "Question is will the DA buy it and take it to a judge."

O'Dwyer, the Chief of Police and Commissioner exited the building and walked down the steps to the podium.

Howe, about to follow, stopped when the Commissioner motioned with his hand.

125

At the podium, the crowd of reporters immediately went nuts with questions. The Commissioner had to beg for silence before he started to speak.

Once the Commissioner began making his statement, Eli tuned him out and found his thoughts had shifted over to Mavis.

Her hair always smelled so good, like freshly cut grass. Her eyes were steel-like grey and the contrast of her eyes and hair made her amazing to look at.

"Hey, Lieutenant, are you listening?" Howe asked.

"No, I'm not," Eli said.

"Tell you the truth, I'm not either," Howe said. "What happened last night after I left the scene?"

"We backtracked and found he came in through the fire escape," Eli said. "Through the window and into the sauna. He couldn't have been inside more than two minutes."

"I'm getting the feeling our man is as smart as he is crazy," Howe said.

"I make him more insane than crazy," Eli said.

"Explain to me the difference," Howe said.

"Crazy means he can't reason," Eli said. "A person can be insane and still reason as well as you or I."

"Who told you that shit, the department shrinks?"

"They just called your name," Eli said.

"Shit," Howe said.

* * *

Eli and Howe sat on a bench in the hallway outside District Attorney Michael Bell's office while the Chief and Commissioner met with Bell inside.

"How do you think I did?" Howe asked.

"At the podium? You did good," Eli said.

"I'm not much of a public speaker," Howe said.

"So you don't plan on a career in politics after you retire?" Eli asked.

Howe grinned. "All I plan on are upstate fishing trips."

"When I was a kid my dad would take me fishing on City Island," Eli said. "We'd fish right off the bridge."

"Great clams on City Island," Howe said.

The door to Bell's office suddenly opened and the Police Chief poked his head out. "Come in and make your case," he said.

Michael Bell was in his late forties and had been Manhattan's District Attorney for eight years. Rumor had it he planned to run for mayor after O'Dwyer's term was up. He sat at his desk and looked at Howe and Eli as they entered his office.

Four chairs were lined up in front of the desk. The Commissioner sat in one, the Police Chief took the chair to his right, leaving the two vacant chairs for Howe and Eli.

They stood and waited for Bell to tell them to sit.

"Captain Howe, Lieutenant Rico, who wants to speak first?" Bell said.

Since Bell didn't tell them to sit, they stood.

"Lieutenant Rico is my lead investigator," Howe said. "I'll let him address you first."

Bell nodded. "Go ahead, Lieutenant."

Eli cleared his throat and spoke for twenty minutes, during which time Bell made notes on a legal pad.

When Eli concluded, Bell looked at Howe.

"Anything to add, Captain?" Bell said.

"I stand by every word Lieutenant Rico said," Howe said. "He's the best damn investigator in the city and I've examined every shred of evidence and agree with his determination and findings."

Bell was silent for a moment as he scanned his legal pad. Then he looked up and said, "Whenever I am challenged with a decision I am just not sure about, I always talk it out. I usually call an assistant attorney to be my sounding board, but Lieutenant Rico will serve nicely."

"Sounding board?" Eli said.

"I'll be you and you can be the federal judge," Bell said. "Shall we begin?"

"Begin?" Eli said.

"Since I'm you, I'll start," Bell said. "Your honor, I need a court order to declassify military records on veterans health records. I believe the murderer of three victims is a former Army Ranger suffering from a breakdown and is targeting men who were 4F during the war. Your turn, Lieutenant."

Eli stayed silent, unwilling to play Bell's *gotcha game*.

"No? Nothing? Allow me to continue then," Bell said. "You see, your honor, I was a Ranger during the war and that makes me an expert on killing. You see, it's impossible for anybody other than an Army Ranger to learn to climb a rope, scale a wall, use a knife or break a neck and therefore our suspect may be military and I request access to government privileged information."

Eli stared at Bell.

"How am I doing, your honor?" Bell said.

"You can go to hell," Eli said. "Sir."

"That will be enough of that, Lieutenant," the Police Chief said.

"Do you know who Edmund Burke was?" Eli asked Bell.

"Enlighten us, Lieutenant," Bell said.

"He was born two hundred years ago in Ireland," Eli said. "He said, and I quote, 'The only thing necessary for the triumph of evil is for good men to do nothing.'"

Bell stared at Eli for a few moments.

Next to Eli, Howe sighed.

"Except for the Lieutenant, clear the room," Bell said.

For a few seconds, nobody moved.

"That wasn't a request, gentlemen," Bell said.

Howe, the Commissioner and Police Chief filed out of the office.

"You have some pair of balls, Lieutenant," Bell said.

"I'd rather have a court order at the moment," Eli said.

"I need a day to prepare," Bell said. "Meet me here at 9:30 tomorrow morning. Be prepared, Lieutenant."

"I will, sir," Eli said. "And thank you."

"Our patience will achieve more than our force," Bell said.

"Sir?"

"Edmund Burke, he said that," Bell said.

Eli grinned. "Yes, sir."

* * *

"Son of a bitch," Howe said when Eli told him the news in the hallway.

"Good work, Lieutenant," the Police Chief said. "I expect a full report afterwards."

"Yes sir," Eli said.

"And on all your progress," the Police Chief said. "This city is in full-blown panic mode."

"Yes sir," Eli said.

* * *

Tyler and Bannon were at their desks when Howe and Eli entered the squad room.

"My office," Howe told them.

The two detectives followed Howe and Eli into Howe's office. Howe sat behind his desk.

"So what do you got on Mr. Boxberger?" Howe asked.

"We checked every square inch of his apartment," Tyler said. "It's clean."

"Except for his sex toys," Bannon said. "You won't believe the shit this guy had."

"His sex toys didn't kill him," Eli said. "What about statements from the janitor and desk clerk?"

"They both knew him as a regular, but no one ever uses their real names," Bannon said. "The janitor said he caught Boxberger giving blowjobs to men in the sauna a few times, but for that place it's nothing unusual. Just the opposite."

"Jesus Christ," Howe said.

"What did he do for work?" Eli asked.

"He owns a small antique store in the West Village," Tyler said.

"I'm sure every queer in the city is a client," Bannon said.

"Can we stick to the facts and what's relevant to his murder," Eli said. "He was killed as the others and that makes three with 4F status. How did our man know Boxberger would be at the bath house ten o'clock Sunday night and how did he know how to gain access?"

"Only one way, surveillance," Tyler said.

"Exactly," Eli said. "So what does that tell us?"

"He's had lots of time to plan his victims," Tyler said.

"Also exactly," Eli said. "That means he's been on the street for a while, maybe even as much as a year."

"So you're saying he has his next victims planned out well in advance?" Tyler said.

"That's what I'm saying and we don't know who they are or when he will strike next," Eli said. "And we won't know unless we catch him in the act and that is very unlikely, or he makes a mistake, which is also unlikely... or, the judge gives us access to military records."

"What are the chances of that?" Bannon asked.

"We'll find out in the morning," Eli said.

"I hate to bring this up, but Boxberger's parents need to be notified," Howe said.

"I'll take care of it," Eli said. "Did we get their address?"

* * *

The Boxberger family lived in a working class neighborhood in Queens. Eli took the Queensboro Bridge from Manhattan to the neighborhood known as Long Island City.

Francis Boxberger, mostly called 'Frank,' was fifty-nine years old and worked for the Sanitation Department. His wife Mary, two years younger, worked as a phone operator for the phone company.

They had two daughters in addition to their son Bruce.

Martha, twenty-nine, and Elizabeth, twenty-seven. Neither daughter was married and they shared the second floor apartment in the Boxberger home.

Two cars were in the driveway when Eli arrived and parked on the street. He had his identification at the ready when he knocked on the door of the first floor.

Mary Boxberger opened the door and looked at Eli.

He held up his identification and badge. "Lieutenant Rico, Mrs. Boxberger," he said. "I need to talk to you about your son."

"My son? What about him?" Mary asked.

"It's better if we talked inside," Eli said.

* * *

"What's this about?" Frank Boxberger asked after he looked at Eli's badge.

"Your son, Mr. Boxberger," Eli said.

"I have no son," Frank said.

"Frank, please," Mary said. "This concerns our son."

"My son is dead to me, stinking faggot," Frank said.

"Mr. Boxberger, I have…" Eli said.

"I told you, my son is dead to me," Frank said.

"Let the Lieutenant speak, Frank," Mary said.

Eli sighed. "There is no good way to say this. Your son has been murdered. Last night around ten o'clock, we…"

Mary fainted and fell to the rug.

* * *

Martha and Elizabeth joined their parents and Eli at the kitchen table. Mary poured coffee, then took a chair next to Frank.

Both daughters cried for ten minutes at the news. Their eyes were bloodshot and swollen.

"I'm not surprised at this news, the way he lived and all," Frank said.

"Frank, our son is dead," Mary said.

"I know he's dead," Frank said. "What I said is I'm not surprised given the way he lived."

"Dad, you don't know how he lived," Martha said. "You haven't spoken to him in nearly ten years."

"He died in a fag bath house, how do you think he lived?" Frank said.

"Frank, please," Mary said and burst into tears.

"Is that it, Lieutenant?" Frank asked.

"Someone will have to identify and claim the body," Eli said.

"We'll take care of it," Frank said. "If there is nothing else, please leave my home."

* * *

Eli sat at the kitchen table and listened to the news on the radio. Boxberger's name as the third victim was still withheld until a positive identification could be made by his family.

He lit a cigarette and took a small sip from his coffee cup. The coffee had gone cold. He stood and dumped it into the sink and filled the cup with lukewarm coffee from the pot.

At the window, he looked at the dark streets and park, sipped and smoked. Without knowing why, Eli reached for the wall phone and dialed the number for Mavis. She answered on the third ring.

"Mavis, it's Eli," Eli said clumsily.

"Is everything all right?" Mavis said. "It's after ten o'clock."

"Rough day," Eli said. "Are you alone?"

"I'm alone," Mavis said. "Something is wrong. What is it?"

"Rough day, rougher tomorrow," Eli said. "I wanted to hear a friendly voice. I'm sorry if I woke you."

"Eli, don't be silly," Mavis said. "Why don't you come spend the night here with me?"

"I have an early meeting tomorrow," Eli said.

"In Manhattan?"

"Yes."

"Which is closer to your meeting, my place or yours?" Mavis asked.

"Yours but..." Eli said.

"I'll see you in about an hour," Mavis said. "Have you had dinner?"

"No, but..."

"Me neither. I'll have something waiting for you," Mavis said.

"Are you sure?" Eli said.

"One hour. Don't be late," Mavis said and hung up.

*   *   *

Eli sat with his back against the rim of the tub. Mavis sat with her back against his chest and she took his arms and wrapped them around him.

"Hungry?" she asked.

"Starved," Eli said.

"I have a meatloaf in the oven," Mavis said. "It will be ready in about fifteen minutes."

"I told you not to go to any trouble," Eli said.

"I was making it anyway," Mavis said. "It usually is good for three meals."

"I remember you told my mother you can cook," Eli said.

"I can do laundry and handle a broom, too," Mavis said. "And in a pinch, I can even do laundry."

"I didn't mean... It's just... "

"I'm teasing you, silly," Mavis said. "Let's get out; I don't want the meatloaf to burn."

*   *   *

They sat opposite each other at the kitchen table, Mavis in her robe, Eli in his underwear.

She cooked the meatloaf the way his mother did when he was growing up, with strips of bacon across the top. There was also a bowl of mashed potatoes, corn and gravy.

Eli sampled the meatloaf. "This is really good," he said.

"Thank you," Mavis said. "I can sew, too."

Eli looked at her. She had a sly grin on her lips that nearly floored him.

"What?" Mavis asked.

"I don't... nothing," Eli said.

"Eat. We can have dessert on the balcony," Mavis said.

* * *

Eli and Mavis ate bowls of chocolate ice cream on the balcony. The lights of the city shone brightly all around them.

"I saw the news on television today," Mavis said. "About the third murder. Is that what's bothering you so much?"

Eli set the empty bowl on the small table and lit a cigarette. "The victim's name has been withheld until a positive identification is made," he said. "I had to tell his family that he died in a homosexual bath house on 28th Street. His mother and two sisters acted as you'd expect, but the father hated his son for being what he was. The man hated his own son."

Mavis reached over and took Eli's right hand in hers. "What time is your meeting?"

"9:30, but I need to be in the office by 8:00," Eli said.

"Then we better get some sleep," Mavis said.

* * *

With Mavis wrapped up in his arms, Eli's world didn't seem so dark and bleak. Maybe that's all love really was, he thought. A person makes another person's world seem better, brighter and worth living in.

Mavis felt Eli drift off to sleep. She rolled onto her side and placed Eli's arm over her chest and closed her eyes.

"I love you, Eli," she whispered ever so softly.

Thirteen

Eli sat across from Michael Bell at the conference table in Bell's office and for ninety minutes they discussed strategy on presenting a request to a federal judge.

"Let's talk about Judge Webb," Bell said. "He was appointed by Roosevelt in '39 and is one of the few holdovers for Truman. He plans to retire after Truman's term is up. He's tough, as tough as they come and he can spot bullshit from a mile away."

"You've presented to him before?" Eli said.

"Many times," Bell said. "Most of the time I've left empty-handed."

"Wait," Eli said. "I read a news story a while back about a request you made for federal warrants against the mafia. That was Webb, wasn't it?"

Bell nodded. "Against Vito Genovese and Webb rejected my request. We see him at one, let's get an early lunch."

*　*　*

They ate at a diner near the federal courthouse.

"Why did Webb reject your request against Genovese?" Eli asked.

"Webb is a purist," Bell said. "He has no wiggle room in his legal decisions. I asked for wiretaps and he refused because my evidence wasn't strong enough. Genovese is the biggest importer of heroin into this country from Afghanistan and Turkey, but I lacked tangible proof in Webb's eyes. He told me to come back when I had additional evidence to present. I'm still gathering so to speak."

Eli sighed. "What are our chances?"

"In the wind, Lieutenant," Bell said. "In the wind."

* * *

Judge Webb was in his mid sixties. His white hair was immaculately cut; his blue eyes were emotionless behind a pair of eyeglasses.

Bell presented first and spoke for thirty minutes.

Webb didn't speak and made notes in pen on a legal pad.

Eli followed Bell and also spoke for about thirty minutes.

Again, Webb didn't speak and took notes.

When Eli concluded, he sat at the table next to Bell.

"Would you both stand," Webb said quietly.

Eli and Bell stood.

"Usually I take time to reflect upon the evidence presented to me," Webb said. "An hour, a day, sometimes as much as a week before I reach a decision. However, in this case I require no additional time to reach a decision. Your request for a court order is denied."

"May I ask why?" Bell said.

"You may," Webb said. "Your evidence, such as it is, is based solely upon a hunch by Lieutenant Rico that the person you seek in the recent string of murders is a former Army Ranger. You have no proof of this, just Lieutenant Rico's hunch and gut feeling that this person is or was an Army Ranger. I can't order the declassification of highly sensitive military records on a hunch and a gut. Bring me actual proof and you can have a court order, but until then your request is denied. That's all, gentlemen."

* * *

Eli and Bell sat on a bench in the small park across the street from the federal building.

Eli lit a cigarette and said, "He knows the only way we can present actual evidence is when we catch him."

"He does, yes," Bell said. "Webb is worried about his legacy as a judge. One bad decision can ruin an entire career on the bench."

"His legacy?" Eli said.

"Welcome to the legal system, Lieutenant," Bell said. "My advice to you is to find some hard evidence we can use and I'll give it another shot."

* * *

Eli stood in front of the map of New York City that hung on the back wall of the squad room.

"What are you looking at?" Howe asked.

"Distances," Eli said.

"Distances? From what?" Howe asked.

"Eighty-First Street to Bleeker is about six miles," Eli said. "West 28th about three and a half."

"From where?" Howe asked.

"Each other," Eli said.

"What are you driving at?" Howe asked.

"How does he get around?" Eli asked. "If you're on your way to kill a victim and you need to be at a specific place at a specific time, how do you travel?"

Howe looked at the map. "Bus, subway, walk," he said.

"That was my thinking," Eli said. "But what if he drove?"

"Drove?" Howe said. "The surest way to be late in this city is to drive."

"Buses get snagged in traffic. Subways always run late. Walking is slow. In all three, your face is exposed to the public," Eli said. "In a car, nobody sees you."

"Okay, so it's possible he drove, what does that mean?" Howe said.

Eli looked at Howe.

"The possibility of a parking ticket," Eli said.

Howe stared at Eli.

Eli looked across the squad room. "Jack, Tyler, the captain's office on the double."

Howe went behind his desk while Eli stood and looked at Bannon and Tyler.

"As many detectives as you need on this," Eli said. "Check a ten-block radius of where each victim was murdered for any cars given parking tickets. Make a list. Go."

Bannon and Tyler looked at each other.

"Someone around here is a fucking genius and it ain't me," Bannon said.

After Bannon and Tyler left the office, Howe said, "Sorry about what happened in court, Eli."

"From his point of view, Webb was correct in his decision," Eli said. "The problem is more men are going to die because of it."

Howe sighed.

"I'll give Bannon and Tyler a hand," Eli said.

* * *

Eli was amazed at the number of tickets given out in a ten-block radius on the night of each murder.

Eleven the afternoon of Tanner's murder.

Thirteen the night of Magrady's murder.

Nine the night Boxberger was killed.

Thirty-three tickets was not a large amount to run down by any means.

By six o'clock, Eli called it quits for the day.

"We'll run down every ticket and see where it goes in the morning," he told Tyler and Bannon.

Alone in the squad room, Eli thought about calling Mavis when the phone rang.

"Lieutenant Rico," Eli said when he answered the call.

"Lieutenant, is Rosa Garcia," Rosa said.

"Hello, Rosa, how are you?" Eli said.

"Fine, but I ask a favor," she said.

"If I can."

"Can you come to the apartment?"

"When?"

"Now."

"Right now?"

"Is important," Rosa said.

* * *

Rosa answered the door wearing a yellow sundress. Her hair was pinned up and she was barefoot.

"Please come in," she said. "I make coffee."

They sat on the sofa and Rosa filled two cups with strong Cuban coffee.

"You help me very much," Rosa said. "I want to say thank you and goodbye."

"Where are you going?" Eli said.

"To Miami," Rosa said. "They tell me many Cuban people live in Miami. I signed all the papers and I'm… how do you say it?"

"Set for life," Eli said.

"Yes. Set for life," Rosa said.

"Good for you," Eli said.

"I rather have Roger, but is nothing I can do about it," Rosa said.

"No, there isn't. It's best to move on and make a life for yourself while you are still a young woman," Eli said.

"That's why I go to Miami, to start new," Rosa said. "The lawyer say many Cuban people have come to Miami to live, so I won't feel so lonely."

"May I offer you a word of advice?" Eli said.

"Of course."

"When you get to Miami, don't let many people know how much money you are now worth," Eli said. "The less people know the better. Live small for a while until you get established."

Rosa nodded. "Good advice."

"Well, I better get going," Eli said.

"I walk you to the door," Rosa said.

At the door, Rosa smiled at Eli. "Maybe in the future you come see me in Miami?" she said. "Is too soon right now, but I like you. You a good man."

Eli smiled. "I'll keep that in mind," he said.

* * *

Eli returned to the squad room and sat at his desk. He was alone and the silence was a bit eerie.

He lit a cigarette and thought about the day's events.

Judge Webb was correct in his decision. He needed more concrete evidence for a warrant and court order. The problem, Eli also acknowledged was another victim or victims had to die to get such evidence and at best that was a maybe.

He crushed the cigarette out in the ashtray, stood, and walked to the door.

Tomorrow was another day.

* * *

The phone was ringing when Eli entered his apartment. He grabbed the phone in the living room.

"Lieutenant Rico," he said.

Mavis laughed. "That's how you answer the phone at home?" she said and laughed again.

Her voice sounded like church bells to Eli.

"Habit. I just came from work," Eli said.

"You left so early this morning I didn't get to say goodbye," Mavis said. "And you left your shirt and stuff behind. I washed them. Now you have an excuse to come see me again."

Eli sat on the sofa and lit a cigarette. "Work is out of control right now," he said.

"I read the papers and watched the news on television," Mavis said. "I think you should come spend the night with me tomorrow. It will take your mind off things."

"I don't think I can," Eli said. "Chances are I'll be working very late."

"I'll wait up," Mavis said.

"I don't think I can," Eli said.

"I would have sworn you really liked me, Eli," Mavis said.

"It's not that," Eli said.

"Then what?"

"I need to be near the phone in case of another call," Eli said. "I can't exactly give the dispatcher your number as a contact, now can I?"

"I see," Mavis said. "No, I suppose not."

"I'll call you in a few days, all right," Eli said.

"Okay, sure," Mavis said and hung up.

Eli set the phone down and sighed.

"Do not fall for a hooker," he said aloud. "Whatever you do, Eli, don't fall for a hooker."

Fourteen

By noon, Eli, Bannon, and Tyler had researched each parking ticket and the owners of each car.

The surprise was that one car the day of each murder was reported stolen. The car ticketed two blocks from The Charter Arms was stolen from Riverside Drive off 120th Street.

The car ticketed one block from the Turkish Bathhouse was stolen from 57th Street and Tenth Avenue.

The car ticketed two blocks from the Jazz Clue came from West End Avenue and 104th Street.

All three stolen cars were Ford sedans, dark blue or black in color.

Eli shared the results with Howe.

"You can bet the next one will also be a stolen car," Howe said. "It's too late now, but the next one gets an overhaul by forensics."

Tyler rushed into Howe's office. "Got another one. The Bronx. Call just came in from Bronx Homicide."

"Tyler, you go with me," Eli said. He looked at Howe. "Feel like getting out of the office?"

* * *

The Webster Avenue Boxing Gym was located in the South Bronx on 167 Street. A dozen uniformed officers were out front, keeping a gathered crowd away from the door.

Eli parked beside a hydrant, tossed his police sticker on the dashboard and he, Howe and Tyler walked to the door.

"Captain Howe, Lieutenant Rico, Detective Tyler," Howe said as he flashed his captain's badge.

"Our Captain is waiting inside," a uniform said.

Howe led the way into the gym. The stink of stale sweat was overpowering.

Captain Davidson of The Bronx Homicide Unit was talking with a few of his detectives.

"Art, how have you been?" Davidson asked.

Howe shook Davidson's hand. "Lieutenant Rico, Detective Tyler," he said.

"Where's the victim?" Eli asked.

"You're gonna love this," Davidson said.

"Before we do anything else, can you have a traffic check done on all cars ticketed within a ten-mile radius of here?" Eli said. "See if any were stolen."

"I can. Why?" Davidson said.

"We believe our man uses a stolen car and leaves it at or near the scene," Eli said.

Davidson turned to one of his detectives. "Go," he said.

*   *   *

The second floor held two small sparring rings and one full-sized boxing ring. Several uniformed officers guarded the main ring. An old black man seated on a stool outside the ring was crying openly.

Inside the ring, dressed in boxing shorts, was the victim.

"Who is who?" Eli asked.

"The negro in the ring is Tyrell Butte, the number nine ranked welterweight boxer in the country," Davidson said. "The old man sitting there is his trainer Eddie Bracken. I guess Butte lived with the old man, who, as you can see is taking this very hard."

Roscoe and Wilson suddenly appeared beside Howe and Tyler.

"Looks like number four," Wilson said.

Eli walked to Bracken.

"Mr. Bracken, I'm Lieutenant Rico. I'd like to ask you a few questions," Eli said.

"Why?" Bracken sobbed. "Why somebody want to do harm to Tyrell? Tyrell never hurt nobody outside the ring. Never."

"Mr. Bracken, I understand Mr. Butte lives with you?" Eli said.

"I practically raised him," Bracken said.

"When did you last see Mr. Butte?" Eli asked.

"Last night around 8:00," Bracken said. "He said he wanted to get some shadow boxing and rope work in. He does that all the time so I didn't think nothing of it."

"You found his body?" Eli asked.

Bracken nodded. "I open the gym at noon every day except Sunday. I didn't realize he was gone from the apartment. He works a regular job at the post office on the Concourse and is usually gone before I get up."

Eli walked to the ring where Wilson and Roscoe were standing next to the body.

"Doc?" Eli said.

"He's number four, no doubt," Wilson said.

"Tyler, check the locker room for his clothes," Eli said.

Eli returned to Bracken. "Mr. Bracken do you happen to know Mr. Butte's draft status?"

"His what?"

"Military status. Did he serve in the war?" Eli said.

146

"He enlisted in '42 after Pearl Harbor, but was turned down on account of his poor eyesight," Bracken said. "He's... what do you call it... far sighted. In the ring all he need to see is sixteen feet away. He wears glasses at work. The Army a different story."

"Was he married, did he have family?"

"Tyrell on his own since he eight and I took him in," Bracken said. "He had a fight in August coming up and after that he was going to spar with Sugar Ray to help him get ready for his next championship fight. Who would do this? Who?"

"Mr. Bracken, does anybody else have a key to the gym besides Mr. Butte?" Eli asked.

"No, nobody," Bracken said.

Tyler returned and said, "Some clothing in a locker, but no wallet."

"Check the front door for signs of forced entry and markings the lock might have picked," Eli said. "Where's the locker room?"

"By the exit sign."

Eli walked to the hallway, past the exit sign and stood in front of the locker room. Howe and Davidson followed him.

"Detective?" Davidson said.

Eli backtracked and pushed open the exit door.

"No lock on this door," Eli said.

He went down the stairs where another exit door was marked Emergency Use Only.

Howe and Davidson followed.

"Unlocked from the inside," Eli said and shoved open the door.

He looked at the metal doorframe.

"Jimmied," Eli said.

"Those marks are fresh," Davidson said.

"This backyard fence faces a side street," Eli said. "He hops the wall, jimmies the lock and goes up to a dark gym where Butte is shadowboxing and that's that. He goes out the same way sight unseen. He abandons the car and grabs the subway or a bus home."

"Why abandon the car and expose himself on the street?" Davidson said.

"By the time of the murder, it's possible the owner reported it stolen," Eli said. "Why risk getting picked up on a stolen car beef when the subway is just a few blocks from here? I'll tell Roscoe to dust this door for prints just in case."

Eli walked up the staircase. Howe and Davidson stayed behind for a moment.

'Your Lieutenant knows his stuff," Davidson said.

"Eli has a natural instinct for this kind of work," Howe said. "Best I've ever seen."

* * *

Late in the afternoon, Eli, Howe, Tyler and Davidson stood in front of the boxing gym while several of Davidson's detectives sealed the door with police tape.

A detective approached Davidson with a report. "On ticketed cars, Captain," he said and gave Davidson the report.

Davidson scanned the report and then looked at Eli. "Stolen car ticketed around the corner from here," he said. "Reported stolen right around the time of the murder. A Ford sedan."

"Stolen from where?" Eli asked.

"White Plains Road off 211th Street," Davidson said.

"East Bronx," Eli said. "Our man knows how to get around the City."

* * *

Howe sat on the edge of Eli's desk as Eli sipped coffee and then lit a cigarette.

"You've been right one hundred percent of the time," Howe said. "And we are no closer than after the first one."

"Our man knows the City," Eli said. "How to get around by subway and bus. An outsider would take years to learn the travel routes he's taken. Our man is a New Yorker or someone who spent years in the City before the war. He's not someone who dropped in for a visit and decided to stay."

"I agree with you, but there is almost eight million people in this city and half are men," Howe said. "Ten percent of that half could fit our man. Even if I had five hundred detectives working around the clock we're talking a year to profile them all."

"We don't have a year, Art," Eli said. "At the rate he's escalating his targets they will be a hundred dead by New Year's Eve. He knows we're pulling all the stops to find him. He reads the papers, listens to the radio and for all we know he has a television."

"I don't even have a television," Howe confessed. "Not at those prices."

"Let's look at what we know," Eli said. "So far his victims have all been men classified 4F. He uses a German bayonet to deliver his message, but kills them with a Ranger Choke Hold. He's very adept at stealing cars and likes Fords. He drives to his victims and uses public transportation to leave the scene. He's smart and skilled and patient and seemingly fearless in that he has no fear of getting caught. His only mistake so far is leaving cigarette butts behind and even that tells us nothing. There must be a half million men in the city that smoke Camels and at least ten percent use a plastic filter."

"How does he avoid blood on his clothes, his shoes?" Howe asked. "Why are there no bloody footprints?"

"He stabs and immediately applies the choke hold," Eli said. "To do that you need to jump back at least three feet. He may have blood on his clothes, but not his shoes."

"As soon as I call the mayor and the chief, I'm going home," Howe said. "I suggest you do the same."

*   *   *

After Howe left and Eli had the squad room to himself, he sat his desk, smoked a few cigarettes and ran things around in his mind one more time.

The question yet to be asked was how was he selecting his victims?

Men don't walk around with their draft status tattooed to their foreheads. That private, privileged information was known to but a select few with classified status.

A doctor, a psychiatrist, a government official with Veterans Affairs, the list was pretty short.

Close to exclusive.

Eli doubted the killer was an employee of Veterans Affairs.

Yet he had access.

How?

A long-term care patient at a military hospital might be able to navigate around the red tape and steal or copy records.

Someone locked up for a year or more, stewing in his own juices, plotting and planning until he's finally released.

The stew bubbled over and there are four dead men whose only crime was being unfit for military service.

How many more military records were in his possession? A hundred. A thousand. More?

The sinking feeling in his gut was that more men would have to die before Eli knew the answer to that question.

*   *   *

Eli parked his car a half block from his apartment and walked. It was hot and sticky and he carried his suit jacket over his right shoulder.

It was dark, and a few hundred feet from his building, Eli spotted someone sitting on the front steps.

That was nothing unusual in the summer months. People sat out all the time.

As he approached the building the person stood up and in the light of a streetlamp he saw it was Mavis. She held an overnight bag in her right hand.

"I called first," she said when Eli reached the steps.

"Work. I've been working," Eli said.

"Can I come up?" Mavis said. "I never got the chance to tell you what I wanted to the other day."

Eli nodded. "Come up," he said.

*   *   *

Eli filled two glasses with ice and then opened a bottle of Coke and poured it over the ice and carried the glasses to the table where Mavis sat. He set the glasses on the table and turned on the wall fan.

Mavis took a sip from her glass. "I'm a bit nervous," she said.

Eli took a chair next to her.

"You? You're nervous?" he said.

"Despite what I did for a living, I'm still a woman and I have feelings, Eli," Mavis said.

"I didn't mean… you said did. What do you mean did?" Eli said.

"Oh Eli, you're so naive when it comes to women," Mavis said. "How could you be this important homicide detective and have no insight when it comes to women?"

"I don't understand. What are you saying?" Eli said.

"Eli, I quit the business nearly two years ago," Mavis said. "I really have been working as a dance coach for new Rockettes. Here, look."

Mavis reached down into her overnight bag and removed a shoebox and set it on the table.

"Open it," she said.

Eli removed the lid. The shoebox was filled with white envelopes. He reached for an envelope. His name and a date were written on it.

"I don't understand," he said.

"Eli, you dolt. That's your money," Mavis said. "Every time you came to see me I put the money in an envelope and set it aside."

Eli looked at the shoe box. There were at least fifty or sixty envelopes.

"Why?" he asked.

"Because, you idiot, I've fallen in love with you," Mavis said.

Eli stared at Mavis.

"You said you were moving home come September," he said.

"I am. Or was. I made the decision to move home because I'm in love with a man who doesn't love me," Mavis said. "But I was wrong. A woman knows when a man loves her and you can deny it all you want, Eli, but you're in love with me, too. There, I've said what I came to say. I've returned your money. Thank you for the Coke."

Mavis stood and picked up her overnight bag.

"Besides the shoebox, do you have clothes in there?" Eli said.

*　*　*

Eli rested his head against the rim of the bathtub and closed his eyes. Mavis sat opposite him.

"It's bad, isn't it?" she said. "The case you're working on."

Eli opened his eyes. "The worst I've ever seen," he said.

"The news on the radio said he was some kind of boxer," Mavis said.

"A welterweight from The Bronx," Eli said. "A few miles south of here."

"What's a welterweight?" Mavis asked.

"He weighed no more than 147," Eli said.

"What do you weigh?"

"225."

"So he was a little guy."

"Yeah, he was a little guy with a bright future," Eli said. "He was going to spar with Sugar Ray."

"I don't know what that means," Mavis said.

"It doesn't mean anything at this point," Eli said. "Not anymore."

"What about... us?" Mavis said. "Is there an us or am I just wasting my time chasing a non-interested man?"

Eli sighed. "Mavis, I haven't been able to get you out of my head since I met you," he said.

"That's encouraging," Mavis said.

"It's just...."

Mavis stared at Eli for a few seconds. "That I was a call girl," she said.

"No, that's not it," Eli said. "It's that I'm a cop and we don't make much money. And the hours are brutal. Sometimes all I come home for is to sleep. What kind of life is that?"

"Do you love me?" Mavis said.

"That's not the issue," Eli said.

"Do you love me?" Mavis said.

"How can something like this work?" Eli said.

"Do you love me?" Mavis said.

"Are you listening to me? Did you hear one word I said?"

"Do you love me?"

"Goddammit, yes," Eli shouted. "Jesus you're a stubborn woman."

"I'm Irish," Mavis said. "Just like you."

* * *

Mavis arched her back so high that Eli nearly fell off the bed. When they finished and Eli rolled off her, Mavis started to laugh.

"What?" Eli asked.

"I don't think you have a problem anymore," Mavis said.

Eli put his head on the pillow and looked at the ceiling. Well, you did it, he thought. You fell for a call girl.

"I'm hungry," Mavis said.

"Me, too."

* * *

"You make a really good omelet," Mavis said.

"In France they often have omelets for dinner," Eli said. "That's where I learned, from watching French chefs make omelets."

"What about tomorrow?" Mavis said. "You go to work; I go back to my apartment, what happens then?"

Eli shrugged. "Let's have dinner with my parents this Sunday."

"That's a start," Mavis said.

"It is," Eli agreed.

* * *

Sitting on the bed with a cup of coffee, Mavis watched Eli go through his morning routine.

"Do you do that every morning?" Mavis asked.

"Most," Eli said. "Sometimes twice a day if I'm really aggravated at work."

"Save a little energy," Mavis said.

Doing push-ups, Eli paused. "For what?"

Mavis shook her head. "For what do you think, silly?"

"Oh," Eli said and continued doing push-ups. Then he paused and stood up. "Oh," he said again and walked to Mavis.

Fifteen

"**Anything new come in** overnight?" Howe asked when he entered the squad room.

"Tyler and Jack are in The Bronx running down leads on Butte," Eli said. "Webster Avenue is a busy street, maybe someone saw something."

Howe nodded. Eli stood and followed Howe into his office.

"I've been thinking, Art," Eli said. "We need access to those medical records."

"The judge will just turn you down again," Howe said.

"What if we went to the State Attorney General?" Eli asked.

"Same thing. Same result," Howe said.

"What about the FBI?" Eli said.

"Even old J. Edgar needs probable cause to get a federal judge to comply," Howe said.

"A whole lot of men could die waiting for a judge to make up his mind, Art," Eli said.

"We don't write the laws, Eli," Howe said. "We just enforce them."

The phone rang and Howe answered the call. He listened for a moment and said, "Hold on."

Eli was about to leave Howe's office when Howe said, "Eli, it's Bannon. They found a potential witness in The Bronx."

* * *

Ronald Jones Jr. sat on the front stoop of his apartment building with his beloved dog, Mooch, seated next to him. Jones was a Back man, sixty-seven years old, a retired bus driver for the City.

Eli picked up a department sketch artist and drove to The Bronx and parked at a hydrant in front of the building. Bannon and Tyler were standing with Jones and his dog.

"Lieutenant, this is Mr. Ronald Jones," Tyler said.

"Mr. Jones, I understand that you have some information concerning Mr. Butte's murder, is that correct?" Eli said.

Jones rubbed his dog's neck as he looked at Eli.

"I drove the number twelve bus for thirty-four years," Jones said. "Three runs a day to City Island. Know where that is, Lieutenant?"

"I fished off the bridge as a kid," Eli said.

"You a Bronx boy?" Jones said.

"One hundred percent," Eli said.

"I usually have tea at this time," Jones said. "Would you care for a cup of tea?"

* * *

Jones filled five cups with brewed tea at the kitchen table. His six-room apartment was spacious, well furnished and cluttered with family photos.

"My wife died two years ago," Jones said as he sat next to Eli. "I retired to take care of her. We were going to enjoy our retirement together, travel, spend time with our kids and grandkids and instead I live alone with my dog Mooch."

Eli looked at the dog at Jones's feet. "He's a fine dog," Eli said.

"He's a mutt," Jones said. "But my wife loved that dog, so I love him, too."

Eli nodded. "So Mr. Jones, what do you have to tell me?"

"I take Mooch for a walk every night at 8:15," Jones said. "Do you know why I call him Mooch?"

"He begs for table scraps," Eli said.

"My wife would feed him right from the table," Jones said. "Can't break him of that habit now."

"So you took Mooch for a walk at 8:15 last night," Eli said.

"I did," Jones said. "We go around the block and walk two blocks over right past the boxing gym. It must have been 8:30 or a bit past when we walked past this white man wearing a hooded sweatshirt, the kind boxers wear when they're in training."

"Can you describe him?" Eli said.

"Big man," Jones said. "Like you. He had the hood over his head so I couldn't see his face all that clearly. It struck me a bit odd that he was wearing slacks and black Army type boots with a sweatshirt. I walked Mooch to the corner and turned around and he was gone. I figure he headed two blocks to Webster to catch the subway."

"Mr. Jones, do you think you can describe him to our sketch artist?" Eli asked.

"I can try," Jones said.

"Tyler, you come with me," Eli said. "Jack, you stay with Mr. Jones.'

* * *

"Mr. Bracken, thank you for coming," Eli said.

"You found something?" Bracken said.

"Too soon to tell. We need to get inside," Eli said.

"When can I open again for business," Bracken asked. "Tyrell wouldn't want me sitting around feeling sorry for the both of us."

"In a few days," Eli said.

Bracken unlocked the door and Eli and Tyler entered, followed by Bracken.

"Where are the lights?" Eli asked.

"I'll get them," Bracken said.

He walked to the wall and flicked several switches.

"Sweatshirts, the kind fighters wear when they warm up," Eli said.

"I keep a rack of them on the second floor," Bracken said. "I have all my fighters wear one when they warm up jumping rope and working the speed bag."

"Show us," Eli said.

They went to the second floor and bracken showed them the long rack of sweatshirts on the wall near the jump ropes.

"Two of every size from small to extra-extra large," Bracken said.

Eli riffled through the sweatshirts and found one extra-extra large and one empty hanger.

"That's odd," Bracken said. "I always have two of each size."

"I believe you," Eli said.

"You think that son of a bitch took it?" Bracken said. "Why?"

"Disguise himself with the hood," Eli said. "Thank you, Mr. Bracken. You'll be notified when you can reopen."

* * *

Walking back to Jones's apartment, Tyler said, "To disguise himself from what? No one knows what he looks like, why disguise yourself?"

"Butte was a small man, about five-foot-five," Eli said. "After he stabbed Butte, in order to apply the choke hold properly he had to bend forward to encircle his neck. He got blood on his shirt. Even in The Bronx, if you get on a bus or subway somebody is bound to notice blood on your shirt."

They reached Jones's apartment.

"Let's see what our artist and Mr. Jones were able to come up with," Eli said.

*   *   *

"This is about as useful as a leaky boat in a flood," Howe said when he looked at the sketch.

"I know," Eli said. "But it's the best Mr. Jones could do."

"All you can see is his jaw line, Howe said.

"But the description fits," Eli said.

Howe looked at the description notes written in pencil next to the sketch. "Approximate height between seventy-two and seventy-six inches, weight between 225 to 250, Broad shoulders. Black combat-style boots."

"It does fit the idea I had in mind," Eli said.

"You can pick up a pair of Army boots at any surplus store anywhere," Howe said.

"I know, but who wants to wear them?" Eli said. "Anybody who served, once your time is done heavy Army boots are the last thing you want to walk around in. Unless you still see yourself as an active soldier."

Howe looked at Eli.

"An active soldier on a mission," Eli said.

"Jesus Christ," Howe said. "Every 4F male in the city is on alert as it is."

"That won't stop him," Eli said. "But maybe a news alert telling men with 4F status to change their habits might slow him down a bit. He's selected his victims based upon their habits, so if they change their habits it makes it that much more difficult for him to strike."

Howe looked at Eli for a few seconds before he picked up the phone and pressed a button. "Get me the mayor," he said.

* * *

O'Dwyer sat at his desk and looked at Howe and Eli.

"I ran your idea past the chief and commissioner, Captain Howe," he said. "We've scheduled a press conference for the six o'clock news on the radio this evening. I would like you to attend and say a few words."

"My lieutenant?" Howe said.

"I don't think it's necessary for him to attend," O'Dwyer said. "You might want to change your shirt and shave. You remind me of Congressman Richard Nixon, who always looks as if he needs a shave."

"Lieutenant Rico is responsible for…" Howe said.

"Don't be late, Captain," O'Dwyer said. "In fact, be early."

* * *

Eli, Tyler and Bannon stayed late in the squad room to listen to the radio press conference.

"Lieutenant, I made a pot of coffee," Tyler said. "Want a cup?"

"I think we all could use one," Eli said.

"Be right back," Tyler said.

Tyler left the squad room and Bannon got up from his desk and went to the radio on the shelf beside the window and fiddled with the knobs.

As Eli lit a cigarette, Tyler returned carrying a tray with three coffee mugs on it. He set the tray on Eli's desk.

Still fiddling with the radio, Bannon said, "Got it," and walked to Eli's desk.

An announcer said that the following was a special news broadcast concerning recent events happening in New York City.

The mayor spoke, followed by the Police Chief, then the Commissioner and the mayor again.

"The Captain didn't speak," Tyler said. "Why was he there?"

"For a photo opportunity," Eli said.

"Eli is the one who should do the talking," Bannon said. "Those assholes don't know if they should wind their ass or scratch their watch."

Eli sighed. "I'm going home."

*   *   *

Eli's phone was ringing when he walked through the door of his apartment. He picked up the call on the phone beside the sofa.

"Eli, it's Mavis," Mavis said. "I saw the report about the killer on the 6:30 news."

"It will probably be the headline on every morning paper in the City," Eli said, sat on the sofa and lit a cigarette.

"I know, but that's not the reason I called," Mavis said. "Tomorrow is Saturday. Are we still on for Sunday?"

"I'm looking forward to it," Eli said.

"Good. So how about you spend Saturday with me like we did last time?" Mavis said.

"Early evening," Eli said. "I have to work on this most of the day."

"6:00?"

"Closer to 7:00."

"I'll have dinner ready."

"I'll have my appetite ready," Eli said.

"See you at 7:00," Mavis said.

After hanging up with Mavis, Eli took a shower and then rummaged around in the kitchen for something to eat. The best he could come up with was a frozen dinner or eggs and bacon.

He fried up a half pound of bacon and did his workout routine while it cooked. Then he scrambled six eggs, made toast and ate at the table with the radio on and the fan blowing cool air on his back.

The soft music paused for the news. It was all about the string of murders. Someone took to calling him the New York City Stalker and provided a special phone number for anyone with information to call.

"That's just what we need, every paranoid nut job in the city calling in with spook stories," Eli said aloud.

He switched off the radio, put the dirty dishes and pans in the sink, lit a cigarette and stood at the kitchen window.

The streets below were dark and quiet. A slight mist had formed and was followed by a soft drizzle of rain.

Sleep beckoned and Eli went to bed.

*　*　*

At twenty past 2:00 in the morning, the phone on the nightstand rang and Eli awoke with a start and reached for it.

"This is Eli," he said, alert and ready for bad news.

"Lieutenant Rico, this is dispatch. We got another one."

"Where?"

"Little Italy. Canal Street off Mott. A social club."

"Tell them I'm on my way," Eli said.

Sixteen

Six police cruisers were parked in front of the Canal Street
Italian Social Club when Eli arrived and doubled parked.

A dozen uniformed officers were on the sidewalk.

"Who is senior man here?" Eli asked.

"That would be me, Sergeant Keys," a uniformed officer man said.

"Anybody inside?" Eli asked.

"Just the victim Jimmy Demore."

"The one they call Crazy Jim?" Eli asked.

"The one and only," Keys said.

"Let's go," Eli said.

Eli and Keys entered the front door. A large window that faced
the street was painted black from the inside.

Face down near a card table was the victim, James 'Jimmy' Demore.

Eli sighed.

"You know who he is, right?" Keys asked.

"Who doesn't?" Eli said.

James Demore, age thirty-four was a made member of the mafia
and the Genovese Crime Family. He was suspected of every crime
in the book, including kidnapping, extortion, drug smuggling,
prostitution, gambling and murder.

Demore was dressed in black slacks, a white sleeveless T-shirt and
black loafers. Eli knelt beside the body.

"Stabbed in the side, broken neck," Eli said.

"Looks it to me," Keys said.

Eli stood. "Is there a phone in here?"

"You know how these guys operate," Keys said. "They use messengers and pay phones."

"Who discovered the body?" Eli asked.

"His wife," Keys said. "I got her in a car."

"Go to your car and call dispatch," Eli said. "Tell them to get Roscoe and Wilson out of bed and down here on the double. Is that an espresso machine?"

Keys nodded and left the club.

Eli went to the espresso bar, turned on the brass coffee maker and brewed two cups of espresso and took them to a table.

Keys returned with the wife of Jimmy Demore. She was a pretty woman in her early thirties with blondish hair and blue eyes. As Keys escorted her to the table, Keys said, "Lieutenant, this is Elizabeth Demore, Jimmy's…"

Elizabeth Demore suddenly darted away from Keys, ran to Demore's body, kicked it and spit. "You filthy pig," she shouted. "You prick son of a bitch good for nothing bastard."

About to kick the body again, Eli grabbed her arm and guided her to the table.

"Mrs. Demore, please sit and tell me what happened," Eli said.

She plopped into a chair and said, "One of his filthy whores finally done him in, the no good bastard."

"I meant, how did you come to discover the body?" Eli said.

"Oh," Elizabeth said. "Is this coffee for me?"

Eli nodded.

Elizabeth picked up the cup and took a sip. "Jimmy, that prick, he didn't think I knew he used this club for his whores. Playing cards with the boys, he would say. Like I'm stupid. I'm home with our

165

three kids and he's over here screwing his whores to all hours of the night."

"Mrs. Demore, I'm interested in tonight," Eli said.

"Oh," Elizabeth said. She took another sip. "Who made this espresso? It's wonderful."

"I did and please answer my question," Eli said.

"I got my mother to watch the kids and took a cab to catch him in the act, the no good bastard prick," Elizabeth said. "The door was unlocked and I walked in expecting to find him humping one of his whores on the table and found him dead on the floor instead."

"What time?"

"I don't know, I forgot my watch."

"She called the police from the pay phone on the corner at ten of 2:00," Keys said.

"Sounds about right," Elizabeth said.

"Mrs. Demore, was your husband classified 4F?" Eli asked.

"He was, but there wasn't a damn thing wrong with him," Elizabeth said. "He paid for his 4F status like the others that belong to Genovese."

"Where do you live?"

"Parkchester in The Bronx. It's a very nice neighborhood."

"Mrs. Demore, I'm going to have an officer drive you home," Eli said. "I will stop by tomorrow to take an official statement."

"You're very kind," Elizabeth said. She stood and as she walked with Keys to the door, she turned and spit again on the body of her husband. "Pig," she said and walked out the door.

While he waited for Roscoe and Wilson, Eli checked the small kitchen and bathroom and found nothing. Off the kitchen, though, was a back door that opened to a small, walled-in courtyard. He measured the wall at six feet high, an easy jump.

Next to the door was a large brick that was used to prop the door open. Since the interior windows didn't open the only fresh air came from propping open the back door.

Eli went inside and pieced together the evening. The card table was set for six players. A half dozen sets of cards were on the table. Ashtrays overflowed with cigarette butts and cigars. Empty espresso cups and empty beer bottles filled the sink.

The card game must have lasted for hours. Demore ended the game probably for the reason his wife suspected, a late night encounter with a woman.

The stalker might have studied Demore's habits and knew a woman was meeting him after the game.

Did she walk in as Elizabeth Demore did and discover the body? If she did, she turned and ran.

If Demore wasn't expecting a woman, why did he stay late after the card game ended?

"Shit," Eli said aloud.

He went back to the courtyard and studied the wall. There were no openings, hinges, hidden doors or gates. The only way in was to jump over it. He placed his hands on top of the wall and in a single, smooth motion went up and over and landed beside a small waste dumpster.

Written in white paint on the side of the dumpster were the words Private Property of The Italian Social Club.

Eli flipped open the lid and looked at the dead body of a blonde woman. Even in the dark he could see her neck had been broken.

*　*　*

Eli, Roscoe and Wilson sat at a table with cups of espresso coffee.

"How do you figure it went down?" Roscoe asked. "The woman surprised him and he had to kill her?"

"I don't think so," Eli said. "He knew Demore would stay late after the card game to meet a woman. He probably figured if she showed up before he finished off Demore that she would be collateral damage."

"Some fucking mind this guy has," Roscoe said.

"He's a cold-blooded bastard for sure," Wilson said.

"Murder is cold-blooded bastard work," Eli said.

"Well, by now the bodies are on the table, so I better get going," Wilson said. "I'll call you later with a report."

Wilson stood and exited the social club.

"Are you all done here?" Eli asked Roscoe.

"I am, but I'd like to finish my coffee," Roscoe said.

Eli grinned. "Me, too."

* * *

"Jimmy Demore?" Howe said. "Crazy Jimmy Demore?"

Eli nodded.

"The old bosses aren't going to take this sitting down," Howe said.

"I don't care what they do so long as they don't impede the investigation," Eli said.

"The shit storm just went from tropical to hurricane," Howe said.

"I'll be back in a while," Eli said. "I told Mrs. Demore I'd stop by and take her statement."

Howe sighed. "I better call the mayor."

On the way out, Eli stopped by Tyler's desk.

"Any identification on the woman yet?" Eli asked.

"Working on it," Tyler said. "The least the guy could have done was leave her purse."

"I suppose it wouldn't do any good to find out who the other five card players were," Eli said.

"They wouldn't talk anyway," Tyler said.

"I'll be at the Demore house in The Bronx," Eli said.

* * *

The Demore home in the Parkchester neighborhood in The Bronx must have cost Jimmy $40,000 or more. Two stories, red brick, big front yard, even bigger backyard with a pool, Jimmy Demore lived well.

"Ma, take the kids outside or something," Elizabeth said. "They're driving me fucking crazy."

"Watch your language, Liz. The children can hear you," Elizabeth's mother said.

"The children are fucking monsters like their father. Now take them outside," Elizabeth said. "I gotta talk to this cop in private."

Eli stood and waited in the living room.

"Let's go to the kitchen," Elizabeth said. "I made fresh coffee."

She pronounced the word as cough-fey as did most Bronx Italians, Eli's father included.

Eli followed her to the large, modern kitchen.

"Take a seat," Elizabeth said.

Eli took a chair at the table for eight. Elizabeth put two cups on the table and poured.

"All day long the fucking phone rings," she said. "One mafia asshole after another. Even Genovese called, that rat bastard."

"Vito Genovese? He called you?" Eli said.

Elizabeth sat and lit a cigarette. "A little while ago," she said. "To offer his condolences and to tell me I'd be taken care of for life. That means when my sons turn eighteen they get recruited into his family. Like father like son, right?"

"Mrs. Demore, about the…" Eli said.

"Liz. Call me Liz. Everybody else does."

"I need a statement from you," Eli said.

"I'm terrible at writing," Elizabeth said. "How about I talk and you write and then I'll sign it afterward."

Eli nodded and took out his pen.

It took a good thirty minutes for Elizabeth to recite and for Eli to copy her words to the report paper.

"Could you read it please and see if you want to make any changes," Eli said.

Elizabeth read her statement and she silently moved her lips as she read. When she finished, she picked up Eli's pen and signed the report.

"Have another cup before you go?" she asked.

"Sure, why not."

"Sweet or not?"

"Not."

Elizabeth refilled the cups and added a little whiskey to hers and then she and Eli lit cigarettes.

"You probably already know, or maybe you don't, but Genovese isn't going to take one of his men getting killed lying down," Elizabeth said.

"I suspect you are right about that, but even Genovese can't interfere with a police investigation," Eli said.

"Genovese has an army of knee-cappers on the street to do his bidding," Elizabeth said. "The police can't stop him even if you tried. I know. My husband was one of his knee-cappers, may he rot in fucking hell."

"Thank you for the coffee and I'll be in touch," Eli said.

"About what?" Elizabeth asked.

* * *

Driving back to headquarters, Eli played the transistor radio in the car. The news was filled with the murder of Jimmy 'Crazy Jimmy' Demore's murder.

Eli lit a cigarette and listened to the broadcaster give a history of Demore's life. Then the radio station shifted to music.

He made a sudden stop at a corner pay phone and grabbed some nickels from the glove box.

Mavis answered the call on the third ring.

"Mavis, it's Eli. I need a favor," Eli said. "Can we switch plans a bit? I need to be near a phone I can answer."

"You mean I stay at your place?" Mavis said.

"Would that be alright?" Eli asked.

"Sure, I understand," Mavis said.

"I'll call you a bit later when I'm done with work," Eli said.

"Eli, be careful," Mavis said. "The news is saying this one is a member of the Italian mafia."

"Was, anyway," Eli said. "I'll try to make it about 6:00, okay?"

*   *   *

"We identified the body of the woman," Tyler said as Eli entered the squad room. "Gloria Phelps. Age is thirty-one. Works as a hat check girl at a nightclub in Little Italy owned by the Genovese family. Her family is going to claim the body."

"Do we know if meeting Demore was a regular thing or something new or what?" Eli asked.

"Does that matter?" Tyler asked.

"It does if you're our stalker and had to plan on killing her in the process to get to Demore," Eli said.

"Right. I'll find out."

Eli went into Howe's office.

"You look like shit," Howe said. "When did you last sleep?"

Eli plopped into a chair and lit a cigarette. "What month is this," he said. "Any blowback on Demore?"

"Personally, I doubt anyone in the department gives a rat's ass a mob goon is dead," Howe said. "But the official statement is we will do our best as with the others."

"Elizabeth Demore feels Genovese will do his own investigation," Eli said.

"That's been discussed," Howe said. "The Chief and Commissioner put a call into old Vito to request a meeting to discuss just that."

"Genovese is going to do what he wants to do no matter what anyone says," Eli said.

"He didn't get to be mafia boss by taking orders," Howe said.

Howe's phone rang. "Hold on a minute," he said to Eli and then answered the phone.

Howe listened for about thirty seconds and then said, "Yes, sir," and hung up. "That was the Commissioner. Genovese agreed to meet with him at 10:00 Monday morning. Genovese requested you and I attend."

"Genovese requested us?" Eli said.

"By name no less," Howe said. "Look, it's Saturday. Go home and get some sleep and I'll see you Monday morning."

"In a bit," Eli said.

* * *

Eli sat at his desk with a cigarette and a mug of coffee that was hours old and tasted harsh.

The more he reviewed the evidence, the more he thought about it, the more convinced he was that the stalker was an Army Ranger.

His athletic ability, his ease of killing using the Ranger Choke

Hold weren't just the only clues that led to that conclusion. Eli was convinced the stalker spent some time, at least a year, maybe more in a veteran's hospital where classified records could be had.

He couldn't have possibly obtained all the records at whatever facility he was a patient at and that meant his list was dwindling. It could be finished for all anyone knew. If it was, would he attempt to gain access to more classified military records?

Would he call it a day and simply fade away, satisfied he fulfilled his lust for revenge?

Eli suspected not.

Around 5:30, he turned off the squad room lights and went to pick up Mavis.

She was waiting for him in front of her building. He left the car and she greeted him with a soft kiss.

"You look like you haven't slept for a week," Mavis said.

"Feel like it, too," Eli said.

He placed her overnight bag in the back seat and held the door for her, then he got behind the wheel.

"Stop by the food market on Second Avenue," Mavis said.

"What do you need?" Eli asked.

"Food, silly," Mavis said almost with a giggle.

Seventeen

Mavis carried a bag of groceries into Eli's apartment, while he carried her overnight bag.

"Turn on the radio and the fan and stretch out on the sofa while I make dinner," Mavis said.

She went to the kitchen.

Eli removed his shoes and turned on both radio and fan and stretched out on the seven-foot-long sofa.

Within a matter of seconds Eli was sound asleep.

Ninety minutes later, Mavis gently shook him awake.

"I must have dozed off," Eli said.

"Dozed off like a bulldozer," Mavis said. "Come on, dinner is ready."

Dinner consisted of breaded pork chops, baked potatoes, rice, greens with red wine and bread.

Eli, once he took a bite of pork chops, realized he was famished and went to town. Mavis, pleased at his appetite, grinned at him.

"What?" Eli asked.

"I'm glad you like my cooking," Mavis said.

"My mother couldn't do better," Eli said. "Although I'd never tell her that."

"Save room for dessert," Mavis said. "We'll take it in the living room."

Mavis made cannolis from scratch using a recipe she found in an Italian dessert cookbook.

"When did you make these?" Eli asked.

"While you were napping," Mavis said. "They're not hard to make. I made just a few to see how they turn out."

"They're wonderful," Eli said.

"I wanted your reaction first before I made a box to bring to your parents tomorrow," Mavis said.

"They'll love them," Eli said.

"I'll make them in the morning," Mavis said. "Right now I feel like soaking in a hot tub. I coached three girls this morning and my feet are killing me."

* * *

Mavis sat opposite Eli in the tub that was filled with hot bubble bath and scented oils that Mavis had in her overnight bag.

Mavis closed her eyes and rested her head against the rim of the tub.

Eli took her right foot and began to gently massage it.

Mavis moaned softly. "That's how a woman knows when a man really loves her," she said. "When he'll give her a foot massage without her asking for it."

"I would think it'd be a bit more complicated than that," Eli said.

"The way to… oh, that's heaven… a man's heart is through his stomach," Mavis said. "The way to a woman's heart is through a foot massage."

"Switch," Eli said.

Mavis moved her feet and Eli took hold of the left.

As he massaged her foot, Mavis said, "Oh… my… God."

*   *   *

"Oh… my… God," Mavis said and arched her back and thrust her hips with so much force that Eli fell completely out of bed.

She immediately sat up. "Eli?"

Eli poked his head up and looked at her.

Mavis stared at him for a second and then broke out into a fit of uncontrollable laughter.

Eli climbed back into bed.

"It isn't that funny," he said.

"Oh… yes… it… is," Mavis said as she tried in vain to regain control.

*   *   *

Halfway across the George Washington Bridge, Mavis suddenly burst into another fit of laughter.

"For crying out loud," Eli said.

"I'm sorry. I'm trying. Honestly," Mavis said.

Mavis looked out her window and regained composure.

"Better?" Eli said.

Mavis nodded.

"Good."

"Your head popped up like a gopher out of his hole," Mavis said and burst into tears.

Eli sighed and lit a cigarette.

*   *   *

Eli's father Salvatore answered the door before Eli had the chance to knock.

"I heard your car," Salvatore said.

Mavis held the bakery box to Salvatore.

"I made cannolis," she said and burst into another fit of laughter.

Salvatore looked at Eli. "What I say?" he asked.

"Nothing. She's a happy person," Eli said.

As Mavis stomped her foot, she said, "Like… a…gopher."

Salvatore looked at Eli.

"Nothing, pop," Eli said. "Give her a minute."

Mavis managed to compose herself through dinner and the table conversation was light and the stalker investigation was never mentioned. Even Eli's sister Sally, warmed up to Mavis and by dessert they were chatting like old college roommates.

"We'll take coffee and dessert in the living room," Michele said. "The old man has a surprise."

"Wait," Salvatore said. "Let me go in first. Give me five minutes."

Salvatore left the dining room and after several minutes he returned.

"Okay, come in," he said.

The entire family, Sally's two children included went to the living room where Salvatore stood in front of a cabinet-sized Philco television.

"Dad, you got a TV," Sally said.

"That's right and we're all going to watch the Ed Sullivan Show," Salvatore said.

"Mavis, be a dear and help me serve dessert," Michele said.

* * *

Later, in his apartment, as Eli removed his pants and looked at Mavis, who was all ready naked in bed, he said, "Let's see if we can do this without you…"

177

And at the sound of his voice, Mavis went into hysterical laughter. "A gopher... out... of his hole," she said nearly in tears.

Eli tossed his pants. "Right," he said.

Eighteen

"**I'm sorry we had** to leave so early," Eli said as he drove Mavis to her apartment in Manhattan. "It's this early meeting I have."

"About the stalker?"

Eli nodded.

"Would you say that we're serious as a couple?" Mavis said.

"I would," Eli said.

"You told me you love me and I know I love you," Mavis said. "So what's the next logical step?"

Eli turned his lead and looked at her.

"Did I just scare you?" Mavis asked.

"No. Don't think I haven't thought about it," Eli said.

"I feel a very large *but* coming on," Mavis said.

"The wife of a homicide cop is a lonely life," Eli said. "Look at the hours I keep. All hours of the day and night and a lot of weekends. Plus the pay is terrible. It's no way to start a marriage."

"We could start over in Ohio," Mavis said. "I told you I had quite a bit of money saved up. Enough to last for years."

"And what am I supposed to do in Ohio?" Eli asked.

"The have police in Ohio," Mavis said. "Even in the country."

"I admit I want to spend my life with you," Eli said. "But I have to finish this case before I can think of anything else."

"Well, that's a start anyway," Mavis said.

Eli slowed his car curbside to Mavis's building.

"I'll call you later tonight," Eli said.

Mavis slid over and kissed him softly.

"Ohio is a good place to raise a family," she said. "Think about that."

* * *

Vito Genovese arrived in a long, black Cadillac sedan that was driven by his personal driver. Two bodyguards also rode in the sedan. Behind the Cadillac a second car, a Ford, was occupied by four additional bodyguards and Genovese's lawyer.

The bodyguards huddled around Genovese and his lawyer from the curb to the revolving doors of the police headquarters building.

The bodyguards were restricted to the lobby, but the lawyer was allowed to accompany Genovese to the Commissioner's office. A uniformed police officer escorted them to the twentieth floor where the office was located.

The officer knocked on the door before opening it. "Sir, Mr. Genovese and his lawyer are here," he said.

After Genovese and the lawyer entered the office, the officer closed the door behind him.

The Commissioner, Police Chief, Howe and Eli were seated at a conference table.

"I am Vito Genovese," Genovese said as he approached the conference table.

"We know who you are," the Commissioner said.

"This is my attorney Edward Green," Genovese said.

"Why did you feel the need for an attorney, Mr. Genovese?" the Commissioner asked. "This is not an official meeting."

Genovese took a chair opposite Eli.

"Everything is official to me," Genovese said. "I understand that you wanted to see me because a man in my employment was murdered by this newspaper stalker. You are concerned that my organization might find this man before you do and if that happens he will never see the inside of courtroom."

"That has occurred to us," the Commissioner said.

"Mr. Green?" Genovese said.

Green snapped open his briefcase and produced a document and set it before Genovese.

"This is a business license for a security company that I own that is fully licensed by the State of New York to conduct investigations," Genovese said. "We will conduct our own investigation and share any findings with the New York City Police Department. Any questions?"

"Mr. Genovese, how does your security company plan to conduct such an investigation and what can you hope to accomplish that the police can not?" the Police Chief asked.

"I'll answer that," Green said. "The Valley Stream Security Company is duly licensed to provide armed security personnel to clients that warrant such protection. In addition, the company employs highly trained investigators licensed by the State of New York to conduct civil and criminal investigations. Most of them are retired police detectives and fully capable of conducting such an investigation. Of course all obtained information will be shared with the police."

"Of course," the Police Chief said.

"That's it, we're done here," Genovese said.

"Before you go, I'm curious as to why you asked for me and Lieutenant Rico to be present at this meeting," Howe said.

"You are the captain overseeing this investigation?" Genovese said.

"I am," Howe said.

Genovese looked at Rico. "And you are the lieutenant doing the field work?"

Eli nodded.

"I wanted to get a look at you," Genovese said. He looked at the Commissioner. "If you feel the need to contact me again, do it through Mr. Green. Good day, gentlemen."

* * *

Eli and Howe stood on the steps of the headquarters building after the meeting with Genovese.

"What do you suppose Genovese meant when he said he wanted to get a look at us?" Eli asked.

"Dammed if I know," Howe said.

"If his people do uncover something you know they'll keep it to themselves," Eli said. "Besides, his security company is just a way for his goons to legally carry guns."

"What makes you think they'll uncover something we won't?" Howe asked.

"Rules," Eli said. "We have them. They don't."

* * *

Eli stopped by Tyler's desk as he entered the squad room.

"What's her name Gloria Phelps has had a thing with Demore for about a year," Tyler said. "So say the staff at the nightclub where she worked."

Eli walked to his desk and Tyler followed.

"They usually met after one of Demore's card games," Tyler said. "Twice a week at least. We found love letters, gifts and canceled checks showing Demore paid her rent."

Eli sat and lit a cigarette. "Our stalker had to case Demore for quite a while to learn these habits," he said. "Take Jack and head over to Little Italy and talk to everybody you can and see if anybody remembers seeing someone on the street that might fit the description of our stalker. Then do the same with the nightclub."

"Right. Check with you later," Tyler said.

After Tyler and Bannon left the squad room, Eli dug out his book of maps. The neighborhood known as Little Italy was fairly large with a population of ten thousand residents. From the nightclub on Canal Street to the social club where Demore was murdered was a distance of seven blocks.

He knew Gloria Phelps would be with Demore. Demore, a made guy would have bodyguards with him whenever he ventured on the streets. The only way to get to Demore was when he was without the bodyguards after the card game. The bodyguards would leave when Gloria showed up and would return when she left, probably in the morning.

He knew he would have to kill Gloria Phelps in order to get to Demore.

And it probably didn't bother him one bit.

Eli sat back in his chair, lit a cigarette and thought for a few minutes.

When he put out the cigarette, he picked up the phone and called Elizabeth Demore.

"This is Lieutenant Rico calling," Eli said when she answered the phone.

"We were just talking about you," Elizabeth said. "When are you going to release the prick's body?"

"I'll have an answer this afternoon," Eli said. "The reason I'm calling is I'd like a few minutes of your time. I have a couple of questions based on some new developments."

"You can't ask on the phone?" Elizabeth said.

"Is your phone secure?" Eli asked.

"Come now," Elizabeth said. "I have a hair appointment at two."

"On my way," Eli said.

After hanging up, Eli went into Howe's office.

"I'll be at Demore's home in The Bronx," Eli said.

*   *   *

Elizabeth Demore answered the door wearing white shorts, the shortest shorts Eli had ever seen on a woman and a sleeveless yellow blouse that was tied off at the ends just above her naval.

She was barefoot and her toenails were painted pink to match her fingernails.

"Do you want coffee or something cold?" Elizabeth asked.

"Cold and can we talk in the backyard?" Eli asked.

"Sure. We'll sit by the pool."

A few minutes later, Eli and Elizabeth sat in pool chairs with bottles of cold soda.

"So what's so secretive?" she asked.

"The questions are delicate," Eli said.

"Any modesty I once had is long gone," Elizabeth said.

"I'm trying to determine a pattern," Eli said. "How the stalker may have known your husband's whereabouts at a certain time."

Elizabeth took a slow sip from the soda bottle, lowered the bottle and said, "So what's your question, Lieutenant?"

"How long have you known about your husband's fling with Gloria Phelps?" Eli asked.

"Flings, Lieutenant. Flings," Elizabeth said. "Jimmy had a lot of whores. If it wasn't one it was another."

"I'm interested in just Gloria Phelps," Eli said.

184

Elizabeth shrugged. "I dunno. A year, maybe."

"Did he always stay out all night?"

"Most of the time. Sometimes he'd come home before the kids woke up."

"Did you know about the card games?"

"Of course," Elizabeth said. "What's all this got to do with him being murdered, anyway?"

"I'm trying to determine if killing Gloria Phelps was planned in advance or something that happened on the spur of the moment," Eli said.

"What difference does that make? Both of them are dead," Elizabeth said.

"Up until now all his victims were alone when he killed them," Eli said. "If he knew Gloria Phelps would be there it means he killed her as collateral damage simply because she was there. Had you been there, arrived thirty minutes earlier, he would have killed you, too."

"I see," Elizabeth said. She took a sip from her soda bottle.

"Why this time?" Eli asked. "Why did you decide to confront your husband this time and not the others?"

Elizabeth sighed. "Something I didn't tell you before," she said. "They have a rule. A silly, stupid rule they live by, these assholes."

"They?"

"The mafia," Elizabeth said. "A made man can fuck around as much as he wants as long as he takes care of his family. Jimmy always took care of me and the kids and his mother. Jimmy whoring around was just part of the life, the way it is. I knew that going in and it never really bothered me so long as he didn't give me the clap or whatever."

"So what changed?" Eli asked.

"This bitch, what's her name Gloria?" Elizabeth said. "She called the house and told me Jimmy was leaving me for her. I can stand for Jimmy whoring around, but not leaving me for another woman. There I draw the line, as do the bosses. So I decided to confront them. I got there late and now I'm damn glad I did."

Eli nodded.

Elizabeth sipped soda and crossed her legs and the white shorts rode up on her thighs even higher.

"Do you like pink?" she asked.

"Pink?"

Elizabeth extended her right leg and placed her foot on Eli's lap and wiggled her toes. "Pink," she said.

Eli looked at her leg.

"See something you like, Lieutenant?" Elizabeth said. "If you do I can show you more sometime."

Eli looked at her.

"Don't be coy, Lieutenant," Elizabeth said. "You've been eye fucking me since we met."

Eli gently removed her leg from his lap and stood up. "Thanks for your time, Mrs. Demore. You were quite helpful."

"I can be even more helpful if you stick around," Elizabeth said.

"Almost forgot," Eli said. "You can claim your husband's body now."

* * *

"Got about forty people that claim they saw someone on the street outside the social club who fits our description," Tyler said. "The sketch artist is working his fingers to the bone."

"What about the nightclub?" Eli asked.

"Two bartenders, a waitress and the cigarette girl say they saw somebody who fits our description," Bannon said.

"By tomorrow we'll have close to fifty sketches," Tyler said.

"Clock out when you're done," Eli said. "It's been a long day."

*   *   *

It was close to seven o'clock when Eli parked his car across the street from his apartment.

A Cadillac sedan was parked in front of his building. Four men wearing dark suits stood on the sidewalk beside the sedan.

Eli crossed the street and walked to his building.

One of the four men stepped in front of Eli. "Mr. Genovese would like a word with you," he said.

"I'll be at my office first thing tomorrow," Eli said.

The rear door of the Cadillac opened. "Just get in," Genovese said.

Eli shrugged and got in beside Genovese and closed the door.

"Drive," Genovese said.

The driver started the engine and guided the Cadillac away from the curb.

"I did some checking on your background," Genovese said. "War hero, Army Ranger, star homicide detective and yet your bosses treat you like a puppet while you do all the work and they get their faces in the newspapers."

"We have a protocol," Eli said. "Same as I suppose you do."

"Protocol my ass," Genovese said. "You asked for a warrant for military records and was refused. Why?"

"That's classified police information," Eli said. He didn't ask how Genovese knew such details. It was no secret Genovese had police and judges on his payroll.

"Sure it is," Genovese said. "You suspect this ghost stalker is former military and you wanted a court order to check military records of mental patients and was refused for lack of evidence."

"Mr. Genovese, what do you want from me?" Eli asked.

"When your phone rings, answer it," Genovese said. "Driver, take the Lieutenant home."

*   *   *

After Genovese's Cadillac pulled away from the curb, Eli sat on the front steps of his building and smoked a cigarette.

There was no point is asking Genovese what he meant by 'answer the phone' because he came to say what he said and wouldn't say anything more after that.

Eli finished the cigarette and went upstairs to his apartment.

He rummaged around for something to eat and then sat in front of the fan and smoked a cigarette while listening to the radio.

The phone on the coffee table rang and he scooped it up. "This is Lieutenant Rico," he said.

"Eli, it's Mavis. You got to quit answering your phone that way," Mavis said.

"Sorry, I'm still in work mode," Eli said.

"Can we have dinner tomorrow?" Mavis asked.

"I don't know," Eli said.

"Eli, I know you're busy with this murder investigation, but you still have to eat," Mavis said. "Do you remember that little restaurant around the corner from my apartment?"

"Sure."

"Call me when you go off duty and we'll meet there for dinner," Mavis said.

"It will probably be late," Eli said. "After 7:00 or so."

"They serve until 9:00."

"Okay, I'll call you when I go off duty," Eli said.

There was a short pause before Mavis said, "Answer a question honestly?"

"Sure."

"I sensed this morning your lack of commitment and I'm wondering if that's due to what I used to do for a living?" Mavis said.

"No, no it isn't," Eli said. "It's exactly what I said it was. My job."

"Jobs are like people, Eli. Both can change."

Eli lit a fresh cigarette and was silent for a moment.

"Is it because I might be recognized in public?" Mavis said.

"No, that never entered my mind," Eli said. "It really is this homicide case right now. I'm tired and stumped. My mind is preoccupied and this is something we should talk about when I'm a little less focused on it and more focused on you."

"I understand," Mavis said. "Call me when you get off duty tomorrow."

"I will. Promise," Eli said.

* * *

Eli stared at the dark ceiling as he tried to fall asleep.

Sleep wouldn't come. Exhausted as he was, his mind wouldn't allow him to rest.

"When your phone rings, answer," Genovese had said.

What did that mean? Who would be calling and for what reason?

Genovese was exceptionally well connected with judges, police and politicians on his payroll, would the call come from one of them?

If not, then who?

There was something else.

Since his return from the war and he was diagnosed with intimacy problems, the only woman he had been able to perform with was Mavis.

Was that because she was a prostitute? If so, now that she was retired from the profession, why was he still able to perform with her?

Because he still thought of her that way?

Or because he actually did love her?

When Elizabeth Demore put her foot on his lap, he felt a stirring in his gut that only Mavis had been able to generate up to this point. He resisted the natural urge, of course, but did it mean that he actually was cured of his problem?

The only way to answer that was to respond to Elizabeth's advances and see what happens.

Even thinking about that riddled Eli with guilt.

Turn it off and go to sleep.

Eli closed his eyes and waited for peace.

Nineteen

After his morning workout, Eli shaved and showered and was toweling off when his phone rang.

It wasn't yet 7:00 in the morning.

He picked up the phone in the bedroom.

"This is Lieutenant Rico," he said.

"Lieutenant, dispatch. We got another one for you," the dispatcher said.

* * *

A swarm of uniformed officers held at bay an even bigger swarm of reporters in front of a three-story brownstone on West 8th Avenue in the Village.

The street was blocked at both ends by mounted police officers and patrol cars.

Eli's car was allowed to pass and he double parked in front of the brownstone.

"Who is senior here?" Eli asked.

"That would be me," a uniformed lieutenant said.

"What the hell is going on here?" Eli asked.

"Don't you know who the victim is?" the uniformed lieutenant said.

Eli shook his head.

"Leland Upton the Third."

"Who is Leland Upton the Third?" Eli said.

"He's the biggest star on Broadway," the uniformed lieutenant said.

"He's an actor," Eli said.

The reporters started firing questions at Eli as they tried to break through the police barrier.

"Keep these people back," Eli said.

"Want to see the victim?" the uniformed lieutenant said.

"Which apartment is his?" Eli asked.

"All of them. This is a private house."

The lobby on the first floor opened up to a massive living room.

"Six sofas, six chairs, full bar, wall-to-wall mirrors and four television sets," Eli said. "This room is bigger than my entire apartment."

"Check out the game room."

The only other room on the first floor was the game room. It held four card tables, two regulation size pool tables, a full bar and a television.

"Upton is or was known for his wild parties," the uniformed lieutenant said.

"How do you know?" Eli asked.

"The gossip page in the newspapers."

"Where is the body?" Eli asked.

"Second floor. Want to walk or take the elevator?"

"Walk. There's an elevator?"

"Check it out."

The elevator door was a polished brass fence. The interior all chrome and mirrors.

"We'll take the stairs," Eli said.

The stairs were covered in thick, plush carpet. The walls were covered in framed photographs of Leland Upton in various costumes and poses from Broadway plays he starred in.

"As you can see Mr. Upton had quite a large ego," the uniformed lieutenant said.

The second floor contained a large sauna, steam room, gym, and showers and massage room on one side. The other half of the floor held a movie theatre with forty seats.

"Mr. Upton wasn't poor," Eli said.

The uniformed lieutenant grinned. "No, no he wasn't."

The body of Leland Upton was in the sauna. He was face down on the hardwood floor. His neck was broken. A visible stab wound was in his left side. A thick towel was wrapped around his waist.

"Who turned off the heat in here?" Eli asked.

"I did. It was a 130 degrees in here when I walked in."

"Who discovered the body and called it in?" Eli asked.

"The housekeeper. Janet Doyle. She a widow. She lives in the basement apartment. She found the body at 6:00 this morning when she was in the kitchen and heard the sauna alarm going off. She went to investigate and found Upton in the sauna."

"Where is the kitchen?"

"Third floor where Upton actually lives."

"Where is the housekeeper?"

"In the kitchen with one of my guys."

"I saw a phone on the first floor," Eli said. "I want you to go downstairs and call my office. Have dispatch send Detectives Tyler and Bannon and notify Captain Howe. Also have them send forensics and the ME. I'll be with the housekeeper."

"You got it, Lieutenant."

* * *

The housekeeper, Mrs. Janet Doyle, age of sixty, had been employed by Upton for ten years. She was a widow since the age of forty-five and lived quite comfortably in the five room basement apartment rent free. Her job as housekeeper consisted of all housework and laundry duties, all meal preparation when Upton was home and preparing food for his lavish dinner parties.

She had been crying earlier, but was somewhat composed when Eli entered the kitchen.

"Mrs. Doyle, I'm Lieutenant Rico," Eli said. "There is no good time to talk about things like this, but I need to ask you some questions."

* * *

Eli, Tyler, Howe and Bannon sat at the kitchen table with mugs of fresh coffee that Janet Doyle made fresh for them. After she poured, she left the kitchen and went to the living room and sat with a uniformed officer.

Eli lit a cigarette and opened his notebook.

"According to Mrs. Doyle, Upton went to dinner with friends at the 21 Club after the show ended, usually six nights a week," Eli said. "The show ends at 9:00 and he always has a reservation for 9:45. He usually returns home between midnight and 12:30. He takes a thirty-minute stint in the sauna, then a shower and gets to bed around 2:00 in the morning and doesn't wake up until 10:00 or so when Mrs. Doyle wakes him for breakfast. She is an early riser and starts her housework before 6:00 in the morning. She always cleans the sauna and shower first because after breakfast, Upton takes another sauna and shower. She said that Upton believed the sauna kept him trim and energized for his busy schedule on Broadway."

"I saw this guy in a play last year," Howe said. "My wife dragged me to it I think last June. Some shit about the Queen of England throwing her cousin in prison. Really boring crap with a lot of thee and thou and thy stuff."

"Mrs. Doyle discovered the body at 6:00 this morning when she went to clean the sauna," Eli said. "Wilson places the time of death between 1:00 and 1:30. Roscoe and his people are combing the building for evidence."

"Do we know how he gained entrance to the building?" Howe asked.

"The rear of the building has a fire escape that runs down to the courtyard garden," Eli said. "The ladder is down. The wall around the garden is seven feet high, an easy jump."

"This fucking guy is not going to stop," Howe said.

"No, but we got something this time," Eli said. "Footprints in the garden. Size fourteen boot."

"Boot? Not shoe?" Howe said.

"Standard Army issue boot," Eli said. "Roscoe's people took photos for the lab to analyze. We should have those by this afternoon."

"What size are you?" Howe asked.

"Thirteen shoe, fourteen boot," Eli said.

Howe stared at Eli for a moment.

"Prints?" Howe finally said.

Eli shook his head.

"The media is going to have a field day on this one," Howe said. "New York's biggest Broadway star murdered in his own home by the ghost stalker. Christ."

"What's his draft status?" Bannon asked.

"4F," Eli said. "Upton was thirty-seven years old last April. To his credit he did try to enlist in January of '42 but was rejected due to his asthma condition."

"Asthma?" Howe said.

"We found his medical records and medicine in his bedroom," Eli said. "And his enlistment reports."

Howe glanced at his watch. "I better head over to the Commissioner's office. He and the Mayor are going to call a press conference for later this afternoon."

"Art," Eli said. "He's running out of time. He's going to step up his pace."

Howe nodded. "I agree," he said.

After Howe left, Eli said, "Jack, hit the neighborhood for witnesses. Tyler, talk to Mrs. Boyle about Upton's habits, friends, women, whatever. Meet me back in the office around 5:00. All the sketches should be complete by then."

* * *

Eli stared at the blow up photograph of the boot print.

"Boot is at least a year old, maybe more," Roscoe said. "I photographed a new boot and compared the prints side-by-side. See for yourself."

Eli took the blown up photograph of the new boot print and compared it to the print found in Upton's backyard.

"I've estimated it would take at least a year of steady wearing to wear down the tread as much as he has," Roscoe said.

"A boot like this can be had at any Army/Navy store anywhere," Eli said. "I wore my boots home and they're still in my closet buried somewhere."

"I know, but it does prove your theory he's a big son of a bitch," Roscoe said. "And I'm no shrink, but by living in those boots I would guess he's living in the past."

Eli looked at the print found in the Upton backyard. "He stepped hard, agreed?"

"Agreed."

"Even worn, Army boots have a deep tread," Eli said. "Why didn't you find dirt from the garden in the house?"

"He took them off on the fire escape before he went in through the window," Roscoe said. "We found dirt on the landing on the first and second floor."

"The window wasn't forced," Eli said. "Hot summer night, the windows were open to vent the hallway. He took his boots off not because he was worried about dirt but because heavy boots make noise on hard wood floors."

Roscoe nodded. "He cased the Upton residence well in advance and knew about the floors before hand," he said.

"He wore gloves, that's a given," Eli said. "What if he removed the gloves to untie the laces on his boots? He may have touched the railing on the fire escape without realizing it. Did you dust the railings?"

"I did not," Roscoe said. "But I will now."

* * *

Eli looked at the body of Leland Upton on Wilson's examination table.

"Six-foot-one, a solid 180 and except for his asthma was exceptionally healthy," Wilson said. "His medical records show he used adrenalin chloride to control his attacks."

"Let me know if you find anything on the body," Eli said.

"The press conference is about to start," Wilson said. "Want to stay and listen?"

"I have work to do," Eli said.

* * *

197

The radio in the squad room was on and the press conference concerning Leland Upton was in full bloom.

"Turn that down, please," Eli said as he entered the squad room.

Tyler switched the radio off.

"What do we got?" Eli asked.

"Couldn't find a single witness anywhere in the neighborhood," Bannon said. "But that neighborhood is pretty quiet after dark, so that doesn't surprise me."

"The housekeeper said Upton didn't have a steady woman in his life," Tyler said. "She said he was always doing a play or rehearsing for one. She said he was a total creature of habit and rarely broke from his daily routine."

"What about the wild parties she mentioned?"

"After parties for opening night," Tyler said. "After a show opened, he would invite the entire cast and crew for a party. Same when a show closed."

"What do we have for sketches?" Eli asked.

"A total of fifty-one," Tyler said.

"Let's look at them," Eli said.

"We can use the table in the interrogation room," Tyler said.

* * *

Tyler and Bannon spread out the sketches on the long table in the interrogation room. Eli looked at each sketch drawn by the department sketch artist.

Eli's eyes scanned each sketch carefully.

As he darted back and forth from sketch to sketch, he locked on one sketch numbered thirty-one.

It was of a large man with broad shoulders, a full beard and long hair under a wool cap. He wore the green Army field jacket Eli was so familiar with.

"Are you all right, Lieutenant?" Tyler asked.

"Him," Eli said and placed his finger on sketch thirty-one. "This is our man."

Tyler and Bannon looked at Eli.

"Who is the witness for this sketch?" Eli asked.

* * *

Mary Pavasi was a sixty-two-year-old widow. She lived alone in the apartment she once shared with her husband and children. Now she shared the apartment with her beloved dog, Elmo.

Her apartment was located one block away from the nightclub on a quiet side street.

"After you called I made tea," Pavasi said.

Neither Eli nor Tyler were tea drinkers, but what the hell?

At the kitchen table, Pavasi filled three cups with the tea.

Eli held the rolled up sketch in his right hand and flattened it on the table.

"Mrs. Pavasi, what can you tell us about the man you described to our sketch artist?" Eli said.

"Like I told your officer here and the artist, I took my dog for a walk around 7:30 in the morning as I always do and he walked past me to the corner," Pavasi said. "He stopped on the corner and smoked a cigarette. The reason I remember so well is it was a fairly warm morning and he was wearing a heavy, green jacket."

"Did you walk past him?" Eli asked.

"Yes, I walked right by him, but he didn't seem to notice," Pavasi said. "I walked Elmo around the block and when I returned to the corner, he was gone."

"Ever see him before or since?" Eli asked.

"No, never."

"Your description said he was around six-foot-two or three," Eli said.

Pavasi nodded.

Eli stood up. "I'm six-three. Was he as tall or taller?"

Pavasi looked at Eli and then stood up. She studied Eli for a few moments and then said, "Taller, but he was wearing some kind of boots. That may have made him appear a bit taller."

Eli took his chair and sipped some tea. "Is there anything else you can remember about this man?" he said.

"No, not that I can think of," Pavasi said. "Except for a slight limp. Did I mention that?

"No, no you didn't," Eli said. "What limp?"

"He walked with a slight limp on the right side," Pavasi said. "His knee must have been bothering him."

Eli and Tyler exchanged glances.

Eli looked at Pavasi. "If you remember anything else, call me at this number," he said and left her his business card.

* * *

Howe sat behind his desk and looked at the sketch of the bearded suspect. "A limp, you said."

"No, Mary Pavasi said it," Eli said. "But it could be a war injury."

Howe sighed. "We took a beating today from the media," he said. "They're calling us incompetent and unqualified. Our department looks bad nationwide."

"The reporters should try doing what we do, they'd write different stories," Eli said.

"Is this sketch good enough to do comparisons from the mug books?" Howe asked.

"It might be," Eli said. "That's an all day task for tomorrow. My guys are beat and I sent them home."

"That's a good idea, Eli," Howe said.

Eli nodded.

He returned to his desk and called Mavis.

"Is it too late?" Eli asked when she answered the phone.

"Not if you go straight to the restaurant," Mavis said.

"Twenty minutes," Eli said.

Twenty

"You look exhausted," Mavis said.

"Long day," Eli said.

"Relax now," Mavis said. "I ordered two steaks and beers on tap."

"You heard the latest?" Eli asked.

"About Leland Upton? Only the whole country has heard the news," Mavis said. "He was a big time Broadway star."

A waitress arrived with two tall glasses of cold beer and set them on the table. "About ten minutes for your steaks," she said.

"Thank you," Eli said.

Mavis took a sip of beer and seemed uncomfortable for a moment. "There is something I need to tell you," she said.

Eli nodded.

"Margo called me this afternoon," Mavis said. "She said…"

"Who is Margo?" Eli asked.

Mavis looked at the table for a moment. "Margo is the redhead I told you about. Remember?"

"I remember. What about her?"

"She called after she heard the news on the radio. About Leland Upton," Mavis said.

"Don't tell me he was a client of hers?"

"No, worse," Mavis said. "She thinks this stalker was."

Eli stared at her. "I have to talk to her right away."

"She'll be at my apartment in one hour," Mavis said. "Enough time for us to eat our steaks."

*   *   *

Margaret Hope went by the name Margo for her clients. She was a few years older than Mavis and had red hair and green eyes. She was a bit shorter than Mavis and slightly heavier in the bosom.

She wore slacks with a teal colored, sleeveless blouse and crossed her legs as she sat on Mavis's sofa.

"Miss Hope," Eli said.

Margo looked at Mavis. "Is he for real?"

"Oh, yes," Mavis said.

"I don't understand," Eli said.

"Call me Margo. Miss Hope makes it sound like you're talking to my mother," Margo said.

"All right, Margo, tell me what you know," Eli said.

Margo opened her bag and removed a pack of cigarettes and lit one.

"The coffee is ready," Mavis said and went to the kitchen.

"I don't pay much attention to the news," Margo said. "I don't read newspapers and never listen to the news on the radio. It's depressing if you know what I mean."

"I do," Eli said. "Please continue."

"I had a… wait, are you at all interested in my outside activities?" Margo said.

Returning with a tray, Mavis said, "Don't be ridiculous, Margo. Eli is a homicide lieutenant and could care less about your activities."

"I have to protect myself, Mavis," Margo said. "The lieutenant may be in homicide but it's all the same playground."

"I assure you I'm not interested in the least about vice," Eli said.

Mavis handed Eli a cup of coffee and then another to Margo.

"I was in a cab this afternoon," Margo said. "The client pays for my cabs because he'd rather see me at his home. He lives way the hell uptown by the Cloisters. Anyway, I'm riding back to my apartment and the cab driver has the news on the radio. He says something like that crazy ghost stalker got another one, some big time Broadway actor. The driver starts going on and on about the stalker, how he uses a bayonet to soften up his victims before he kills them. I asked him what a bayonet is and he tells me it's this big knife they use in the Army. I didn't think anything of it until later when I got home. That's when I called Mavis."

"Because?" Eli asked.

"Six months ago, maybe seven, this guy calls me up for a date," Margo said. "He said he got my number from the desk clerk at his hotel and…"

"What hotel?" Eli asked.

"Oh. The Fleming in Times Square. A real flea bag if you know what I mean," Margo said. "He said his name was Bill Carson. I told him to call back in five minutes. I called the desk clerk and checked to see if there was a Bill Carson staying there and he said yes. So when he called back we made a date. I went to him. Guy turned out to be a real freak."

"What did he look like?" Eli asked.

"He was a big guy like you," Margo said. "Around your age or so. His hair was real long and he had a bushy beard. His right leg looked like it was caught in a fence or something. He said it was from a German twenty-five, whatever that is."

"Eyes?" Eli said.

"Dark. Almost black."

Eli nodded. "So tell me why he was a freak and why you think he might be the stalker?"

"Well, he… "Margo paused and leaned in to whisper in Mavis's ear.

Mavis nodded. "It's okay, tell him."

Margo took a breath. "He got naked in the bathtub and wanted me to pee on his bad leg," she said. "I had to drink two beers first."

"And did you?" Eli asked.

"Pee on his leg? Yes. That's what he paid for, that's what I did," Margo said. "But get this. The whole time I was… peeing on his leg, he had this huge knife in his hand and kept saying 'The fucking Nazis did this to me; the fucking Nazis did this to me.' Like that, over and over again."

"While holding the bayonet?" Eli said.

Margo nodded.

"Did he say anything else?" Eli asked.

"No. Wait. Yes," Margo said. "He mumbled something about Goddamn draft dodgers. He didn't want sex, so I beat it the hell out of there and took a cab home."

"Miss Hope. I mean Margo, can you look at some sketches for me?" Eli said.

"You mean go to the police station?" Margo asked.

"My office is at headquarters," Eli said.

"Do I have to?" Margo said.

"It's important," Eli asked.

Margo whispered in Mavis's ear again. Mavis nodded.

"Some of her clients… you know," Mavis said.

"Not at this time of night," Eli said. "Just one of my men and he's no client of yours, trust me."

Margo nodded. "Okay."

*   *   *

Eli and Margo met Tyler in the interrogation room shortly after 11:00 pm. Tyler had spread out the fifty-one sketches across the table as Eli requested.

"Now, Margo, please look at each sketch carefully and see if any match the description of the man you told me about," Eli said.

Margo nodded. She walked the length of the twelve-foot-long table as she inspected each sketch. When she reached the second row of sketches, she paused and placed her finger on the sketch labeled number thirty-one.

"Him," Margo said. "This is him."

"Are you sure?" Eli asked.

Margo nodded. "I'm sure. This is him, the freak."

"Thank you," Eli said. "I'll drive you home."

* * *

Eli and Mavis soaked in a hot tub full of scented oils and bubble bath.

Eli closed his eyes and rested his head against the rim of the tub.

"So what now?" Mavis asked.

"We scour the city until we find him," Eli said.

"Scour?" Mavis said.

"I heard them say that on the radio show Boston Blackie," Eli said.

Mavis smiled. "Will Margo have to be mentioned? She's worried about her name coming up in the newspapers."

"Not if I can help it," Eli said and opened his eyes.

"Did she... say anything else?"

"She suggested she come back to your place for what she called a threesome," Eli said.

"Oh, for God's sake," Mavis said.

"I told her yes. She should be here any minute," Eli said.

Mavis nudged Eli with her left foot. "Keep talking, big boy," she said. "You'll talk yourself out the door."

"He's out there," Eli said. "I'll find him."

"I know," Mavis said.

Eli closed his eyes again.

"Water's getting cold," Mavis said. "Let's get out. I'll fix us a snack."

Eli, breathing softly, didn't respond.

"Eli?" Mavis said.

* * *

"I have to go," Eli said.

"Your shirt, socks and underwear are in the drier," Mavis said. "Be about another fifteen minutes. You might as well have some breakfast."

They had just finished making love and both were still naked in bed.

"When did you wash them?" Eli asked.

"While you were still asleep. I got up early. Feel like some eggs?"

By the time Eli was dressed, Mavis had prepared omelets with hash browns and toast and coffee. They ate at the kitchen table.

"Thank you," Eli said.

"For breakfast?"

"For Margo," Eli said. "It's the first real break we've had."

"I'm helping my own cause," Mavis said.

Eli looked at her.

"You said you needed to finish this to concentrate on us," Mavis said. "I did my part, now go do yours and finish it."

Twenty-One

"Bill Carson?" Howe said as he looked at the sketch. "You're kidding."

"It's a fake for sure, but this is our guy, Art. No doubt," Eli said.

Howe picked up Eli's written report and scanned it quickly. "Because this hooker Margaret Hope stepped forward and said he was a client of hers?"

"He had a bayonet and a damaged right leg," Eli said. "She said she heard him say from a German twenty-five."

"Twenty-five caliber machine gun," Howe said.

"On D-Day the beachheads were protected by hundreds of them," Eli said. "She said he also mumbled something about draft dodgers."

"This hotel, the Fleming, it's a dump," Howe said. "I can tell just by the address."

"Tyler and Jack are there now questioning the staff," Eli said.

Howe sat back in his chair and looked at Eli. "Are you sure this just isn't a hooker seeking publicity? Looking to be come the next starlet."

"She wants her name left completely out of it," Eli said. "Apparently some of her clients are cops. Besides, she described the guy to a T and knew about the wounded leg. She's on the level, Art."

"I'll go see the Chief," Howe said.

* * *

208

Eli was at his desk when the phone rang. He thought it was either Bannon or Tyler calling with an update.

It wasn't.

"Lieutenant Rico, this is District Attorney Michael Bell calling."

"Well, I have to say this is a surprise," Eli said.

"Yeah, well, I got another one for you," Bell said. "Meet me in court in thirty minutes."

*   *   *

Bell and Eli stood before the desk of Federal Judge Webb in his chambers at the courthouse.

"After careful consideration I've decided to review your request and grant you a court order," Webb said.

Webb signed a two page long document and handed it to Bell.

"I expect results for my investment," Webb said.

"You'll get them," Bell said.

*   *   *

Eli and Bell stood on the courthouse steps and smoked cigarettes.

"What the fuck just happened?" Bell said almost giddy.

"I answered the phone," Eli said.

"What?"

"Nothing. Let's take a walk over to Veteran's Affairs," Eli said.

*   *   *

John Rook looked up at Bell as he tossed the court order onto Rook's desk.

Rook picked up the document and scanned it quickly.

209

"I'll need to see my supervisor," Rook said.

"You do that," Bell said.

Rook stood up and was gone for about ten minutes. When he returned he was not alone.

"This is Deputy Director Shaw," Rook said.

"Your request will take some time," Shaw said.

"How much time?" Bell asked.

"At least twenty-four hours," Shaw said.

"We'll be back at 1:00 tomorrow afternoon," Bell said.

* * *

Eli and Bell sat next to Howe in the Commissioner's office. The Police Chief stood to the Commissioner's left.

"I must say that this is a bit of good luck," the Commissioner said. "Tomorrow you will transport all records from the VA to the Chief's office where he will assume command of the investigation. Captain Howe will assist and assign his men accordingly. It's about time we got a break on this case."

"I don't think so, Commissioner," Bell said.

"Excuse me?" the Commissioner said.

"I'm the Manhattan District Attorney, not you," Bell said. "That makes me top cop in the room. This goes as I say it goes. The records will not leave my office. Lieutenant Rico will supervise the investigation and pick his own team to assist him. Captain Howe will be kept in the loop but will serve no function besides consultant. Am I clear on this?"

"You're crazy. You can't pull a stunt like this and..." The Commissioner said.

"It's a well known fact that the Chief here couldn't find his dick in the dark with a flashlight," Bell said. "And you're just a civilian

210

appointee. This investigation is under my wing now. As of noon tomorrow, Lieutenant Rico is under my jurisdiction until this case is closed. Deal with it. "

Howe glared at Eli for a moment.

"If you'll excuse me, I have work to do," Bell said.

* * *

"I didn't know about that, Art," Eli said. "Bell never said a word about his plan after we left the judge."

"It figures," Howe said. "Bell wants to run for mayor and eventually for governor. He figures being known as the man who solved the ghost stalker case would jump-start his career in the public eye."

"It probably will," Eli said.

"And yours," Howe said.

"Mine? I have no political ambitions, Art. Never have," Eli said.

"Maybe not politics, but Captain Rico before age forty is quite an accomplishment," Howe said. "Unheard of in the department."

"Is that what you think? That I would pull a stunt like this for personal gain," Eli said.

Behind his desk, Howe sighed. "No. No, I don't," he said. "I think you'd work just as hard if you were still a patrolman. That said, opportunity knocks but only once."

Eli nodded. "I better talk to Bannon and Tyler."

* * *

"We'll need more than just the three of us," Tyler said.

"Maybe," Eli said. "We'll see how it goes. If we need more men, I'll pull some of the guys."

211

"Where do we work out of?" Tyler asked.

"DA's office starting noon tomorrow," Eli said.

"How does the Captain feel about this?" Bannon asked.

"He's okay with it," Eli said. "We need to keep him advised though. Now how did you make out at the hotel?"

"They have a high turnover," Tyler said. "Only one employee, the night desk clerk goes back more than six months. Guy's a doper, but he was able to pull records going back a year. We found a Bill Carson registered and stayed for two weeks."

"We got the registration cards," Bannon said. "No prior or forwarding address, but we have his handwriting sample and prints for comparison."

"Good work," Eli said. "We might get lucky and find a sample of his handwriting in his medical reports."

The phone on Eli's desk rang and he walked to it and answered the call.

"Lieutenant Rico," he said.

"You have one month," Genovese said. "After that, I take over. Am I clear?"

Before Eli could respond, the line went dead.

* * *

Tyler entered the interrogation room with three mugs of coffee and set them on the table in front of Eli and Bannon.

"Thanks," Eli said.

"Fifty copies of the sketch will be ready in about an hour," Tyler said.

"Good. We'll need them," Eli said.

The phone in the interrogation room rang and Eli scooped it up. "Lieutenant Rico," he said.

"Eli, it's Roscoe," Roscoe said. "No prints on the fire escape."

"It was worth a shot," Eli said.

"But, we got a beautiful set of prints off the outside window," Roscoe said.

"Get them over here. Fast," Eli said.

"Already on the way," Roscoe said. "You can thank me later with a steak."

Eli hung up. "Roscoe got a set of prints off the window. Where are the prints from the registration card?"

"On my desk," Bannon said.

"As soon as the messenger arrives with Roscoe's set, take them to the print technicians for comparisons," Eli said.

Bannon nodded.

Eli lit a cigarette, sipped coffee and then said, "Why the Fleming?"

"It's a dump. It's cheap," Tyler said.

"That's not what I mean," Eli said. "Say you've just gotten out of prison or in this case, a VA hospital. You're short on funds so where do you go until you get back on your feet?"

"A fleabag," Bannon said.

"For two weeks," Tyler said. "Long enough to get your finances in order and move out."

"It's doubtful he found a job," Eli said. "So he has another means of support.

"Welfare or disability?" Bannon said.

"Possibility," Eli said. "Whatever it is will leave a paper trail for us to follow."

There was a knock on the door. It opened and a uniformed officer stepped inside. "Set of prints for you, Lieutenant," he said.

Bannon took the prints. "Be right back,"

Gone for just a few minutes, Bannon returned with the prints lifted off the reservation card from the Fleming Hotel.

Eli, Bannon and Tyler examined both sets of prints under a magnifying glass.

"If these aren't a match, I don't know what is," Tyler said.

"Get them over to the lab for verification," Eli said.

* * *

"I picked the two best men I have, Tyler and Bannon," Eli said.

"If we need more, my staff is qualified," Bell said. "Meet at my office at noon and we'll walk over to the VA."

"Okay," Eli said.

"By the way, any blowback from Howe?"

"He thinks you want to be governor."

"I do. See you at noon."

Eli hung up and called Mavis.

"Pack a bag," he said. "We're going to my place."

Twenty-Two

"What are we celebrating?" Mavis asked.

After picking Mavis up, Eli drove them to Nick's Italian Restaurant in the Little Italy neighborhood in The Bronx.

"I don't…"Eli said.

"Wait, where are the menus?" Mavis asked.

"There aren't any," Eli said. "What I was saying…"

"How do you know what to order?" Mavis asked.

"The waiter stops by and tells you what the chef feels like cooking," Eli said. "Later, the waiter tells you what he feels like charging you. Now what I was…"

"What if the waiter doesn't like you?"

"He charges you more," Eli said.

Mavis nodded. "What were you going to say?"

"I don't think I can live in Ohio," Eli said. "But I can try living in upstate New York or New Jersey if you're willing."

Mavis stared at Eli for several seconds. "Did you… did you just ask me what I think you did?"

"If you think I asked you to marry me then you think right," Eli said.

Mavis stared at Eli for several seconds. "Of course I will marry you," she said. "But why now? We just talked about…"

"I saw something today I didn't like," Eli said. "My boss thinks I

215

stabbed him in the back and the man who gave him that idea is more interested in his political career than the victims. I don't want to wind up that way in ten years, looking over my shoulder to advance my career by stepping on the careers of others."

"I won't pretend to know anything about police work, but didn't you have to bust you ass to become a homicide lieutenant?" Mavis said.

"Like breaking rocks with a rubber hammer," Eli said.

"How long have you been a cop, Eli?" Mavis asked.

"Eleven years, minus time in the Army."

"That's not long enough to get a pension, is it?"

"No, but I can cash it out and put a down payment on a place in the country," Eli said. "I can return to school and get a law degree and work part time. There are lots of things I can do. The truth is I'd rather be your husband than a cop."

Mavis had to bite her lower lip to keep from crying.

"Of course, I don't expect you to say yes until I have a proper ring first," Eli said.

"Of course," Mavis said, choking back tears.

A waiter stopped by the table. "What will you have?" he asked.

"What do you got?" Eli said.

"The chef feels like making stuffed pork chops and veal Parmesan tonight," the waiter said.

"We'll have one of each," Eli said.

"For the lady as well?"

"She can eat me under the table," Eli said. "And a bottle of red wine."

*   *   *

"Do you know what I'm afraid of?" Mavis said.

They were naked on Eli's bed, covered with sweat after making love even though the fan blew directly on them.

"What?" Eli asked.

"My past."

"I don't care about the past," Eli said.

"Maybe not now, but later," Mavis said. "I'm afraid that one day you'll wake up and resent what I did for a living."

"What you did for a living is what helped me through an emotional problem and healed scars from the war," Eli said. "How could I ever resent that?"

"I just want you to be sure," Mavis said.

"I've never been surer of anything in my life," Eli said. "I want to finish this case and then I'll tender my resignation."

"I have a fair amount of money saved up," Mavis said. "We won't need to worry about that while you go to school. And I can still coach the girls in my spare time like I do now. I'll need to learn how to drive if we live in the country."

"We won't need your... you can't drive?" Eli said.

"My folks always drove me and in Manhattan nobody drives," Mavis said.

"Get a permit and I'll teach you," Eli said.

"So, what kind of ring did you have in mind?"

"A small one," Eli said. "Remember, I'm on a cop's pay."

"I don't care if it's so small you can't even see it," Mavis said.

"I'm still in the mood," Eli said. "But, I don't think it's that small."

Mavis looked down. "I didn't mean that, silly," she said.

* * *

"Don't you have to go to work?" Mavis asked.

Eli flipped pancakes and said, "I'm going in late today. Noon."

217

"So we have time for a hot bath after breakfast?"

The phone on the wall rang and Eli handed Mavis the spatula. "Keep flipping," he said. "And watch the bacon."

Eli grabbed the phone. "This is Eli," he said.

"Lieutenant, it's Jack," Bannon said. "I came in early because I wanted to check on the fingerprints. The prints from the window match the reservation card."

"Bring them to Bell's office," Eli said. "I'll see you at noon."

Eli hung up and returned to the stove where Mavis was placing bacon on a sheet of wax paper.

He kissed her on the back of the neck.

"Breakfast is ready," she said.

* * *

"Where do I get a learner's permit?" Mavis asked as Eli pulled curbside to her building.

"Forty-Forth and 8th," Eli said. "I'll call you later."

* * *

Rook had eight large cartons waiting for Bell.

Bell, Eli, Bannon and Tyler removed two cartons at a time and loaded them into Eli's car.

"I'll see you at your office," Eli told Bell.

By 3:00 in the afternoon, the cartons were broken down by alphabetical order in Bell's very large conference room.

"Jack, where are the handwriting samples?" Eli asked.

Bannon had made copies of the hotel reservation card.

"I'm due in court in twenty minutes," Bell said. "I should be back by 5:00."

After Bell left, Eli said, "Well, let's get to work."

"Lunch, Lieutenant," Bannon said.

"Good idea," Eli said. "I'll hit the coffee shop across the street."

* * *

Bell returned at 5:20.

"Jack, take five and grab us some coffee," Eli said.

"We have a well stocked break room," Bell said. "You can make a pot there."

Bell went behind his desk. Eli took a chair opposite it.

"We started with the letter C," Eli said. "And eliminated every Carson that received care at the VA hospitals and clinics. We figured Bill Carson was a fake name, but it needed to be checked."

"Will you need additional manpower?" Bell asked.

"Yes. At least two, maybe three," Eli said.

Bell nodded. "I'll assign two people in the morning. Plus myself. I freed my calendar."

"We plan to knock off around 8:00," Eli said. "And start at 9:00 tomorrow."

"I have an appointment at 6:00," Bell said. He reached into a desk drawer and produced a small cash box. "Send out for a decent dinner," he said and produced five twenty-dollar bills. "And get a receipt."

* * *

"Lieutenant, I can't see straight anymore," Tyler said.

Eli looked at his watch. It was twenty minutes to 9:00. "You know what, I can't either. Let's pick this up at 9:00 tomorrow morning."

"You don't have to tell me twice," Bannon said.

219

* * *

"I took a chance you might still be up," Mavis said when Eli answered his phone.

"I actually just got in," Eli said.

"Now? It's after 10:00."

"I know. Tomorrow will be just as bad."

"I went to the Motor Vehicle Department today," Mavis said. "I have to take a written test to get a learner's permit."

"That's standard," Eli said. "Listen, I probably won't have an ounce of free time the rest of the week, but if you want you can stay over Saturday and have dinner with my parents on Sunday?"

"I'd like that very much," Mavis said. "I love you and try to get some rest."

* * *

Why use the name Bill Carson?

There were nine William Carsons that received VA treatment for wounds suffered during the war. How many with that name served, were killed or arrived home in one piece.

Of the nine, two were Rangers. Both were killed in '44. None of the remaining seven received treatment for mental issues.

Did the stalker choose the name Bill Carson at random, or did he serve with a Bill Carson and simply used the name because it came to mind?

There was only one way to be certain why the stalker used the name Bill Carson and that was to catch him.

"Easier said than done," Eli said and turned off the bedside lamp.

Twenty-Three

"**We are looking for** men who suffered from mental issues and received VA treatment," Eli said. "Men treated for breakdowns, violent tendencies, resentment of any kind and other such issues. He's also a big man, tall and broad, so we can eliminate men shorter than, say, five-ten."

Eli, Tyler and Bannon were at the conference table with Bell and his two investigators, Sergeant Vail and Sergeant Thomas.

"We'll work alphabetically from A to Z," Eli said. "Questions?"

"Do they have to be local?" Thomas asked. "I mean from the Tri-State Area?"

"No, but our man knows the City backwards and forward, so he's probably local, or spent a great deal of time in the City," Eli said.

"Does it matter if he's left handed?" Vail asked.

"Jack, give them the registration cards," Eli said. "Our man is right-handed all the way. Department experts studied his handwriting and determined he's a righty."

"Mr. Bell briefed us yesterday," Vail said. "You believe our man was a Ranger. Is it possible he wasn't and learned this stuff on his own?"

"You were in?" Eli asked.

"3rd Army," Vail said.

"Do you know what a Ranger Choke Hold is?" Eli asked.

"No, no I don't," Vail said.

"Anymore questions?" Eli asked.

"Can we take our ties off?" Thomas said.

"Let's go to work," Eli said. "Minus our ties."

*   *   *

"Let's break for lunch," Bell said. "It's after one."

"Good idea," Eli said, stood and stretched.

"Write down what you want and I'll call for delivery," Bell said.

"I'll make a pot of coffee," Eli said.

While they waited for lunch to arrive, they sat at the table with cups of coffee.

"Something I want to toss around," Eli said. "Why use the name Bill Carson?"

"It's a common name, easy to remember," Vail said.

"Easy to spell, easy to write, easy to remember," Thomas said.

"So is John Doe, John Smith and any first name with Jones," Eli said. "I think he might have served with someone named Bill Carson and Carson was killed in action."

"Two Rangers named Carson, both dead," Tyler said.

"Go back and pull those files and see who they served with, when and where," Eli said. "Including officers and medics and engineers."

"Tyler and Bannon stood up.

"After lunch, guys," Eli said.

Bell looked at Eli. "What do you do, lie awake at night and think about this?"

"The Lieutenant is much smarter than he looks," Bannon said. "He's a deep thinker."

The phone on Bell's desk rang and he went to answer it. "Send him right up," he said and hung up. He returned to the table. "Lunch," he said.

* * *

Close to 3:00 in the afternoon, Bell's phone rang again. He went to his desk and answered the call. "I thought I told you to hold my calls," he said. He listened for a moment and then said, "Lieutenant, for you."

Eli went to the desk and took the phone. He listened carefully for a moment and then said, "No, I'll take it. Ask Howe to meet me there. Thanks."

"Lieutenant?" Tyler said.

"We got another one," Eli said.

Tyler and Bannon stood up from the table.

"No, keep working," Eli said. "Art will meet me there."

"I'd like to tag along if you don't mind," Bell said.

Eli nodded. "Alright," he said.

* * *

Joseph Tully ran a newsstand on Broadway outside the 79th Street subway station. He was twenty-nine-years old and lived alone in a small, third floor apartment on Eighth Avenue and 51st Street in Hell's Kitchen.

Wilson, after examining the body said, "He's been dead thirty-six hours, maybe more."

Bell stared at the dead body of Tully and choked back the bile rising up in his throat.

"It's different than being in a courtroom, isn't it," Howe said.

"Roscoe, he came in through the window in the kitchen where the fire escape is located," Eli said. "Dust everything."

"He's blind in the left eye," Wilson said. "What do you want to bet he's 4F?"

"The building superintendent called it in, where is he?" Eli asked.

"In his apartment in the basement," a uniformed officer said.

* * *

"He has this kid that works for him at the newsstand," Jose Torres, the building superintendent said. "He came by around 2:00 this afternoon and said Mr. Tully didn't show for work yesterday or today. I got the key and went in to check. I found him that way on the bedroom floor and I called the police."

"Did you touch anything besides the door?" Eli asked.

"I used the phone in the living room to call the police," Torres said.

"Do you know his habits?" Eli asked. "When he left for work and got home, women, girlfriends, anything like that?"

"I don't know much about Mr. Tully," Torres said. "I know he leaves for work early, 3:00, 4:00 in the morning, something like that."

"The kid who worked for Mr. Tully, where can I find him?" Eli asked.

"He's at the newsstand, I think," Torres said.

"Art, can you supervise upstairs?" Eli asked. "I want to speak to the kid."

"I'll go with you," Bell said.

* * *

"They call me Jake. My real name is John, but nobody calls me that except for my Ma when she's mad at me."

"How long have you worked for Mr. Tully?" Eli asked.

"Since I'm sixteen," Jake said. "Four years now. I attend classes at NYU during the day and take over for Mr. Tully at four. The evening papers are delivered at 5:00 and I stay open until they're all gone usually around 8:00 or so."

"What happened yesterday?" Eli asked.

"I show up and the stand was closed. All the newspapers were still on the sidewalk in bundles," Jake said. "People had ripped them open and helped themselves to whatever. I called his apartment but he didn't answer. I came by early and when he didn't show today I knew something was wrong and walked over to his apartment and talked to the superintendent Mr. Torres."

"Did you know Tully was blind in his left eye?" Eli asked.

"Of course," Jake said. "Everybody knew that."

"Will you open the newsstand tomorrow?"

"I think so," Jake said. "Mr. Tully wouldn't like it being closed."

* * *

"Wilson said he'd call with his report later tonight or tomorrow morning," Howe told Eli when he and Bell returned to Tully's apartment.

"Roscoe?" Eli said.

"He dusted every square inch of this place but said he found nothing on the window or fire escape," Howe said.

"Art, can you have our guys handle this one?" Eli asked. "Anything they find send over to Bell's office."

"I can do that," Howe said.

* * *

It was after 7:00 by the time Bell and Eli returned to Bell's office. Tyler, Bannon, Thomas and Vail were still working.

"How did it go, Lieutenant?" Tyler asked.

"We have our next victim," Eli said. "How about here?"

"We're compiling a list of possible candidates," Bannon said.

"Knock off for tonight," Eli said. "All of you."

After the four detectives left, Bell removed a bottle of bourbon from his desk and two water glasses. He splashed an ounce into each glass and sat in his chair.

Eli sat in the chair opposite the desk.

"The *Times*, *News* and *Mirror* will have a field day with tomorrow's headlines," Bell said.

Eli took a sip from his glass. "Don't they understand he reads the papers and listens to the news just like everybody else," he said. "Why feed his appetite?"

"Sex, murder and movie stars caught with their pants down sell newspapers," Bell said.

"I understand that, but for all we know the stories written about him just makes him want to kill even more," Eli said. "It's definitely increased his pace."

"Then so do we," Bell said. "I'll bring in another four men in the morning."

Eli nodded. "I think I'll go home," he said and tossed back his drink.

* * *

Eli felt his frustrations mounting and decided to go through his workout routine before settling on something to eat.

It was a warm night and he turned on the fan and aimed it on the floor.

He started with sit-ups and did two sets of one hundred.

Sweat rolled off his back.

Next he did six sets of pull-ups on the bar in the bathroom door frame. The first set was twenty reps, the last an even dozen.

Drenched in sweat, Eli ran the cold water in the bathroom sink and stuck his face and head into the basin to cool off.

Still frustrated and angry, Eli got on the floor and did push-ups. He cleared his mind and kept careful count of the repetitions.

As he passed the fiftieth rep, his shoulders began to ache. By the time he closed in on seventy-five, his arms burned. Near one hundred, his chest, arms and back were on fire.

He pushed the limit and collapsed at the 111th push-up.

On his back, Eli needed several minutes to regain his breath. Then he took a quick, hot shower, toweled off and tossed on shorts and a T-shirt.

There wasn't much in the refrigerator in the way of food. He improvised by frying up a half pound of bacon and making a six-egg omelet. As he ate at the table, Mavis called.

"Tomorrow is Friday," Mavis said.

"I didn't even realize that," Eli said.

"You sound exhausted."

"I am."

"Stay over tomorrow night," Mavis said. "I miss you."

"We had another one."

"I heard on the radio."

"I'll have to work Saturday."

"I know, but a good night's sleep and some good food won't hurt you," Mavis said.

"Let's reverse that," Eli said. "I need to be near the phone."

"Okay. I'll do some food shopping before you pick me up," Mavis said.

"It probably won't be until 7:00."

"I'll be ready," Mavis said. "Call me before you leave work."

"I will."

After hanging up the phone, Eli placed the dirty dishes and pans in the sink, turned on the radio, lit a cigarette and settled in on the sofa.

A few songs played and then the news came on. A broadcaster gave details of the latest 'Ghost Stalker' murder. "As the body count grows, an entire city lives in fear and the police seem powerless to stop the carnage," he said.

Eli switched off the radio.

"Carnage," he said aloud. "Try storming a beach on D-Day if you want to see carnage, asshole."

Frustrated, angry, Eli went to bed.

Before he turned off the lamp on the nightstand, he looked across the room at the dresser. Weeks ago he placed the shoebox Mavis brought him on the dresser and never gave it a second look.

He got out of bed, went to the shoebox and removed the lid and took the box to the bed. He dumped the envelopes and opened each one. Sixty twenty-dollar bills.

Twelve hundred dollars.

"Sure, why not?" he said aloud.

Twenty-Four

Bell was at his desk when Eli entered the office. Bell had copies of the morning papers.

"They're crucifying us," Bell said.

"We expected it," Eli said. "Okay if I use the phone?"

"Go ahead."

Eli used the phone on the conference table and called Howe.

"Art, it's Eli. Anything new on Tully?" Eli said.

"Identical MO according to Wilson," Howe said. "No prints according to Roscoe. I have a couple of men interviewing tenants of his building for witnesses."

"I'm going to talk to the kid Jake again," Eli said. "I'll call you later."

Eli hung up and returned to Bell's desk.

"Have the men pick up from last night," Eli said. "I'm going to talk to that kid Jake again. I won't be long."

* * *

Eli parked in front of a hydrant and stuck his police card on the windshield. He took the sketch with him as he walked the half block to the newsstand on 79th Street and Broadway.

The newsstand was open and Jake was inside behind the counter.

"Hello, Jake," Eli said.

Jake nodded. "I opened like you said. I figured Mr. Tully would want it that way. He was very dedicated to his customers."

"I'm sure he was," Eli said. "I would have showed you this yesterday except that I didn't have it with me."

Eli unrolled the sketch and placed it on the counter.

"Have you ever seen this man before?" Eli asked.

Jake stared at the sketch for a few seconds and then looked up at Eli.

"Are you kidding with me or what?" Jake said.

"No, I'm not. Why?" Eli said.

"He was like just here," Jake said. "About an hour ago. He bought the morning papers. *The Times, News* and *Mirror.*"

"Are you sure? Take another look," Eli said.

"I'm sure," Jake said. "You can't miss the guy. He's big, like you, with the long hair and beard like the jazz freaks in the Village. Like I said, he bought the papers."

"How did he pay?"

"Let me think," Jake said. "He gave me two one-dollar bills. I gave him his change and he left."

"Which way?"

"I didn't notice. There was a bunch of people buying papers to take on the subway."

"Ever see him before today?"

Jake shook his head. "I'd remember a guy like that."

"Do you still have those dollar bills?"

Jake shrugged. "I have a lot of dollar bills this time of day."

"Don't touch them," Eli said. "Put new dollar bills in a separate place. I'll be right back."

Eli went to the pay phone on the corner and called Roscoe.

*   *   *

Roscoe dusted forty-one one-dollar bills. Forty of them produced no clear-cut sets of prints. One had a perfect thumb and first-finger print.

"Run this over to Art, Roscoe," Eli said.

"I have to account for that dollar," Jake said.

Eli gave him a dollar from his wallet.

"Thanks, Jake, you've been a big help," Eli said.

*   *   *

Eli entered Tiffany's shortly after they opened at 10:00 in the morning. A small crowd entered the famous jewelry store with him.

Eli went straight to the main counter.

"May I help you, sir?" A clerk asked.

"What kind of engagement ring can I buy for twelve hundred dollars?" Eli asked.

"A decent one," the clerk said.

*   *   *

"The son of a bitch showed up at Tully's newsstand this morning and brought the papers," Eli said.

Bell, Tyler, Bannon, Vail and Thomas were at the conference table.

"You're kidding?" Bell said.

"He paid with two one-dollar bills and Roscoe lifted his prints off one of them," Eli said.

"He's a fucking vulture, this guy," Bannon said.

"With balls like King Kong," Thomas said.

231

"We know he's in the City and we know he's close," Eli said. "How are we doing here?"

"Just started the E pile," Vail said.

"I got a question, Lieutenant," Thomas said. "Say this guy is as you say, a Ranger with a giant chip on his shoulder, how does he get access to classified military records on draft status? It's not like they leave them laying around a hospital."

Eli stared at Thomas for several long seconds.

"Lieutenant?" Thomas said.

"Eli?" Tyler said.

"Mr. Bell, you come with me," Eli said. "Everybody else keep on working."

* * *

"Oh, good, my headache wasn't bad enough," Rook said as Eli and Bell approached his desk.

"Do you have many veterans working for the VA?" Eli asked.

"Many," Rook said.

"How many?" Eli asked.

"Spread out over the five boroughs, a hundred. More. Why?" Rook said.

"Get their records," Eli said.

"I'll need to see my supervisor," Rook said.

"Then see him," Eli said. "We'll wait."

Eli and Bell took chairs in the waiting area and after ten minutes, Rook returned with Shaw.

"What's all this about?" Shaw asked.

"We need to talk privately," Bell said.

* * *

"Do you really think this Ghost Stalker works here at the VA?" Shaw said from behind his desk.

"Not anymore," Eli said. "But say he did, how easy would it be to go through draft status records and find records on men classified 4F."

Shaw stared at Eli.

"What do you want to see?" Shaw asked.

"Anybody who worked here during the past year who served, was wounded, who stayed at a VA hospital and probably doesn't work here any longer," Eli said.

Shaw sighed. "This will take a while," he said.

"We have a while," Eli said.

*   *   *

Eli and Bell were on the front steps of the VA building. Both had deli containers of coffee and were smoking cigarettes.

"You have great instincts, Lieutenant," Bell said. "I want you to head up my investigative staff. It's quite a prestigious position and a captain's shield comes with it."

"I have to think about it," Eli said.

"Is there a woman you have to discuss it with?"

"Yes."

"There always is," Bell said. "But I'm sure she wouldn't mind a prestigious promotion and the money that comes with it. Besides, being a captain's wife is nothing to sneeze at in its own right."

"I'll talk to her about it," Eli said.

"Good," Bell said. "Well, let's go see if they met our request."

*   *   *

"Eighty-seven veterans working for or worked for the VA during the past year," Rook said. "Do you want copies of all the files to take with you?"

"Just the use of an office," Bell said.

"How about a conference room?" Rook said.

The conference room table was large enough for Bell and Eli to spread out the eighty-seven files and dig right in.

They read files for half an hour.

"There must be a place to get some coffee in this building," Eli said. "I'll be right back."

There was a cafeteria on the second floor and he got two containers of coffee to go. When he returned to the conference room, Bell was deeply engrossed in a file.

"Lieutenant, have a look at this," Bell said.

Eli set the containers on the table and took the file.

Justin Riddick. Age listed as Thirty-two. Height listed as six-foot-five. Served in the Army from '42 through early '46. Joined the first squad of Rangers in '43. Wounded several times, the last time in March of '45 and was sent to London.

After Germany fell, Riddick was sent stateside and spent two years at the VA Hospital on Long Island.

In early '47, while still recovering from wounds inflicted by a German .25, Riddick's wife filed for divorce long-distance from their home in Rhode Island.

Riddick had a son that he hadn't seen since the boy was six months old.

After receiving the divorce notice, Riddick spiraled downward into a deep depression and suffered a total breakdown.

Two years of treatment were required to bring Riddick back to mental health and in December of '48 he was pronounced fit enough to be released from the hospital.

In late December he applied for a position with the VA in Manhattan and was employed as a night custodial worker. His address was listed as the Fleming Hotel.

In April, Riddick stopped coming to work. His supervisor tried to contact Riddick at the Fleming Hotel, but was told no one by that name had ever registered.

Eli set the folder aside and looked at Bell.

"This is our man," he said. "I'm sure of it."

* * *

"The night cleaning crew supervisor doesn't come in until 8:00 in the evening," Shaw said.

"Are you shitting me?" Bell said. "Call the fucking guy up and get him down here on the fucking double."

Shaw used his office phone to call the supervisor at home.

"He used the name Bill Carson to register at the Fleming," Eli said. "He was already planning this before he left the hospital. What better way to obtain classified information than to work at night when no one is around."

Shaw hung up the phone and looked at Eli and Bell. "He'll be right down. He lives in Queens, so give him an hour."

"You have records of men with 4F status kept where?" Bell asked.

"In our records room," Shaw said.

"Show us," Bell said.

* * *

"It looks like the library," Eli said.

The large room was wall-to-wall with catalogue files.

"It is similar in that we use an index card system. Of course, we only have records of men living in New York State," Shaw said. "Going back to the beginning of World War One. On file here and in Washington. It helps to prevent fraud, mislabeling an individual and so forth."

"Mr. Shaw, did you serve?" Eli asked.

Shaw shook his head. "I have a condition known as rapid heartbeat."

"Is your card in here?" Eli asked.

"Of course," Shaw said. He looked at Eli and Bell. "Oh dear God," he said.

Shaw rushed to the file marked S and pulled out the sleeve marked SH and began rummaging through cards.

Eli and Bell stood behind him.

Shaw suddenly stopped and slowly turned around. His face had gone ashen. "It's… not here," he said.

"Aren't you glad we just happened to come along," Bell said.

* * *

From behind his desk, Shaw drank a glass of water with visibly shaking hands.

"I'm on his list, aren't I?" Shaw asked.

"It would appear so," Bell said.

"Are you a family man, Mr. Shaw?" Eli asked.

"Wife and two kids," Shaw said.

"Where do you live?" Eli said.

"New Jersey."

"He hasn't crossed the river yet," Eli said. "But I would call my wife and make temporary arrangements to stay elsewhere until he is caught. And don't come to work. If you need it, we'll clear it with your boss as part of our investigation. How do you commute?"

"Train and subway," Shaw said.

"I'll have an officer drive you home," Eli said.

* * *

Dominick Lumia, a veteran of World War One, was into his twenty-first year working for the VA in Manhattan. He started as a janitor and worked his way up to supervisor.

"Yeah, I remember Riddick," Lumia said. "Guys that size you don't easily forget."

"What did he do here?" Eli asked.

"Floor buffer," Lumia said. "He operated the buffing machine."

"What can you tell us about him?" Eli asked.

"Not much, really," Lumia said. "He knew how to handle a buffer for sure. He said they let him buff the floors at the hospital. He was quiet for so large a man. Graceful like, if you know what I mean. He kept to himself and then one night didn't show for work. I've never seen him since."

"Did he ever talk about the war or the hospital?" Eli asked. "His friends or women?"

"Not to me," Lumia said. "I have twenty men I supervise every night, I don't have time for small talk."

"Did he ever speak about his leg, his wound in the war?" Eli said.

Lumia shook his head. "I never asked him. I figure a man is entitled to his privacy. It never interfered with his work, though."

"Mr. Lumia, how do you get paid?" Eli asked.

"Fifteen years ago in cash," Lumia said. "Now by check. Most of us have an account at the VA Savings and Loan on Sixth Avenue. I know Riddick cashed checks there because on Friday we'd show up early and walk over."

* * *

Eli and Bell sat at a table in the cafeteria with cups of coffee.

"We know who he is, how do we find him in a city of eight million?" Bell said.

"Two possibilities," Eli said. "Check the DMV for a driver's license. We know he drives, maybe he does it legally."

Eli paused to light a cigarette.

"What's the second?" Bell asked.

"If you're paid by check you have to go to a bank to cash it," Eli said. "If you have an account, you need an address to open it."

Bell looked at his watch. "Banks are closed until Monday and we'll need another court order for both."

"First thing Monday we get one," Eli said. "In the meantime we can check his medical reports at your office."

* * *

At Bell's office, Eli skipped ahead to the R pile and found Riddick's very thick file and took it to the conference table.

"This is our man," Eli said.

Tyler read the name. "Justin Riddick," he said.

The next hour, Eli, Bell and the four detectives read Riddick's medical reports from the VA hospital.

Struggling to recover from his leg wounds, Riddick spiraled into depression when his wife of six years broke off contact with him. His condition worsened when she filed for divorce and later remarried.

Riddick became angry, violent and reclusive. He struggled with depression and violence for several years until a breakthrough finally came and he slowly regained his mental health.

"He bullshitted them into releasing him," Bannon said.

"I'm missing something, though," Tyler said. "Why take all this shit out of men who are 4F? They have nothing to do with it."

"I'll verify it in the morning, but who wants to take bets that Riddick's wife married a man who is 4F?" Eli said.

"Shit," Tyler said.

"Everybody pack up and go home," Eli said. "And hope he doesn't kill again before we find him."

"Want we should brief Howe?" Bannon said.

"I'll do that in the morning," Eli said.

* * *

Bell took out his bottle and poured two small drinks and gave one to Eli.

Eli sat in a chair and lit a cigarette.

"You're one hell of a cop. Lieutenant," Bell said. "It would be an injustice to this city if you didn't take command of my Special Crimes Unit. Homicide is great, don't get me wrong, but here we do it all and you'd do it as a captain. Oh, and unless otherwise dictated, my guys work nine-to-five, Monday through Friday."

"It's something for me to think about," Eli said.

"It is. Talk it over with your girlfriend over the weekend," Bell said. "We'll meet Monday in court. I don't think we'll have any problem obtaining warrants this time."

Twenty-Five

Mavis was waiting for Eli in front of her building. She had an overnight bag and two large bags of groceries.

She greeted Eli with a warm hug and kiss when he got out and loaded the bags into the back seat.

"You look as if you had a long day," Mavis said as Eli pulled away from the curb.

"A good day," Eli said.

"Can you talk about it?"

"No, not yet, but there is something related to it we need to discuss," Eli said.

"Okay."

"Later, when we get to my place," Eli said.

* * *

"That chicken you put in the oven smells wonderful," Eli said.

"It needs another thirty minutes," Mavis said. "And now that we're both relaxed, what did you want to discuss?"

They were in the tub filled with bubble bath and oils. Mavis had turned off the bathroom light and lit several candles on the sink before getting in opposite Eli.

Earlier, when they walked through the door to Eli's apartment, both were consumed with their desire for each other and had their clothes off before they reached the sofa. They were so nutty with lust that they didn't realize until later the grocery bags were left in the hallway.

"I've been offered a promotion to the DA's office," Eli said. "It comes with a captain's badge and a captain's pay grade. Best of all, it's nine-to-five and no weekends unless there's an emergency. I could take a few night classes a week and you could still coach the dancers."

Mavis sat up in the tub. "Would you have to live in the City?"

"No. It's not a restriction. Half the force lives in Westchester."

"Before I get too excited, throw my arms around you and cry with happiness, what else?" Mavis said.

"Nothing else," Eli said. "Unless you count I put a deposit on a ring for you as something else."

Mavis stared at Eli for several seconds. "Wait. You're not supposed to tell me that. You're supposed to surprise me."

"I know, but we already talked about it and besides, I don't know your ring size," Eli said.

"Seven and one half," Mavis said. Then she rolled her eyes and said, "Let's not play too hard to get, shall we Mavis."

"Tomorrow, I plan on just half a day," Eli said. "I can pick you up around noon and we can head to the City and get it sized."

"I promise you you'll never regret one day in all the day's we will be married," Mavis said.

"I know that," Eli said. "Now if we can eat that chicken in the oven before my skin shrivels to a prune I would be a happy man right now."

*   *   *

"Are you afraid?" Mavis asked.

241

"I thought you were asleep," Eli said.

The room was dark and cool from the fan blowing across the bed.

"I'm too excited to sleep. So, are you?"

"Am I what?"

"Afraid. Of commitment, of marriage."

"I chase murderers for a living after spending four years in a war, there isn't much I'm afraid of anymore," Eli said. "Except maybe spiders. They give me the creeps."

"Spiders?"

"Especially when you find one in the shower."

"Don't worry, if you find a spider in the shower I'll protect you," Mavis said. "So now that you've evaded my question, maybe you'd like to take a crack at it again."

"Of course I'm not afraid of commitment to you, or marriage for that matter," Eli said. "I just hope I'm a good enough husband."

Mavis sat up in the dark. "What? Are you kidding me? I'm the one who should be… what are you doing?"

"What's it feel like I'm doing?" Eli said.

"It feels a lot like you're feeling me up," Mavis said.

"Since neither of us can sleep," Eli said.

Mavis rolled on top of Eli.

"Waste not, want not," she said.

* * *

Eli dropped Mavis off at her apartment and told her he would pick her up around noon. Then he drove to his office to meet Howe.

On the way, Eli stopped for coffee and bagels.

At his desk, Howe munched on a bagel as he read the files on Justin Riddick.

242

"If ever there was a suspect, this is our man," Howe said.

"Now all we got to do is find him," Eli said. "Monday we get court orders to check the bank where he cashed his pay checks and the DMV for a license. We'll find him. One way or the other."

Howe sat back in his chair. "Bell doesn't have enough men to cover this. Take from me whatever you need."

"Thanks, Art," Eli said. "Right now I have to call Rhode Island."

"What about the mayor and chief?" Howe said.

"I'll let Bell handle that," Eli said.

Eli waited about an hour for the Rhode Island State Police to call him back. While he waited, Eli and Howe killed time in Howe's office over cups of coffee and the latest department gossip.

When the call finally came back, it was as Eli suspected. Riddick's wife, after divorcing him, married a wealthy Providence banker with 4F status.

"Congratulations, Eli, your motive is official," Howe said.

"Thanks, Art. I have to call Bell," Eli said.

Bell had given Eli his home number and Eli shared the news when Bell answered the phone.

"Monday morning, Lieutenant, start getting fitted for a captain's badge," Bell said.

After Eli hung up, Howe was on the way out and Eli said, "Art, a minute please."

Howe sat on the edge of Eli's desk.

"Bell has offered me to head up the DA's squad," Eli said. "It's a good opportunity and I think I'm going to take it. I want you to understand why."

"I'm listening," Howe said.

"I'm going to get married," Eli said. "It's basically a nine-to-five position. That will make it much easier on my wife."

"Jesus, Eli, I didn't even know you had a steady girlfriend," Howe said. "My two cents says you're doing the right thing. I'm invited to the wedding, right?"

"Of course," Eli said. "Front row seat."

"As much as I hate to lose you around here, you're doing the right thing for your wife and future," Howe said. "When do I get to meet the lucky girl?"

"Soon," Eli said. "Right now I have to meet her for lunch."

* * *

"A perfect seven and one half," the salesman at Tiffany's said as he measured Mavis's ring finger.

"How soon before it's ready?" Eli asked.

"Next week," the salesman said.

"I don't get to see it until then?" Mavis asked.

"Nope. Let's go to lunch," Eli said.

"Can I pick the place?" Mavis asked.

"Sure."

* * *

"This is the last place I would have thought you'd pick for lunch," Eli said.

They were at an outdoor table at the main restaurant at The Bronx Zoo.

"Silly, but in the ten years I've been in New York I've never been to the zoo," Mavis said.

"I used to come here all the time when I was a kid," Eli said. "I think admission was a quarter back then."

"Wouldn't it be something to take our child to the zoo on weekends," Mavis said.

"Yes, yes it would," Eli said.

"What do we tell your parents tomorrow?"

"Nothing. Let's wait until you have the ring and see if they notice," Eli said.

"Maybe not your dad, but your mother will notice right away," Mavis said. "Let's walk around and see the animals."

* * *

As Eli and Mavis held each other in the dark and waited for sleep, Mavis said, "What was it like for you in the war?"

"Did I have another nightmare?" Eli asked.

"No, but if we're going to be together for the rest of our lives I'd like to know all there is," Mavis said.

Eli sighed softly. "I stopped counting how many men I killed when it reached one hundred," he said. "After that it seemed pointless."

Mavis gasped no louder than a whisper.

"It's why I don't talk about it," Eli said.

"Don't hide things from me is all I ask," Mavis said. "Especially the bad."

"I won't," Eli said. "Now let's get some sleep."

* * *

The ease at which Mavis fit into Eli's family made it appear she had been part of it for years instead of weeks.

She helped Eli's mother set the table and serve the meal. After dessert, Mavis taught Eli's sister Sally how to do the famous Rockettes leg kick. Eli's father owned a movie camera and he filmed them kicking their heels.

Driving home after 10:00 at night, Mavis said, "I want to stay at your place tonight."

"I have to leave early," Eli said.

"I know, but I want to anyway," Mavis said. "How early is early?"

Twenty-Six

"This is getting to be a habit with you two," Judge Webb said.

Bell set the file on Webb's desk. "You wanted results," Bell said.

Bell and Eli took chairs while Webb read the file. When he was done, he closed it and said, "I'll grant your request for warrants for the bank and the DMV. Catch this bastard. Put an end to it."

"We'll need a warrant to search his premises," Bell said.

"If you obtain an address, come back. I'll grant you one," Webb said.

* * *

After reading the court order, the bank president told Eli and Bell to have a seat while he checked records.

After twenty minutes, the bank president returned with an index card.

"As I suspected, Mr. Riddick never opened an account with us," he said. "However, he did need to fill out this required card in order to cash his paychecks. His last check was cashed sometime back in April."

Eli took the card. The handwriting was Riddick's. The address was on Fifty-Third Street between Eighth and Ninth Avenue.

"Thank you," Eli said as he pocketed the card.

* * *

Webb studied the bank index card. He nodded and signed the search warrant and handed it to Bell.

"Good luck," he said. "The City needs a break in this."

"Thank you, Judge," Bell said.

"That address, that's the neighborhood they call Hell's Kitchen?" Webb said.

"It is," Eli said.

Webb nodded. "Be careful, Lieutenant."

"I will," Eli said.

* * *

Eli loaded three speed-loaders and put them into his right jacket pocket.

"Do you think we should bring some uniformed officers?" Bell asked.

Checking his revolver, Tyler paused. "You don't get to the field much, do you Mr. Bell?"

"I don't... oh, you mean on a manhunt?" Bell said.

"What he means is an army of uniformed officers might just tip our hand that we're, you know, coming," Bannon said.

"Yes, yes, of course," Bell said. "There are five of you, is that enough?"

"Eli counts as two, so there are six," Tyler said.

"Stay in the car, you'll be fine," Eli told Bell. "If we're ready, let's go."

* * *

Eli drove Bell and Tyler to the curb on the corner of Fifty-Third and Eighth Avenue. Behind him, Bannon drove Thomas and Vail and parked directly behind Eli.

"Stay in the car unless I say otherwise," Eli said to Banner.

"My hands are sweating," Bell said.

Tyler grinned. "If it makes you feel any better, so are mine."

"Let's go," Eli said.

Eli and Tyler left the car and waited on the sidewalk for Bannon, Thomas and Vail to join them.

"Keep your weapons holstered until we enter the building," Eli said. "We don't want to alert or frighten any civilians on the street."

As they walked from Eighth to Ninth Avenue, Eli spotted a lone figure across the street, walking toward them.

The figure was large.

Imposing.

He carried two brown bags of groceries.

He wore heavy boots and a green Army jacket.

His hair and beard were long, shaggy.

In the center of the block, he paused and looked across the street at Eli.

Eli stopped and stared across the street at the figure.

For a split second, nothing else existed except the man staring back at him.

"Jesus Christ, it's him," Eli said, softly.

"What?" Tyler said.

"Riddick," Eli said.

Riddick dropped the grocery bags, turned and ran to Eighth Avenue.

Eli raced across the street, dodging cars and ran to Eighth Avenue just as Riddick turned the corner.

Riddick had a full block lead on Eli. Pedestrian traffic was heavy and that didn't help as Eli had to bob and weave through people walking to work.

At Fifty-Second Street, Riddick turned east. Eli turned the corner and spotted Riddick a block ahead of him. With his six-foot-five stride, Riddick ate up ground and opened the lead slightly.

While Eli's shoes were not the best for running, Riddick's heavy boots would eventually slow him down. The question was when?

Eli dodged foot traffic and raced against red lights to keep Riddick in sight. He still had a full block lead, although it hadn't increased.

Eli removed his tie and opened the top two buttons on his shirt so he could breathe better.

Riddick crossed over to Broadway and headed south. Pedestrian traffic was heavy and Eli watched him knock a woman to the ground.

A crowd formed.

"Police! Police!" Eli yelled. "Out of the way, please."

The heavy boots were starting to slow Riddick down a bit and Eli gained a good hundred yards on him.

It wasn't enough.

A man pushing a garment rack across the street was knocked down by Riddick and the rack struck a cab, causing a three-car accident.

All around Eli, horns blared.

He ignored them, ignored the fire in his lungs and kept running.

That's how you get to be a Ranger, by ignoring the pain and pushing your body beyond ordinary limits.

Focusing your mind to a point where pain and exhaustion no longer mattered.

Only the task at hand existed.

Eli had a clear line of sight to Riddick as most people on the street had gotten out of the way of the running giant.

The gap had closed to half a block.

Eli widened his stride and sucked in massive amounts of air. The gap closed a little bit more.

Then, just like that, Riddick vanished.

At first, Eli thought Riddick might have tripped, but when he didn't reappear he knew it was something else.

Gasping, sucking in air, Eli raced even harder and reached the spot where Riddick had vanished. A true Ranger at heart, Riddick ignored the pain in his leg and the fire that had to be burning in his lungs, and forced his body to perform when other men would quit.

Times Square.

The subway.

The crossroads of the world.

A crowd was walking up the steps to the entrance on Forty-Third Street. Eli pulled his badge and yelled, "Police emergency, make way," and rushed down the stairs.

There were six turnstiles that lead to the platform. Eli jumped one and rushed to the southbound platform.

Several hundred people were waiting for a train. Riddick wasn't among them. Eli looked across the platform to where Riddick was trying to hide in a crowd.

Eli looked southbound and the train was still minutes away. He jumped down to the tracks and ran across four lanes and jumped onto the northbound platform.

People around him screamed.

"Police emergency, get out of the way," Eli yelled.

Riddick was off and running to the end of the platform.

Eli took of after him. "Police, out of the way," he shouted.

Riddick jumped down to the tracks and ran into the northbound tunnel.

Eli ran to the end of the platform, pocketed his badge and jumped down onto the tracks and raced into the dark tunnel.

He ran several hundred feet and stopped when Riddick was nowhere in sight. Eli pulled his revolver and walked slowly to the end of the tunnel where it opened up to six sets of tracks.

In the distance, he saw the lights of an approaching train.

Walking a safe distance from the third rail, Eli scanned left and right for signs of Riddick hiding in the shadows.

As he walked past an iron beam, Eli was struck on the back of the head with something blunt and he dropped to his knees. As his revolver fell from his right hand, Eli was struck again and fell face down onto the tracks.

"I didn't want this, not this way, detective," Riddick said. "But so be it."

Riddick reached down to take Eli by the throat just as footsteps sounded and Riddick looked back at Tyler and Bannon, who were running through the tunnel towards him.

"Freeze! Police!" Tyler yelled.

Riddick dropped Eli and took off running to his left and vanished in the dark.

By the time Tyler and Bannon reached Eli, the approaching train was just seconds away and they grabbed Eli and jumped onto another set of tracks to safety.

As the train whisked to the platform, Tyler said, "Jesus, Christ."

* * *

Bannon held the battering ram and looked at Eli.

"Kick it in," Eli said.

"I always hated this part," Bannon said.

"I rather enjoy it," Tyler said.

Bell looked at the back of Eli's head. "You need to go to the hospital," he said.

"It's a bump on the noggin," Eli said. "Jack, go."

Bannon hit the door three times with the battering ram before the frame cracked and the door flew inward.

Eli, Bannon, Tyler, Bell, Thomas and Vail entered the apartment of Justin Riddick. Tyler flicked a wall switch and they looked at the living room. There was a sofa, coffee table and a lamp and nothing else.

"I like what he's done with the place," Tyler said.

"Check everything," Eli said.

The kitchen was basic, with a small table, one chair, small appliances and minimal food. The bathroom held the usual stuff except for prescription bottles of pain medication.

"Issued by the VA," Eli said. "His leg bothers him."

The bedroom didn't have a bed, just a mattress on the floor. A desk littered with notebooks stood beside the window.

"Get some boxes," Eli said. "We'll take all this to the office."

* * *

When Eli took his jacket off at Bell's office, the back of his white shirt was covered in dried blood.

"Lieutenant, I'm taking you to the hospital and that's an order," Bell said.

Eli nodded. "Get started on this," he said. "I'll be back as soon as I can."

* * *

"You have a slight concussion," a doctor in the emergency room told Eli. "We're keeping you overnight for observation."

"Doctor, I have a job to do," Eli said.

"So do I," the doctor said. He looked at Bell. "Who are you?"

"For the moment, I'm his boss," Bell said.

"Then tell him he's staying the night," the doctor said.

Bell looked at Eli. "You heard the man."

"For crying out loud," Eli said.

* * *

Mavis gasped when she entered Eli's hospital room and saw the bandages on his skull.

"It's not as bad as they made it out to be," Eli said. "It's just a bump on the head."

Mavis sat in the chair beside the bed and took Eli's hand. "Is this what it's like, the wife of a cop?" she said.

"I've never fired my gun in the line of duty," Eli said. "And when I transfer over I'll be a glorified paper pusher."

Mavis looked at the bandages. "Jesus, Eli," she said.

"I'm fine and I'm starving," Eli said. "There's a cafeteria on the second floor. Maybe you could get me a couple of cheeseburgers and fries?"

"Maybe I could give you another bump on the head, too?" Mavis said.

"And a Coke," Eli said. "With ice."

Mavis sighed. "I'll be right back," she said.

Ninety minutes later, a nurse entered the room and told Mavis visiting hours were over.

"I'll be out of here tomorrow," Eli said. "I'll call you in the morning."

* * *

Just as Eli was beginning to doze off, a doctor stopped by his room to check up on him.

The doctor used a small flashlight to check Eli's eyes and then asked him to follow his finger.

"I see no signs of concussion," the doctor said. "You were lucky, detective, but I wouldn't go bouncing around too much for the next few days. That's still a nasty bump you have on your head."

"I'll be sitting mostly for the next few days anyway," Eli said.

"Good," the doctor said. "Get some sleep and I'll check you in the morning."

Twenty-Seven

By the time the doctor changed the bandage on Eli's head and released him, he didn't reach Bell's office until 10:00 in the morning.

Bell and the crew had already been working since 8:00.

"How is your head?" Bell asked.

"Fine. What do we got?" Eli asked.

"Some pretty amazing stuff, Lieutenant," Tyler said.

"Thirty notebooks," Tyler said. "Each one devoted to a single victim. Detailed information on each victim, their habits, when the best time to strike, all of it outlined in pencil."

Bannon brought Eli a fresh cup of coffee as Eli took a chair at the conference table. "We got his German bayonet and Roscoe says it's a perfect match."

"Thanks," Eli said. "So we got his notebooks and his pain meds and his bayonet, what does he do now?"

"He can't walk into a VA and ask for more, that's for sure," Tyler said.

"And we know who the next victims were supposed to be and each has been contacted by now," Bannon said.

"Did we find any cash in the apartment?" Eli asked.

"No, not a nickel," Thomas said.

"He either has money stashed somewhere else or on him," Eli said. "Have you requested stop payments on his disability checks?"

Bell stared at Eli for a moment, then stood, went to his desk and picked up the phone.

Tyler grinned at Eli. "Good to have you back, Lieutenant," he said.

"So, what does Riddick do next?" Eli said.

"Leave the City if he's smart," Vail said. "Go into hiding."

"Cut his hair, shave the beard, pick up some new clothes and get lost," Bannon said. "It would be the smart move."

At his desk, Bell hung up and then immediately answered the phone when it rang. "Lieutenant, it's for you."

Eli went to the desk and took the phone.

"Eli, It's Art," Howe said. "Margaret Hope called this morning. She asked you give her a call. She said she remembered another detail she wanted to tell you, but she refused to talk to anybody else. Take down her number."

Eli wrote the number on a slip of paper, sat and dialed. It rang twice and Margaret Hope answered the call.

"This is Margo," she said.

"Miss Hope, Lieutenant Rico," Eli said.

"Lieutenant, I remembered something else," Margo said.

"I'm listening," Eli said.

"I have a… client. Can you meet me for a cup of coffee? It's something I have to show you," Margo said.

"Where?"

"Automat on West Forty-Seventh," Margo said.

"Alright, I'm on my way," Eli said.

He hung up and returned to the conference table. "I have to see Margaret Hope for a few minutes. She remembered something about Riddick. I won't be long."

* * *

Margo was already seated with two cups of coffee when Eli entered the automat. He went directly to her table and took a seat.

"I appreciate you meeting me," Margo said. "I have to be somewhere in twenty minutes. Umm, what happened to your head?"

"It's okay, just a bump, So what did you remember?"

Margo opened her small purse and withdrew a folder piece of paper. "He had a tattoo like this on his right shoulder blade. I drew this from memory."

Eli opened the paper and looked at the lightning bolt that had the word Rangers written across it. "That's a Special Forces tattoo, a Rangers tattoo," he said.

"Does it help you?"

"A great deal," Eli said. "You can't hide a tattoo. Thank you."

"You know, I have to admit you're something," Margo said.

"How do you mean?" Eli asked.

"Most men would never forgive their girl for sleeping with his boss, but with you it rolls off your back," Margo said.

"My boss?" Eli said.

"Captain Howe," Margo said. "He's a client of mine. He used to be a client of Mavis, but she sent him over to me. Listen, I have to go. Glad I could help."

After Margo left, Eli sat for several long minutes.

He felt a sickness rise up in his gut that he had to choke down hard. Finally, he stood and felt his stomach revolt and he rushed to the men's room and vomited into a toilet. He heaved until his stomach was empty and cramped.

Then he went to a sink and ran the cold water, removed the bandage and dunked his face into the water.

When he stood up, he grabbed a paper towel from the dispenser and dried his face. "Ah, Jesus," Eli said aloud.

*   *   *

When Mavis opened her door she was surprised to see Eli standing there.

"Eli is everything...?" she said.

Eli smacked her across the face with so much force he knocked her to the floor.

"With my boss?" Eli shouted.

Mavis gasped and rolled over and looked up at him. Her head rang for several seconds and her eyes watered. Slowly, she stood up.

"With my fucking boss?" Eli said and smacked her a second time.

Mavis hit the floor again and smashed her nose against the hard wood.

Eli grabbed her and yanked Mavis to her feet.

"With Art Howe?" Eli said and made a fist.

"I couldn't tell you," Mavis said. "How could I tell you that? Please, Eli, listen to me. Why do you think I sent him to Margo? I love you."

Eli's face was a mask of fury, but he looked at his fist and then lowered his hand. Then he shoved Mavis and she fell backward and hit the floor.

"Fucking whore," he snarled.

Eli turned and left the apartment, slamming the door.

"Eli, wait," Mavis cried.

*   *   *

Eli used a pay phone on the corner to call Bell.

"Margaret Hope identified a Special Forces tattoo on Riddick's right shoulder blade," Eli said. "He can change his appearance, but he can't change that."

259

""I'll go back and check his medical records," Bell said. "I don't recall mentions of a tattoo."

"His service records would have that," Eli said. "Listen, my head is pounding. I'm going home and lay down for a while."

"Maybe you should check back into the hospital?" Bell said.

"No, it's just a headache," Eli said. "I'll be fine tomorrow."

* * *

When Eli walked into his apartment the phone on the coffee table was ringing. He ignored it and went to the kitchen where the wall phone continued ringing.

He grabbed a bottle of soda from the refrigerator, sat at the table and lit a cigarette. The phone rang several more times and then stopped.

Eli quietly smoked and sipped.

A few minutes later, the phone rang again. Eli ignored it and lit a fresh cigarette. The phone rang a dozen times and then stopped.

Eli drank some soda and then the phone rang again. Eight, nine, ten times and as it rang for the eleventh time, Eli jumped from his chair and grabbed the phone.

"Fuck!" he screamed and yanked on the phone. "Fucking… fuck you, motherfucker!" he screamed and pulled the phone from the wall and slammed it to the floor where it shattered.

In the living room, the second phone continued to ring.

Eli sat at the table and waited for it to stop.

Finally, it did.

Eli went to the bedroom, stripped down and entered the shower. As he turned on the water he could hear the phone ringing again.

As he toweled dry, the phone rang another dozen times and then stopped.

Eli dressed, clipped his gun to his belt, tossed on a windbreaker and left the apartment. As he closed the door, the phone rang.

He crossed the street and found a bench in the park and watched kids play a game of baseball. There was a lot of shouting and fighting involved and as he watched them shout and roll around, Eli started to cry.

"Aw, Jesus," he said softly.

* * *

Around ten o'clock, Eli took the phone in the living room off the hook and went to bed. He knew he wouldn't sleep, but he didn't know what else to do. After tossing and turning for an hour or so, Eli heard a knock on the door.

The knocking went on for several seconds and then Howe said, "Eli, I know you're home, your car is parked downstairs."

Eli got out of bed and went to the living room, opened the door and punched Howe in the jaw, knocking him backwards against the wall.

Eli turned and crossed the living room to the small table against the wall where a bottle of Scotch and glasses rested. He poured an ounce of Scotch into two glasses and waited for Howe to enter the apartment.

Howe was bleeding from the nose and lips.

"Damn you, Eli," Howe said.

Eli handed Howe a glass.

"Look, my wife can't… she's… Mavis retired two years ago from the business," Howe said. "She told me she had fallen in love with you. What was I supposed to do, tell you that? If you were smart, which I know you are, you'd put this behind you and go running to that woman."

"How did you know I found out?" Eli asked.

"She called me at home two hours ago," Howe said. "She told me what happened and said she's been trying to call you all night."

Eli sat on the sofa, reached for his cigarettes on the coffee table, lit one and sipped Scotch.

Howe sat next to him. "Christ, my lip, Eli."

"You deserved it," Eli said.

"No, I didn't," Howe said. "I was a client of hers, nothing more and she quit two years ago when she fell in love with you. It's in the past. It has nothing to do with now. She loves you and that's all that counts."

Eli sighed. "I'll get you some ice," he said.

"I'll get it," Howe said.

Howe went to the kitchen and returned with a dishtowel filled with ice. He sat and held the towel to his lip. "She's probably still up worried about you, why don't you give her a call," he said.

"I can't."

"Why not?"

"I hit her, Art. I hit her."

"Fist?"

"No, but a couple of really hard slaps, though."

Howe sighed.

"I don't know, I just lost control," Eli said.

"Look, the fact that she's been calling you all night and then called me means she's forgiven you for that already," Howe said. "Call her and you'll see I'm right."

"I think I should apologize in person," Eli said. "In the morning, I'll go over to her apartment hat in hand."

"You do that," Howe said. "In the meantime I've got to figure out an explanation to my wife about this fat lip."

* * *

After many sleepless hours, Eli drifted off and through the haze of sleep heard the phone in the living room ringing.

He bolted awake, looked at the clock that read 6:00 in the morning and dashed into the living room to answer the phone.

"Mavis?" Eli said.

"Hardly," Riddick said.

"Who is this?" Eli said.

"I was going to kill you on the subway tracks, but it's better this way."

"How did you get my number?"

"Your name was listed in the newspaper story," Riddick said. "Your number's in the book."

"You said it's better that way, what are you talking about?"

"I can't finish my work now, but that doesn't really matter," Riddick said. "People will know why I did what I did and remember. The cowards who stayed behind while we fought and died will be marked men for life. It will make other men think twice about faking their draft status in the future."

"You're a sick man, Riddick. I can help you," Eli said. "Tell me where you are and I'll come to you alone. I promise."

"You shouldn't have beaten up your girlfriend, Lieutenant," Riddick said.

"What?"

"I've been following you around for a month now, Lieutenant," Riddick said. "While you've been hunting me all this time I've been right behind you. I know all about your sweet little Mavis, your parents, too."

Eli was stunned into silence.

"I'm going to give you the chance to be a hero," Riddick said.

"Otherwise I'm going to kill her in cold blood."

"Mavis has done nothing to you, Riddick," Eli said.

"Very true," Riddick said. "Nonetheless, I'm going to kill her unless you do exactly as I say. Agreed?"

"How can I trust you?"

"You've no choice," Riddick said. "I could kill her right now and let you listen to her screams on the phone."

"Alright, I agree," Eli said. "What do you want me to do?"

"At eleven o'clock tonight, answer your phone," Riddick said and hung up.

Twenty-Eight

"How is your head, Eli? Bell asked.

"Still have a bit of a headache," Eli said. "I should be alright to come to the office tomorrow."

"Take your time, Eli," Bell said. "The men are working the notebooks and by now Riddick has probably left the city."

"I'll see you tomorrow," Eli said.

* * *

"Hi, Ma," Eli said.

"What's wrong," Michele asked. "You never call this early during the week."

"Nothing is wrong, Ma," Eli said. "I just felt like saying hi. I'll see you at dinner on Sunday."

"Make sure you bring Mavis," Michele said. "I feel like she is part of the family."

"I will, Ma. Bye."

* * *

Eli stripped down and went through his entire workout twice, leaving him exhausted, burned out and hungry. He grabbed a

265

shower, dressed and went downstairs and walked to the Grand Concourse.

He picked up the newspapers and entered the coffee shop on 190th Street. He sat at the counter. They were still serving breakfast and he ordered a double order of scrambled eggs, bacon, home fries and toast. With orange juice and coffee.

Eli ate slowly and read the newspapers. He rarely paid attention to politics, but there were a few interesting stories about Truman. In sports, the Yankees were a lock to return to the World Series, even with DiMaggio hurt most of the season.

After his plate was empty, Eli asked the waitress for a refill on the coffee and a slice of apple pie. He read the funnies while he ate the pie and lingered over the coffee.

He paid the bill and doubled the tip and then walked to the park and sat on a bench. A ball game was in progress and he watched until the one ball they had got lost and the game was called.

As the kids walked past Eli's bench, Eli said, "How much is a new ball?"

"Ninety-five cents," one of the older boys said.

Eli dug out his wallet and handed the kid a dollar bill. "Go get a new one," he said.

"Thanks, mister," the kid said.

* * *

Back in his apartment, Eli took a nap with the bedroom fan blowing on him. He awoke around 6:00 in the evening. He made a pot of coffee and drank a cup in the living room while listening to the radio.

Then he shaved carefully and took a long, hot shower. He usually didn't bother much with selecting his clothing. White shirts for work, comfortable slacks and jacket.

He went through his closet for the loosest fitting pair of slacks he owned. He matched it with a white long-sleeved shirt and set them on the bed.

In the kitchen, Eli found a roll of heavy duct tape in a drawer.

There was nothing to do now but wait. He dumped the stale coffee and made fresh and took a cup to the living room, sat on the sofa and lit a cigarette.

The volume on the radio was low and soft music played in the background.

News came on, but Eli didn't hear one word of it. Then music resumed.

Time inched along. Each second seemed a minute, each minute seemed like ten.

Finally, the phone rang.

Eli moved forward on the sofa and lifted the receiver and placed it to his ear.

"This is Eli," he said.

"Are you familiar with The Whitestone Bridge?" Riddick said.

"I live in The Bronx," Eli said.

"On The Bronx side of the bridge in Throggs Neck right off the beach is a strip motel being renovated," Riddick said. "One hour. No need to tell you to come alone and unarmed."

"No, no need," Eli said.

"One hour," Riddick said and hung up.

Eli stood and went to the kitchen for the roll of tape and took it to the bedroom. He left his service revolver and backup piece on the dresser. He picked up his switchblade and pushed the button. Instantly the five-and-a-half inch long blade extended.

He closed the knife and ripped off two long strips of duct tape and taped the knife to his left bicep.

Then he dressed in slacks and long-sleeved shirt. He took his wallet, badge and keys and left the apartment.

It was a beautiful night.

Twenty-Nine

The beach in Throggs Neck was deserted. It was dark and quiet when Eli parked in front of the strip motel. It was in the process of being gutted. A large dumpster was filled with trash.

Eli parked beside the dumpster. He got out of his car, closed the door, walked a few feet and waited.

The door to room six opened and Riddick slowly emerged and walked toward Eli. He held a flashlight in his left hand and a .45 pistol in his right.

"Walk," Riddick said.

Eli took several steps forward.

"Stop," Riddick said.

Riddick aimed the flashlight at Eli.

"Arms up, turn," Riddick said.

Eli held his hands up and turned.

"Stop. Pull up your shirt," Riddick said.

Eli pulled his shirt out of his pants.

"Turn," Riddick said.

Eli turned and faced Riddick.

"Show me your ankles," Riddick said.

Eli lifted his pants.

"Roll up your sleeves," Riddick said.

Eli rolled up his sleeves to the elbow.

"Show me your chest," Riddick said.

Eli opened three buttons to expose his chest.

"Satisfied?" Eli said.

Riddick cradled the flashlight while he removed a bottle of aspirin from his pocket and spilled a half dozen tablets into his mouth. He replaced the bottle and aimed the flashlight at Eli.

"You didn't bring my pain killers by any chance, did you?" Riddick said.

Eli shook his head. "Sorry, you didn't ask," he said.

"Alright, let's get this done," Riddick said.

"It's not too late to let me help you," Eli said.

"Help me, help me how?" Riddick said. "Can you make my leg healthy again? Can you bring back all the friends I lost in the Invasion? What can you do to help me?"

"Murdering innocent people won't help you," Eli said.

"Innocent!" Riddick shouted. "Innocent a what? Cowards hiding under their beds while others bled and died for them."

"Being 4F doesn't make you a coward," Eli said.

"Enough chatter," Riddick said. "Get inside."

Riddick stepped to his right as Eli passed him.

"There is a battery lantern on the floor," Riddick said. "Turn it on."

In the doorframe, Eli bent over, felt for the lantern and turned it on. The room had been stripped bare except for the radiator under the window ledge.

"You said Mavis was here, where is she?" Eli asked.

"The bathroom. Take a look," Riddick said.

Eli picked up the lantern and walked to the bathroom. Mavis was roped to the radiator under the window. She was still in pajamas. Her ankles and wrists were tied with rope and her mouth was taped closed.

She looked at Eli and nodded.

Eli turned around just as Riddick cracked him on the back of the neck with the heavy .45 pistol.

Unable to scream, Mavis kicked about on the floor.

Riddick pointed a finger at her. "Hush," he said. "Hush."

On all fours, Eli was hurt but not out.

Riddick stuck the .45 into his belt. "I'll be leaving town because of you," he said and kicked Eli in the stomach with his boots.

Mavis thrashed about on the floor.

Riddick turned to her, grabbed the .45 from his belt and aimed it at Mavis. "I told you to shut up," he yelled. "I won't tell you again."

"Let her go," Eli gasped. "You got me, you got what you wanted."

Riddick kicked Eli in the ribs. "Now I got to go somewhere else and start all over again because of you," he said.

"You don't have to," Eli rasped. "I can help you."

Riddick ignored Eli. "First fucking thing is kill that bitch wife of mine and her new husband. Talk about cowards. All he did was make money during the war while I bled for them. Well, no more. No fucking more."

"Look, all of us who returned from the war have ghosts," Eli said. "This is not the way to…"

Riddick kicked Eli in the ribs several more times. "What do you know about it? Huh, what?" he screamed.

Eli started to cough up blood.

"It's your own fault, you know," Riddick said. "Being such a hotshot cop and all."

Riddick kicked Eli in the jaw and he rolled onto his back, dazed and dizzy.

"Ranger to Ranger, brother to brother," Riddick said and tucked the .45 into his waistband.

As Eli tried to roll onto his stomach, Riddick grabbed him and spun him around. Riddick encircled Eli's neck with his left arm. He lifted Eli to his feet and as Riddick brought his right arm around to take hold of his left wrist Eli reached into his shirt and tore away the switchblade, pushed the button and shoved the blade into Riddick's left forearm to the handle.

Riddick released Eli and screamed as Eli yanked the knife free from Riddick's flesh and stepped back.

With his right hand, Riddick reached for the .45 in his waistband. Eli lunged forward and shoved the switchblade into Riddick's chest.

The .45 fell from Riddick's hand to the floor. He looked down at it and then up at Eli. Defiantly, Riddick took hold of the switchblade and pulled it from his chest and tossed it to the floor.

Blood streamed down from Riddick's arm and chest.

He looked at Eli and nodded.

"Ranger to Ranger," Eli said. He stepped around Riddick, encircled his neck with his left arm and then clasped his left wrist with his right hand. "Brother to brother," Eli said.

Mavis watched in horror as Eli thrust his legs backward, bending Riddick at the neck, cracking his neck and spine.

Eli released Riddick and he fell at Eli's feet.

Eli looked at Mavis. She stared at him wide-eyed. He took a few steps forward and fell to his knees and picked up the switchblade. Then he inched his way on his knees to Mavis and used the switchblade to cut the rope binding her wrists.

"You're going to have to do the rest," Eli told Mavis and passed out on the floor.

Thirty

Richard Bell, Mayor O'Dwyer, the Police Chief and the Commissioner answered questions from the front steps of New York Hospital.

"The terror that has gripped New York City all summer is finally over thanks to the heroic actions of Homicide Lieutenant Eli Rico. Lieutenant Rico suffered non-life threatening injuries in the confrontation with the suspect and is resting in an undisclosed room until he is fit for medical discharge. In the meantime, we will take questions."

As reporters fired questions, Art Howe waited behind the hospital in his car for the delivery door to open.

Finally, the door opened and Michele walked out, followed by Mavis. Mavis held the door open and Salvatore wheeled Eli out in a wheelchair. Eli's neck was in a stiff brace. The left side of his jaw was broken and his ribs were wrapped because three of them were broken.

Salvatore wheeled Eli to Howe's car where Howe opened the rear door.

"Can he stand?" Howe asked.

"My son can stand," Salvatore said with pride.

Eli braced his hands against the armrests of the wheelchair and slowly stood up. Michele kissed Eli on the cheek. Salvatore shook

Eli's hand.

Eli nodded and slowly got into the back seat.

Howe closed the door.

"Thank you, Captain," Salvatore said.

Michele hugged Mavis warmly. "You take care of my son," she said.

"Don't worry, we'll be coming for Sunday dinner in no time," Mavis said.

"That's a beautiful ring," Michele said.

Mavis looked at the diamond ring on her left ring finger. "Yes, yes it is," she said.

Howe got behind the wheel and Mavis sat next to him.

"What time is your flight?" Howe asked.

"Three hours," Mavis said.

Howe grinned as he started the engine.

"How is the weather in Ohio this time of year?" Howe asked as he feathered the gas.

About the Author

Al Lamanda is a native of New York City. In addition to his many mysteries, he also writes Western novels under the name Ethan J. Wolfe. He has been nominated for many awards, and won the Nero Wolfe Award for Best Mystery of the Year for his novel, *With 6 You Get Wally*, book five in the John Bekker Mysteries. The series continues with *Who Killed Joe Italiano?* (Encircle Publications, 2018), and *For Deader or Worse* (Encircle Publications, 2019). Al is always working on his next novel. Watch for more titles—including John Bekker #8—coming soon!

For more exciting new fiction, visit encirclepub.com!

And if you enjoyed reading this book, please consider writing your honest review and sharing it with other readers.

Thank you,
Encircle Publications

Join us at:
Facebook: www.facebook.com/encirclepub

Twitter: twitter.com/encirclepub

Instagram: www.instagram.com/encirclepublications

Sign up for Encircle Publications newsletter and specials:
eepurl.com/cs8taP

CPSIA information can be obtained
at www.ICGtesting.com
Printed in the USA
LVHW111504140121
676487LV00005B/258